Tru Blue

New York Times Bestselling Author
MELISSA FOSTER

MF

ISBN-10: 1941480594
ISBN-13: 9781941480595

This is a work of fiction. The events and characters described herein are imaginary and are not intended to refer to specific places or living persons. The opinions expressed in this manuscript are solely the opinions of the author and do not represent the opinions or thoughts of the publisher. The author has represented and warranted full ownership and/or legal right to publish all the materials in this book.

TRU BLUE
All Rights Reserved.
Copyright © 2016 Melissa Foster
V1.0
Rev. 1, 6.2.20

This book may not be reproduced, transmitted, or stored in whole or in part by any means, including graphic, electronic, or mechanical without the express written consent of the publisher except in the case of brief quotations embodied in critical articles and reviews.

Cover Design: Elizabeth Mackey Designs

WORLD LITERARY PRESS
PRINTED IN THE UNITED STATES OF AMERICA

A Note to Readers

I have been thinking about Truman and Gemma for a very long time, and I'm so happy to bring you their story. While *Tru Blue* is a stand-alone romance, if you've read my other books, you may recognize a few characters in Peaceful Harbor. An excerpt of *River of Love*, the story in which the Whiskeys were first introduced, is included at the end of this book.

To ensure you never miss a release, sign up for my newsletter:
www.melissafoster.com/news

If this is your first Melissa Foster book, then you have a whole collection of loyal, sexy, and wickedly naughty heroes and sassy, smart heroines waiting for you. All of my novels may be enjoyed as stand-alone romances, or as part of the larger bestselling Love in Bloom series.

For more information about Love in Bloom, or my darker, sexier books, *Wild Boys After Dark* and *Bad Boys After Dark*, visit my website:
www.MelissaFoster.com

Melissa Foster

Visit Melissa's Reader Goodies page for…

www.melissafoster.com/reader-goodies

- FREE Love in Bloom ebooks
- Downloadable reading order, series checklists, and more

CHAPTER ONE

TRUMAN GRITT LOCKED the door to Whiskey Automotive and stepped into the stormy September night. Sheets of rain blurred his vision, instantly drenching his jeans and T-shirt. A slow smile crept across his face as he tipped his chin up, soaking in the shower of *freedom.* He made his way around the dark building and climbed the wooden stairs to the deck outside his apartment. He could have used the interior door, but after being behind bars for six long years, Truman took advantage of the small pleasures he'd missed out on, like determining his own schedule, deciding when to eat and drink, and standing in the fucking rain if he wanted to. He leaned on the rough wooden railing, ignoring the splinters piercing his tattooed forearms, squinted against the wetness, and scanned the cars in the junkyard they used for parts—and he used to rid himself of frustrations. He rested his leather boot on the metal box where he kept his painting supplies. Truman didn't have much—his old extended-cab truck, which his friend Bear Whiskey had held on to for him while he was in prison, this apartment, and a solid job, both of which were compliments of the Whiskey family. The only family he had anymore.

Emotions he didn't want to deal with burned in his gut, causing his chest to constrict. He turned to go inside, hoping to outrun thoughts of his own fucked-up family, whom he'd tried—*and failed*—to save. His cell phone rang with his brother's ringtone, "A Beautiful Lie" by 30 Seconds to Mars.

"Fuck," he muttered, debating letting the call go to voicemail, but six months of silence from his brother was a long time. Rain pelleted his back as he pressed his palm to the door to steady himself. The ringing stopped, and he blew out a breath he hadn't realized he'd trapped inside. The phone rang again, and he froze.

He'd just freed himself from the dredges of hell that he'd been thrown into in an effort to *save* his brother. He didn't need to get wrapped up in whatever mess the drug-addicted fool had gotten himself into. The call went to voicemail, and Truman eyed the metal box containing his painting supplies. Breathing like he'd been in a fight, he wished he could paint the frustration out of his head. When the phone rang for the third time in as many minutes, the third time since he was released from prison six months ago, he reluctantly answered.

"Quincy." He hated the way his brother's name came out sounding like the enemy. Quincy had been just a kid when Truman went to prison. Heavy breathing filled the airwaves. The hairs on Truman's forearms and neck stood on end. He knew fear when he heard it. He could practically taste it as he ground his teeth together.

"I need you," his brother's tortured voice implored.

Need me? Truman had hunted down his brother after he was released from prison, and when he'd finally found him, Quincy was so high on crack he was nearly incoherent—but it didn't take much for *fuck off* to come through loud and clear. What Quincy needed was rehab, but Truman knew from his tone that wasn't the point of the call.

Before he could respond, his brother croaked out, "It's

Mom. She's really bad."

Fuck. He hadn't had a mother since she turned her back on him more than six years ago, and he wasn't about to throw away the stability he'd finally found for the woman who'd sent him to prison and never looked back.

He scrubbed a hand down his rain-soaked face. "Take her to the hospital."

"No cops. No hospitals. *Please*, man."

A painful, high-pitched wail sounded through the phone.

"What have you done?" Truman growled, the pit of his stomach plummeting as memories of another dark night years earlier came rushing in. He paced the deck as thunder rumbled overhead like a warning. "Where are you?"

Quincy rattled off the address of a seedy area about thirty minutes outside of Peaceful Harbor, and then the line went dead.

Truman's thumb hovered over the cell phone screen. Three little numbers—*9-1-1*—would extricate him from whatever mess Quincy and their mother had gotten into. Images of his mother spewing lies that would send him away and of Quincy, a frightened boy of thirteen, looking devastated and childlike despite his near six-foot stature, assailed him.

Push the buttons.

Push the fucking buttons.

He remembered Quincy's wide blue eyes screaming silent apologies as Truman's sentence was revealed. It was those pleading eyes he saw now, fucked up or not, that had him trudging through the rain to his truck and driving over the bridge, leaving Peaceful Harbor and his safe, stable world behind.

THE STENCH OF urine and human waste filled the dark alley—not only *waste* as in feces, but *waste* as in drug dealers, whores, and other deviants. Mud and graffiti streaked cracked and mangled concrete. Somewhere above, shouts rang out. Truman had tunnel vision as he moved swiftly between the tall buildings in the downpour. A dog barked in the distance, followed by the unmistakable yelp of a wounded animal. Truman rolled his broad shoulders forward, his hands fisted by his sides as memories hammered him, but it was the incessant torturous wailing coming from behind the concrete walls that had him breathing harder, readying for a fight. It sounded like someone—or something—was suffering inside the building, and despite his loathing for the woman who had brought him into the world, he wouldn't wish that on her—or wish the wrath he'd bring down on whoever was doing it on anyone else.

The rusty green metal door brought the sounds of prison bars locking to the forefront of his mind, stopping him cold. He drew in a few deep breaths, pushing them out fast and hard as memories assailed him. The wailing intensified, and he forced himself to plow through the door. The rancid, pungent scents of garbage and drugs filled the smoky room, competing with the terrified cries. In the space of a few heart-pounding seconds, Truman took in the scene. He barely recognized the nearly toothless, rail-thin woman lying lifeless on the concrete floor, staring blankly up at the ceiling. Angry track marks like viper bites covered pin-thin arms. In the corner, a toddler sat on a dirty, torn mattress, wearing filthy clothes and sobbing. Her dark hair was tangled and matted, her skin covered in grit and dirt. Her cheeks were bright red, eyes swollen from crying. Beside her a baby lay on its back, its frail arms extended toward the ceiling, shaking as it cried so hard it went silent between wails. His eyes landed on Quincy, huddled beside the woman on the floor. Tears streaked his unshaven, sunken cheeks. Those big blue eyes Truman remembered were haunted and scared, their once vibrant color now deadened, bloodshot with the sheen of a soul-stealing high. His tattooed arms revealed the demons that had swooped in after Truman was incarcerated for the crime his brother had committed, preying on the one person he had wanted to protect. He hadn't been able to protect anyone from behind bars.

"She's..." Quincy's voice was nearly indiscernible. "Dead," he choked out.

Truman's heart slammed against his ribs. His mind reeled back to another stormy night, when he'd walked into his mother's house and found his brother with a bloody knife in his hands—and a dead man sprawled across their mother's half-naked body. He swallowed the bile rising in his throat, pain and anger warring for dominance. He crouched and checked for a pulse, first on her wrist, then on her neck. The pit of his stomach lurched. His mind reeled as he looked past his brother to the children on the mattress.

"Those your kids?" he ground out.

Quincy shook his head. "Mom's."

Truman stumbled backward, feeling cut open, flayed, and left to bleed. His siblings? Living like this?

"What the hell, Quincy?" He crossed the room and picked up the baby, holding its trembling body as it screamed. With his heart in his throat, he crouched beside the toddler and reached for her, too. She wrapped shaky arms around his neck and clung with all her tiny might. They were both featherlight. He hadn't held a baby since Quincy was born, when Truman was nine.

"I've been out for six months," he seethed. "You didn't think to tell me that Mom had more kids? That she was fucking up their lives, too? I could have helped."

Quincy scoffed. "You told me…" He coughed, wheezing like he was on his last lung. "To fuck off."

Truman glared at his brother, sure he was breathing fire. "I pulled you out of a fucking crack house the week I got out of prison and tried to get you help. I *destroyed* my life trying to protect you, you idiot. *You* told *me* to fuck off and then went underground. You never mentioned that I have a sister and—" He looked at the baby, having no idea if it was a boy or a girl. A thin spray of reddish hair covered its tiny head.

"Brother. Kennedy and Lincoln. Kennedy's, I don't know, two, three maybe? And Lincoln's…Lincoln's the boy."

Their fucking mother and her presidential names. She once told him that it was important to have an unforgettable name, since they'd have forgettable lives. Talk about self-fulfilling prophecies.

Rising to his feet, teeth gritted, his rain-drenched clothes now covered in urine from their saturated diapers, Truman didn't even try to mask his repulsion. "These are *babies*, you asshole. You couldn't clean up your act to take care of them?"

Quincy turned sullenly back to their mother, shoving Truman's disgust for his brother's pathetic life deeper. The baby's shrieks quieted as the toddler patted him. Kennedy blinked big, wet, brown eyes up at Truman, and in that instant, he knew what he had to do.

"Where's their stuff?" Truman looked around the filthy room. He spotted a few diapers peeking out from beneath a ratty blanket and picked them up.

"They were born on the streets. They don't even have birth

certificates."

"Are you shitting me?" *How the fuck did they survive?* Truman grabbed the tattered blanket that smelled like death and wrapped it around the babies, heading for the door.

Quincy unfolded his thin body and rose to his feet, meeting his six-three brother eye to eye. "You can't leave me here with *her*."

"You made your choice long ago, little brother," Truman said in a lethal tone. "I begged you to get clean." He shifted his gaze to the woman on the floor, unable to think of her as his mother. "She fucked up my life, and she clearly fucked up yours, but I'll be damned if I'll let her fuck up *theirs*. The Gritt nightmare stops here and now."

He pulled the blanket over the children's heads to shield them from the rain and opened the door. Cold, wet air crashed over his arms.

"What am I supposed to do?" Quincy pleaded.

Truman took one last look around the room, guilt and anger consuming him. On some level, he'd always known it would come to this, though he'd hoped he was wrong. "Your mother's lying dead on the floor. You let your sister and brother live in squalor, and you're wondering what you should do? *Get. Clean*."

Quincy turned away.

"And have her cremated." He juggled the babies and dug out his wallet, throwing a wad of cash on the floor, then took a step out the door. Hesitating, he turned back again, pissed with himself for not being strong enough to simply walk away and never look back. "When you're ready to get clean, you know where to find me. Until then, I don't want you anywhere near these kids."

CHAPTER TWO

PEACEFUL HARBOR WAS supposed to be Truman's clean slate. The bridge into Peaceful Harbor marked the line between his old life and his new one. But tonight as he headed over the bridge toward home, his past clung to him in the form of a baby, fast asleep on his shoulder, and a toddler buckled in beside him and resting on his arm. Only these babies weren't part of his past—but they sure as hell would be part of his future. Anger coiled dark and tight inside him—at their mother, their brother. At *himself* for not somehow knowing Kennedy and Lincoln existed, which was really messed up considering the circumstances. He didn't even want to think about what they'd been through, or if his mother had stopped using while she was pregnant, the way she had with Quincy. That had lasted until the week after he was born, when she dove back into the underworld.

With the baby against his shoulder, he grabbed the diapers, unlatched Kennedy's seat belt, and lifted her into his arm. "Come on, princess."

She snuggled in against his neck with a gentle sigh, tugging at heartstrings he thought he'd lost long ago. He put the awful blanket over the kids to shield them from the rain, which had slowed to a drizzle, and carried them up to his sparsely furnished apartment. He had no idea what he was doing. The last thing he wanted to do was wake them and start a cry-fest again, but their diapers were ready to explode, and they desperately needed baths.

He carried them into his bedroom and laid Kennedy down on his bed. Her little eyes popped open, her dark lashes sweeping repeatedly over her cheeks. Her face scrunched up, and her lower lip twitched, the edges forming a frown. She began whimpering, and he scooped her against him again.

"Shh. Shh. Shh. It's okay. I've got you." He sat on the edge of the bed, holding one sibling against each shoulder. Kennedy continued whimpering, and every sad sound clawed at those strings he thought he no longer possessed like a cat batting at a toy. He caught a glimpse of himself in the mirror, and for the first time, he tried to see himself through someone else's eyes. Tattoos covered his hands and arms, snaked out from beneath his collar and up his neck. He hadn't shaved in at least a week, maybe longer, and his dark, rain-soaked hair was plastered to his head.

He considered himself to be hard, maybe even cold to some people, and that had never bothered him. But knowing he probably looked scary as hell to the baby sister he had no idea existed until tonight? That made his insides ache in a new and unfamiliar way.

He laid the baby on the bed and pushed his hair away from his face, hoping Kennedy might see that he wasn't a bad guy. She lifted her head from his shoulder, her eyes filled with more worry than a child her age should know. He forced a smile, wanting to ease her fear and knowing damn well that what she'd witnessed tonight was probably just the tip of the iceberg of the scary shit she'd seen in her short life.

"I'm your brother," he said softly, swallowing past the lump in his throat at the thought of the brother they'd just left behind. "My name's Truman, and I'll take care of you from now on."

Her lower lip trembled again, her eyes welling with tears. He had no idea if those tears were caused by their fucked-up evening, her life in general, or *him*, but he expected it was a combination of the three. He pulled her to his chest again.

"Shh. I know this is all new, but I promise things will get better now." He hoped to hell it was the truth. "But first we need to get you cleaned up. Okay?"

He was afraid to leave Lincoln unattended. He carried the sleeping baby, a clean blanket, and Kennedy into the bathroom. He spread out the blanket on the bathroom floor, laid Lincoln down, and filled the bathtub. His mind traveled to dark places. God only knew what their mother would have allowed to happen to his baby sister. He peeled the dirty clothes from Kennedy's body, silently praying for the precious little girl to be free from scars and bruises, though he knew her real scars would never be visible to the naked eye. He stripped off the heavy, soiled diaper, cringing at the redness peppering her tender skin, and felt sick knowing Lincoln was probably in the same shape.

"Okay, princess, time to get you cleaned up." He lifted her to set her in the tub, and she dug her nails into his arm, wildly kicking her feet.

"No! No baf!" she cried, pulling her little knees up to her chest to avoid the water.

"Okay," he said quickly, and gathered her against him as Lincoln stirred. Renewed anger rose to the surface. What the hell had happened to her? He shushed her, holding her shaking body safely against him and ignoring the urine and feces now covering his arm and shirt.

"No baf!" she cried. "No baf! Scawy!"

Lincoln began to cry.

"Shh, okay." None of this was *okay*, but he couldn't let her sleep in her own shit.

He reached for Lincoln, who was now in full-blown screaming mode, and held him in his other arm, smearing his sister's shit all over the front of the baby's already disgusting clothes.

"Baby hungy," she said, and patted Lincoln on the back.

Of course he was. Truman didn't know much about babies, but everyone knew they needed to eat every few hours. He needed to buy food, and clothes, but first he had to clean the shit from their bodies. He offered the only thing he could to try to calm Kennedy.

"I'll hold you in the bath. Then I need to get food for your brother. What does he eat?"

She pushed off his shoulder and stared at him like he was speaking a foreign language. Christ, how long had it been since they'd eaten? Upon closer inspection, he could see grime under her fingernails. Her hair wasn't just tangled and matted, it was layered in grease, and he could see her ribs. He had no choice but to do this the hard way, and he knew her rash would hurt like hell when it touched the water. Better to do this fast than mess around and prolong the torture.

"Okay, princess, this is the deal." He set her on his leg, laid Lincoln down, and quickly stripped off the baby's diaper, revealing a worse rash on his bottom than Kennedy's. He carefully took off the baby's shirt, and nearly lost his mind at the sight of a big fucking bruise on the baby's upper arm. He ground his teeth together to keep from cursing whoever put it there. He held Lincoln against his chest, feeling sick to his stomach. Fighting tears of anger and empathy, he whispered, "Never again, little guy. I promise you. Never again."

Truman took off his own soiled shirt and set Kennedy on her feet so he could take off his jeans and boots, leaving on his briefs. "We need to get you two cleaned up. Then we're going down to the corner to get you and your brother some food and warm clothes."

"No baf!" She clung to his legs.

Tru closed his eyes for half a second to get his emotions in check. He was still waiting for the impact of finding his dead mother to hit him, but she'd already been dead to him for a very long time. That didn't stop the night from hell from burning under his skin. Between the screaming baby and the stubborn girl, he should be fit to be tied, but it wasn't their fault they were born to an unfit and uncaring mother.

He picked up Lincoln and climbed into the bath. Lincoln kicked his feet, crying as Truman washed him. Meanwhile, Kennedy held on to the side of the tub watching them.

"Baby no like baf."

"He's doing okay," he assured her, holding on to the baby as he poured body wash into his hands. "You're okay, right, little bro?" He kissed the baby's head. "Doesn't it feel good to get clean?" Lincoln's cries quieted, and Kennedy cocked her head to the side, her little brows tightly knitted.

"I think he likes the bath now, princess," Truman said.

"Me like baf." She put her arms around the side of the tub and tried to throw her leg over the top.

"Whoa." He lifted her onto his lap with one hand, wishing he had a third arm.

A short while later, he diapered them, dressed each in one of his clean, soft shirts, grabbed a few crackers for Kennedy to eat in the car, and drove to Walmart.

GEMMA WRIGHT TOSSED a third pint of ice cream into her basket and reached for a jar of hot fudge from the display beside the freezer. She stopped short, eyeing the caramel topping and rainbow sprinkles, and decided to get all three. It was after midnight, and calories didn't count after midnight. That was her night-owl rule and she was sticking with it. Especially after some jerk hit her car and took off. Tonight she deserved the biggest ice-cream sundae known to man.

She headed over to the children's aisle to check out the new bodysuit tutu her friend and employee Crystal had told her about. As the owner of Princess for a Day Boutique, she was always on the lookout for cute outfits. She spotted a rack of pastel bodysuits with bright fluffy tutus.

"Thank you, Crystal!"

Lifting a pink outfit with a white tutu from the rack, she felt the familiar pang of longing wriggling deep inside her. Some girls dreamed of white weddings, expensive gowns, and knights in shining armor—or billionaires in Armani suits and lavish honeymoons. Gemma didn't need a fancy wedding, or even a gallant husband, for that matter. She did quite well on her own. She had her dreams. They were just a little different from most girls'. All her life she'd sat on the sidelines, first listening to girls complain about menstrual cramps and, later, watching women's bellies grow with new life. But Gemma was born without a uterus, and oh how she used to wish she could experience those dreadful cramps to determine if they really were as horrid as her friends had claimed and to use them as an excuse to miss gym class. Gemma's dreams had nothing to do with lavish weddings or *anything* other than being lavished with love. She dreamed of little chestnut-haired babies and a loving, stable man to father them. A man who knew how to love, not throw money and gifts at them, hoping it made up for his absence. A man who wouldn't desert his family for all the wrong reasons.

The sound of a baby crying brought another pang of longing. She gazed in the direction of the noise as the wailing grew louder, and carried her basket to the edge of the aisle, peering around the corner. Her heart nearly stopped at the sight of an impossibly tall man with thick dark hair and untamed scruff holding the crying infant while he paged through a magazine. His heavily tattooed, thickly muscled arms swallowed the child, like he was afraid the baby might slip away if he didn't hold every inch of it. A little girl sat in the cart with her back to Gemma, surrounded by just about every type of baby food and formula there was. Alarm bells went off in Gemma's head. Why were these babies out so late? And why was he reading a magazine while the baby was screaming? Gemma had a naturally inquisitive mind, and she was used to it running in crazy directions. She began weaving a story about the guy—his wife left him, and he was a single dad for the first time, totally lost. Or maybe he'd abducted the kids. That was her imaginative side taking over. The side that made up stories when she was younger to get through her treacherously lonely life and wrote the newsletter for her boutique, which included a made-up story for the kids and something interesting and local for parents to check out. She ducked around the aisle again, clutching her basket, mentally figuring out how she could ease that wailing baby's sadness without seeming too nosy.

The baby let out a bloodcurdling cry, and she pushed that

adventurous, crazy, story-seeking part of herself aside and peered around the aisle again, this time checking out the man more closely. The magazine he was looking at slipped to the floor, and he kissed the baby's head, murmuring something she couldn't hear. His big hand covered the breadth of the baby's back like a football. He had deep-set eyes that were currently focused on the unhappy baby. The sleeves of his dark T-shirt clung to his massive biceps, making her wonder what he did for a living. Did they have lumberjacks around here? His jeans clung to powerful thighs, hanging low over black boots. He was sexy in that badass, hardcore way Crystal loved so much. He caressed the little girl's cheek so gently Gemma could feel it on her own cheek. He pressed a kiss to the top of the little girl's head, then held her tiny hand, quieting the alarm bells in Gemma's head.

"He's okay, princess. Just hungry. We'll feed him as soon as we get a few more things and pay for the formula." He spoke softly to the little girl, his voice full of concern.

Princess.

His eyes darted from the baby to the little girl, then back to that sweet little guy in his arms. "Don't worry, buddy. We'll get one of everything."

She watched him grab one of every size diaper and set them in the cart around the girl, and then he stuffed the ones that wouldn't fit beneath the cart. She might not have a uterus, but she had ovaries, and they'd just exploded at the love emanating from the slightly intimidating dichotomy of darkness and light before her.

CHAPTER THREE

TRUMAN FELT THE unmistakable heat of a stare before he lifted his gaze and saw the long-legged babe watching him. Strands of brown, gold, and just about every color in between fell in loose waves around smooth ivory skin and plump crimson lips—lips he imagined doing all sorts of erotic things. He saw her in brush strokes, imagined painting her delicate chin, her long, slender neck, slim shoulders, and trim waist, and sexy-as-sin curvaceous hips. His body flamed with awareness. Lincoln wailed, jerking Truman's big head into gear, overriding the greedy little one below his belt, and he stepped between the stranger and Kennedy.

Her green eyes skittered over his cart. "I guess your baby eats a lot?"

Her voice was like liquid heat, flowing over his skin, soft and warm like the summer sun, but the thread of curiosity it carried caused him to stand up taller and square his shoulders. He didn't need anyone slowing them down.

"He's starved," he said gruffly. He grabbed the handle of the cart and bounced Lincoln against his shoulder, trying to quiet him.

"So *feed* him." Her eyes never left his, like a cat that owned whatever territory it crossed, piercing and challenging at once.

He gave her a deadpan look that he knew translated to, *No shit, really?*

"Right." He pushed the cart past her and she grabbed the side of it. His hand shot out and circled Kennedy. The woman's eyes dropped to the little girl, eyeing her skeptically.

"Is it dress like Daddy day?" Her fingers curled around the cart as she reached for a package of formula.

"Something like that," he said, watching her open the package and tear the protective cover off of one of the ready-made bottles of formula. She put on the nipple, shook it up, and handed it to him.

He looked at the bottle, then at her. "I haven't paid yet." The last thing he needed was to get harassed for using something he hadn't paid for. His plan had been to get in, get out, and get home, not get hung up with a pushy little know-it-all, regardless of how hot she was. Lincoln hiccupped between cries, and she thrust the bottle into his hand.

"It's not like they'll arrest you for feeding a hungry baby."

"Baby hungy," Kennedy piped in.

Truman's chest constricted. He reluctantly took the bottle and held it to the baby's mouth. Lincoln sucked, then cried, sucked, then cried.

"You should cradle him." She set down her basket and motioned with her arms like she was cradling a baby.

He shifted Lincoln in his arms. The woman stepped closer. She must have seen wariness in his expression, because she stopped a few inches from him and reached across the short distance. Her hands were soft and warm as she lowered Truman's elbow, angling Lincoln's head higher than his feet.

"There," she said tenderly, smiling at Lincoln. "That should help."

Sure enough, Lincoln drank the formula. Kennedy beamed at the woman, who was looking at Truman like she was trying to figure him out. That was his cue to leave.

"Thanks," he said, and took a step toward the front of the cart.

"Do you know how to burp him?" She glanced in the cart again. "Because it looks like this is Daddy's first day care assignment."

"They're my *siblings*," he said flatly. "And yeah. I can burp him. *I think*."

"Do you have burp rags?"

He cocked a brow.

She rolled her eyes and smiled at Kennedy. "Time to educate your big brother." She began weeding through the formula and diapers in the basket. "Too big, too small. Wow, big brother will spare no expense to diaper you guys. I like that in a man." She smiled up at him as she set the inappropriately sized diapers on the shelf and tossed in a few others. She stretched to reach a high shelf, the edge of her expensive blouse lifting just enough to reveal a sliver of tanned, taut stomach.

She might be pushy, but there was no ignoring the effect her curvy body had on him. *Great, flash a little more skin and I'll be juggling a baby and a hard-on*. It took all of his willpower to look away.

"They size these by weight," she explained. "But they're always off. So I'd try Swaddlers and Cruisers for him, and are you in pull-ups yet?" she asked Kennedy, who simply blinked up at her.

"Diapers," Truman answered, though he had no idea what pull-ups were.

"Soon enough," she said, and patted Kennedy's head. She

loaded up the cart with several packages of diapers. "Now, about these formulas. There are all types. How old is he?"

"I don't know. A few months." How the hell did she know he was a boy?

Hands on hips, she eyed him skeptically. "Thought they were your siblings."

"They are," he growled, reminding himself she was trying to be helpful and she was easy on the eyes. This was also the happiest Lincoln had been since he'd rescued him from that hellhole. Even though he hated asking for help—*ever*—he could use a little guidance on this messed-up night.

"Sorry," he said more kindly. "I'm not sure exactly how old they are." *Because I had no clue they were alive until tonight.*

She leaned over the cart and smiled at Kennedy again. "How old are you, sweetie? Two? Three?"

Kennedy leaned away, her eyes darting up at Truman.

"Oh, you're a shy little one," the woman said. "Well, I'm Gemma Wright, and I was a shy little girl, too. Let's get you what you need." She set her hands beside Truman's on the cart handle and set those riveting emerald eyes on him again. "You obviously can't push the cart *and* feed your baby brother. What else do we need?"

"We?"

She sighed, as if she was tiring of his attitude, and picked up the magazine he had dropped earlier. "*Parenting*. Good choice." She looked at his white-knuckled grip on the cart. "Are you afraid I'll steal her? Seriously, just chill a little so we can get your babies out of here and they can get some sleep."

She glanced at the *Parenting* magazine, then leaned in closer, filling his senses with the faint scent of vanilla and *woman*. He'd never paid much attention to vanilla, but he knew he'd never look at it the same again.

She lowered her voice. "Obviously you're trying to be a good big brother. I can walk away and leave you to fumble and juggle your way around Walmart, or you can chill out and take advantage of an offer from a night owl who enjoys helping scary-looking men."

"Why would you help someone who's scary-looking?" he asked gruffly.

She raked her eyes down his body with more than a hint of interest, licking her lips as her eyes drifted up again. She caught him watching her and rolled her eyes. He'd obviously misread her. What did he know about women like her? She was dressed in slacks and a blouse that probably cost more than his monthly rent.

"You're not *that* scary. Besides, I can see you're a softy by the way you treat the kids." She brushed her fingers over Lincoln's head. Then she grabbed a bag of something from the shelves and tore it open, laying a white cloth over Truman's shoulder. "Put him on your shoulder and burp him so he doesn't get a tummy ache."

Truman eyed Lincoln, who was nearly asleep, with the bottle hanging on his lower lip. He set the bottle in the cart beside Kennedy, who was struggling to keep her eyes open, and lifted Lincoln to his shoulder, patting him until he let out an airy burp. This pushy chick knew what she was talking about.

"What's your name?" she asked.

"Truman."

"Truman. I like it," she said, as if he needed her approval. "And the kids?"

He eyed the children, feeling territorial.

"They must have names," she coaxed.

"Kennedy," he relented, then brushed his cheek over the baby's and said, "Lincoln."

Her eyes brimmed with amusement. "Does your mother have a thing for presidents?"

Before he could think of an appropriate response, she wrapped her fingers around the handle of the cart and said, "Okay, then. Let's get your stuff. What do we need?"

There were worse things than being helped by a hot chick with a sense of humor. He picked up her basket and said, "Clothes, food, car seats, and a bed."

"A bed?"

"For him." He nodded at the baby.

"A *crib*. And car seats? You have no car seats? How did you get them here?" When he didn't respond, she said, "Lordy, what was your mother thinking? She could have given you a few lessons in childcare."

That might be hard, considering she's dead.

GEMMA PUSHED THE overloaded cart into the dark parking lot, while Truman carried both sleeping babies like they were additional appendages. They left a second cart holding the crib and the playpen Gemma had convinced Truman to buy, along with a few other essentials, in front of the store for him to pick up after the kids were settled in his vehicle. She was curious about why the kids were dressed in his shirts, and why at least Kennedy didn't have shoes on, but every time she pried—which she'd done often over the past hour—he changed the subject. He was so protective and loving toward them, she let it go, despite her curiosity.

"This is my truck." He stopped beside an old blue truck, the type with front and rear seats. "How do you know so much about kids?"

She lifted a shoulder. "I own a princess boutique. You should bring Kennedy down for social hour sometime. It might help bring her out of her shell." She met his sharp, serious gaze. His eyes were the bluest of blue, and beyond compelling, but they were also haunted and wary, moving stealthily over the parking lot.

"Princess boutique? I'm not even going to try to guess what that is." He unlocked the door and laid Kennedy on the seat. She stirred, and he leaned in, whispered something, and brushed a kiss to her cheek.

Everything he did with the children was touching and tender. When they were shopping, he hadn't gotten irritated when Kennedy got whiny. He'd simply lifted her into his arms and soothed her. She'd seen parents less patient with their own children, and these were only his siblings. She wondered why he had them, and for how long, given all the things he'd had to purchase. She was glad she was there to help, or he'd have forgotten shoes and baby wash and other things big brothers didn't ever think about.

"Want me to hold Lincoln while you get the car seats ready?" She reached for the baby and he bristled. "Truman, do you seriously think I'd help you buy all this stuff and then do something harmful to your baby brother? I'm offended."

A pained expression washed over his face. He lowered Lincoln from his shoulder and kissed his cheek. Love thickened the air between him and the baby, and it was just about the most beautiful thing Gemma had ever witnessed. It lasted only a few seconds, but in those seconds she knew this big, burly man's heart was wrapped around his two precious siblings.

"I'm sorry." The edges of his mouth tipped up in a small smile, the only smile she'd seen that wasn't aimed at the children. It was the slightest shift in his expression, but it softened all his rough edges, and when he set those emotive blue eyes on her, her stomach tumbled.

"I appreciate all of your help. I'm just not used to..." His jaw clenched. "I just want to be careful with them." Careful didn't begin to describe how he was with them. *Attentive, protective, and loving* might scratch the surface. When he'd told her about their diaper rashes, the pain in his voice and expression had nearly taken her to her knees.

"I'll be *extra* careful," she assured him.

When he set the baby in her arms, the familiar longing reared its needy head. And when she got a whiff of Lincoln's sweet baby scent, it soothed that ache. Truman's hands cradled her forearms as the baby settled into them, and Gemma checked out his tattoos. Why were they all blue? And what did they mean? She'd never been interested in men with tattoos or guys who were hard. Truman was a mysterious mix of many things, and because of that he came across as a little dangerous, but there also was something genuinely tender about him that made Gemma's heart beat faster.

He made quick work of unloading the bags into the back of the truck and unboxing the car seats, his muscles flexing and bulging with his efforts. Since Kennedy was sleeping on the passenger side, he carried the baby seat around to the driver's side and set it in the middle of the bench seat.

"You should really put that in the backseat. He'll be safest there."

"The back? What if he chokes or something?" He lowered

his voice, glancing at Kennedy, still fast asleep on the passenger seat. "I won't be able to see him. I'd rather have him up front."

"Then you have to turn off the airbags. Infant car seats are made to *only* face backwards. You have to hook in the base with the seatbelt, and then the bucket snaps into it." His perplexed expression told her he had no idea what she meant. "Here. Hold Lincoln and I'll show you."

He took the baby from her and watched as she climbed into the truck and proceeded to give him instructions on turning off the airbags once the truck was started, and hooking the base to the infant seat in place. She knelt on it and tightened the belt. "You have to make sure it's secure."

She shifted into the driver's seat and he stretched across her lap and carefully set Lincoln in the car seat. His arm brushed her breasts, sending heat coursing through her body, but he was so focused on the baby she didn't think he noticed.

He turned and smiled, bringing their faces so close she could feel his breath. She drank in his handsome features, seeing past his wild scruff. His cheekbones were chiseled and strong. His lips were a darker pink than most and bowed in a way that made her want to kiss them. His eyes swept over her face with an expression of concern—*for the baby*. As it should be.

"Can you show me how to hook him in?"

"Um, yeah. Sure." *Let me just reel in these crazy hormones.* She showed him how to hook the belts and secure the baby, then turned to climb out of the truck, and he was *right there*.

His thick arms stretched over his head, his hands resting on the frame of the truck, blocking her exit, and those piercing blue eyes locked on her. Her pulse skyrocketed.

"You know a lot about babies."

She breathed a little harder. "I'm a woman. We know

things."

His eyes searched hers for what felt like a very long time, and then he cleared his throat and turned away, leaving her with heart palpitations. She watched him circle the truck and lift Kennedy into his arms, settling her against one shoulder as he retrieved the other car seat and set it in the truck.

Realizing he probably didn't know how to secure that seat either, she hurried after him. "Here, let me."

She climbed onto the runner so she could reach over the car seat and buckle the seat belt, and felt his very large, very hot hand press against her lower back. She bit her lower lip, equally turned on by his touch and nervous that he really could be dangerous. *Dangerously loving toward these babies. Okay, I'm going with turned on.*

And maybe a little nervous.

He peered around her as she secured the car seat into place and explained the steps to safely buckle Kennedy into it. When she turned to step down, he wrapped one thick arm around her waist, lifting her from the runner. For the briefest of seconds she felt all his hard muscles pressed against her, and her body flooded with heat again. He set her on her feet and placed Kennedy into the car seat, completely oblivious to the sparks he'd ignited.

How is that even possible?

He closed the truck door and grabbed her bags from the cart, glancing around the parking lot. "Where are you parked?" His eyes landed on her Honda Accord, parked two rows away beneath a streetlight. "Oh, man. Someone got sideswiped."

"That would be me," she said, reaching for the bags. "Some jerk hit me when I was at work and drove off. My insurance company will increase my rates if I file another complaint."

"Another…?" Amusement filled his eyes.

"I'm a bad-driver magnet. I've been hit twice. Well, three times if you include the latest one."

"Bring it by Whiskey Automotive tomorrow after you get off work. I'll fix it for you free of charge. No need for the insurance company to get on your case, and it's the perfect way for me to thank you for your help."

"That's way too much for the little help I've given you." Was he crazy? It was at least a few hundred dollars' worth of work, if not more.

He stepped closer, and her heartbeat quickened again. He seemed even taller and broader against the light of the moon, and so stably rooted he made her feel defenseless and vulnerable. He was studying her, and he wasn't exactly smiling, but he no longer had that guard-dog look he'd had when she'd first seen him.

"You saved me hours of wandering around Walmart and hundreds of dollars from almost buying the wrong diapers, foods, baby clothes, and God knows what else. Bring your car by the shop tomorrow." He said the last sentence with staid calmness, leaving no room for negotiation.

She wanted to take her car in, if for no other reason than to see him again, but it felt wrong accepting something so big for the little help she'd given him. "But—"

He pressed a long finger to her lips, successfully disarming her with his sudden and arresting smile. "Bring it by the shop when you get off work. I'll fix it over the weekend so you have it by Monday morning. It should only take a few hours, but we have loaners at the shop, so you won't be without a car."

"Truman, that's too much," she insisted. "Won't it need to be painted?"

"I don't think so."

"But how…?"

"I can't tell you all my secrets. You're very good with baby stuff. I'm very good with my hands." A glimmer of heat sparked in his eyes. "Bring it by tomorrow. Now get out of here so I know you're safe before I take the kids home."

She nodded and took a step away, turning back to say, "Remember not to lay Lincoln on his stomach when he sleeps. And use the ointment on their rashes. That'll help a lot."

"I've got it," he said, watching her unlock her door. "Thanks again. See you tomorrow."

She felt his steady gaze watching over her as she climbed into the driver's seat, just as he'd stood sentinel over his siblings. As she drove out of the parking lot, her ice cream long ago forgotten, she'd never been so happy for a hit-and-run.

CHAPTER FOUR

TRUMAN WAS CONVINCED he'd just experienced the longest morning of his life, following the longest night of his life. He'd put the kids to sleep in his bed last night, put the groceries away, then set to work putting together the crib. Lincoln had woken up what seemed like ten minutes later, but in reality was probably an hour, and two hours after that he'd woken up hungry again. This morning was a mad rush of feeding, changing, bathing, and changing again—a far cry from the lackadaisical mornings he was used to, when the biggest rush he'd faced was getting downstairs to the shop by seven thirty. He hadn't even taken a shower because he was afraid to leave the kids. How did single parents manage?

Tomorrow he'd take a shower right after Lincoln's crack-of-dawn feeding, when his little brother went back to sleep.

It was seven forty-five and here he was feeding Lincoln again, this time in the shop. The kid was an eating machine. Meanwhile, Kennedy was playing happily in the playpen, but he knew she was too big to stay in there for long. He'd have to figure out some sort of schedule. Hell, he'd have to figure out some sort of life.

The door to the office opened and Dixie Whiskey poked her head into the garage, her red hair and wide smile lighting up the garage. "We're here, Tru—" Her eyes widened, and she breezed into the garage, her spike heels tapping out a fast beat across the concrete floor. Her older brother, Bear, followed her in. "Aw! Whose baby is that?"

The Whiskey family owned the garage as well as Whiskey Bro's, the bar down the road. Bear and Dixie worked days in the auto shop office and some evenings at the bar.

"Mine, now." Truman pulled a burp rag from his back pocket and tossed it over his shoulder, then shifted Lincoln and patted his back. This morning the baby had spit up all over his shirt when he'd forgotten the burp rag. Gemma would probably roll her eyes at that, too.

Bear flashed a wise-ass grin. "Thought you couldn't have conjugal visits in prison."

"They're my *siblings*," Truman said sharply. Lincoln let out a loud burp. "That's a good boy."

"What do you mean they're your siblings?" Dixie crouched by Kennedy. "And what's this precious girl's name? Hi, sweetie. I'm Auntie Dixie."

Kennedy frowned as Dixie picked up a toy from the playpen.

"It's okay, princess," Truman reassured her. "Aunt Dixie has funny hair, but she's nice."

Dixie stuck her tongue out at him and Kennedy giggled.

"That's Kennedy, and this little guy is Lincoln." He met Bear's serious gaze and lowered his voice so Kennedy wouldn't hear him. "My brother decided to resurface last night. Our mother overdosed. He was a mess, and these two were living in a crack house. Last night was a nightmare. You don't mind if I keep them here in the shop with me, do you? Just until I get things under control?"

"Hey, your family is our family. Whatever you need." Bear ran a hand through his thick dark hair. He and his siblings, Dixie, Bullet, and Bones, were part of the Dark Knights motorcycle club, and with the exception of Dixie, the names they used were their biker names. Bear had once wrestled a bear, and he had the scars to prove it. Bullet was ex-Special Forces, and Bones was a doctor.

Truman had grown up in the next town over, and he'd met Bear at a classic car show when he was just sixteen. Bear had taken Truman under his wing, given him a job, and taught him how to work on cars. He'd worked around whatever schedule Truman had been able to keep and had knocked the sense back into him every time he'd strayed even slightly from the straight-and-narrow path, like by skipping school to work. He'd even allowed Truman to bring Quincy with him to the shop, since their no-good mother was never around to take care of him. Once Truman had learned to drive, Bear had lent him a car, eventually selling him the truck he now used, and they'd been close as brothers ever since. The Whiskeys were the nicest, most reliable people Truman had ever known, and he was proud to be considered part of their family.

"What's the plan?" Bear asked. "And how's Quincy?"

Truman sighed. No matter how hard he tried, he couldn't stop wondering that himself. He'd called his brother before going to sleep last night, but hadn't heard back.

"My plan? Make sure their lives don't suck, and as far as Quincy goes, I already threw years of my life away so he could *have* a life."

"And…?" Bear knew him so well. Unlike Truman's no-good mother, Bear had visited him weekly when he was in prison, and he'd brought Quincy a time or two. But Quincy had stopped returning Bear's calls, and eventually he'd fallen completely off the radar. Truman knew how hard Bear had tried to find Quincy and get him on a cleaner path, but users knew how to disappear, and Quincy had learned from the best.

"I tried to call him last night," Truman admitted. "He hasn't returned my calls, but in fairness, I told him to stay away from the kids until he's clean. I'll help him when he's ready, but, man..." He cradled Lincoln in his arms and kissed his cheek. "They don't even have birth certificates. He never even told me they existed, and the way he let them live..." He ground his teeth together in an effort to bury the anger simmering inside him. "He can't be trusted around them."

Bear put a hand on his back. "I hear ya, bro."

"Listen, do you think Bones can get a pediatrician to check them out, no questions asked? Just until I get my arms around what to do. If I bring them in to a doctor, they'll ask all sorts of questions, and there's no way I'm letting them get tied up with Social Services. I just need a little time to figure things out, but I have to know they're healthy."

"Of course. I'll call him in a sec. Just let me..." Bear scooped Lincoln into his tatted-up arms and rubbed noses with the baby. "Love the way babies smell."

"Gemma helped me pick out baby wash and baby shampoo and about a million other baby things."

"Gemma?"

Just hearing her name made him smile. He didn't even want to think about how it had looked last night, two kids out with him at midnight, dressed in his shirts, while he stocked up on everything under the sun. He was surprised she'd even offered to help. She'd probably thought better of it this morning and would stay as far away from this end of Peaceful Harbor as she could. *My loss.* But he couldn't help wondering what might have happened if they'd met under different circumstances. *Different lifetimes.*

Kennedy reached for him, bringing his mind back to the moment. "Come here, princess." *Princess. What is a princess boutique anyway?*

Bear and Dixie were looking at him expectantly, and he realized they were still waiting for a response about who Gemma was.

"I met her last night at Walmart when I was out buying all this shit." He looked at Kennedy and corrected himself. "*Stuff.* She helped me find everything—clothes, food, bottles, diapers. Man, there's so much that they need. I'm not complaining, just saying. I never realized how much work babies were. This is all so messed up. Thursday morning I was checking in with the parole office and thinking about how I only had thirteen more months of *that*..." He glanced at Kennedy again. "Fifteen hours later, and thirteen months feels like a flash in the pan."

"There *are* other ways to handle this," Dixie said carefully. "You don't have to raise them, and it wouldn't make you a failure or mean you're a bad person."

Truman had thought about that when he was wiping shit off his hands at four o'clock in the morning and then again at seven when he realized that even taking a piss was a group process. But they were his blood, and he wouldn't turn his back on blood.

"I failed Quincy. I'm not going to fail these two."

"I JUST DON'T see what you're worried about." Crystal

pushed her jet-black hair over her shoulder and heaved the other end of the box she and Gemma were carrying to the storeroom. She was in full goth-princess mode, from her dark lipstick to her chunky black leather boots and black lace stockings, tutu, and blouse. "Were the kids clean?"

"They appeared to be freshly bathed." Gemma pushed the door open with her butt, holding it for Crystal to get a foot through, before inching into the room. They'd just received the new stock of rebel-princess clothes, and she was excited to see them. She'd dressed carefully this morning, choosing her *Brave* princess outfit, a short blue velvet dress with a thick gold belt and strappy leather sandals. She wasn't normally nervous around men, but with Truman, she needed all the courage she could muster.

"Were they afraid of *him*?" she asked as they set the box down with a *thump*.

"No, but I got a little chill from him, which was nothing compared to the holy-shit-this-guy-is-all-man vibe he gave off. He wore testosterone like aftershave. It just seemed weird, that's all. Kennedy had no shoes on. It was like he'd taken them out of bed, only he didn't even have a crib for the baby."

Her heart warmed with thoughts of Truman soothing Lincoln and the sweet way he'd caressed Kennedy's face and spoken so reassuringly to her. "He loves them. That much was clear. But the rest is curious, don't you think?"

Crystal pulled a box cutter from a shelf and sliced open the top. Her hair veiled her face, and she gave Gemma a you-know-what-I-think glance through the thick strands as she yanked open the box. Withdrawing a little black leather vest, she held it up with a gratified smile. "Being a rebel princess myself, I would have dropped off my car first thing this morning, gotten my fill of those glorious tattoos you described, a scorching-hot kiss—or ten—and I'd have left him wanting more. You're the story seeker, the pushy girl no one sees coming. I'm surprised you didn't march right in and interrogate him to get all those lingering questions answered. You even wore your princess *Brave* dress. So what's the deal?"

She laughed. Crystal was the leather to Gemma's lace. She was brash where Gemma was pushy. Gemma had rebellion in her, but while her favorite rebellious outfit was a pink and black schoolgirl type miniskirt, lace-up black high heels, a frilly white shirt, and distressed leather jacket, Crystal was full-on biker dark—leather pants, boots, and bustier showing as much cleavage as possible. Still, they clicked like a seat belt and always had each other's backs.

"I don't *interrogate*."

Crystal set her hand on her hip and glared at her.

"Okay, maybe I do, but I *didn't* with him. There's something about him that stopped me. I could kick myself right now because I *almost* did what you said this morning, but something about him made me become this…" She plucked out a pretty pink princess dress from another box.

"Aw, Gem. That's because you might usually be Princess Confidence, but something about this guy has unearthed the fatherless girl who worries that everyone has hidden emotions, hidden agendas, or that they'll just plain let you down. And from what you told me about how protective he was, I think that's scaring you, too, because it's what you always wished you'd had."

Chills feathered over Gemma's skin. Her parents had lavished her with all the things they wanted *for* her, protected her with a gated community, nannies twenty-four seven, and a smothering, rigid schedule. As she got older she realized that her parents were incapable of giving her the only thing she'd ever wanted—the type of love that couldn't be bought, security and comfort that was born from that love, and the freedom that went along with loving someone so much you wanted to see *their* dreams fulfilled.

"Which explains, Gemma girl," Crystal teased, bringing her back to their conversation, "why you're still here at almost seven o'clock on a Friday night when we closed an hour ago and Mr. Hotter than Hell is waiting for you to drop off your car, which we all know is code for Bring That Sexy Bod Over."

Gemma rolled her eyes, although the thought had entered her mind.

Crystal's eyes widened. "Oh my God. Could it be? After all this time of going out with guys you have zero interest in, you've finally met a guy who makes your heart go pitter-patter? Or even better, makes your coochie tingle and throb, and—"

Gemma threw the pink dress at her and she dodged it with a laugh.

"That's it! You like this tattoo-covered badass. The 'you're just asking for trouble' type of guy you're always warning me about. You like that über-alpha growl and testosterone-laden cold shoulder." She sauntered out of the stockroom blowing on her fingernails, then swiping them up and down the center of her chest. "My work here is done."

Gemma groaned and followed her out. "God, you're annoying. Why did I hire you again?" They'd met in a coffee shop in Peaceful Harbor when Gemma was scouting areas to move to after college. Crystal was a straight shooter like her, which was why they'd clicked from the moment they'd met. Crystal might be brasher and darker in looks and dress, but they both held strong to the no-bullshit attitude that made the business—and their friendship—a success.

"Because you love me." Crystal fluttered her lashes. "And because I'll give it to you straight." She set her hands on Gemma's shoulders and said, "Go forth, sweet maiden, and conquer your Neanderthal."

Gemma couldn't help but laugh.

"That's just it. I *do* like him. He intrigues me in a way I can't ignore. But you know me. I never like guys this fast. And despite the tattoos and grunts, he's *not* a Neanderthal. Neanderthals don't have hearts that practically climb out of their chests." She warmed just thinking about the way he'd held the children, the way he'd spoken to them and looked at them. And when she thought of the way he'd looked at *her*, her body went white-hot. She grabbed her purse from behind the counter and a bag of goodies she'd packed earlier and headed for the front door. "Wish me luck."

"I wish you long-hard-cocks-and-balls-of-steel luck. Promise me you will *stop* overthinking and rebury the unearthed worries, because otherwise you'll never give him a chance."

"I promise," she said over her shoulder, hoping she really could.

"I want complete details! And don't give me any of that *we didn't do anything* bullshit, because in your head, you already have. I see it in your eyes!"

Gemma headed out the front door, careful not to glance back and reveal the other sexy thoughts she was currently having.

CHAPTER FIVE

WHISKEY AUTOMOTIVE WAS located just outside of the main part of town, near the bridge that led out of Peaceful Harbor. A bridge Gemma had rarely crossed in the four years she'd lived there. She liked the comfort of the small close-knit community in the seaside town, which was so different from the exclusive gated community in which she'd grown up. Through her shop, she'd become a member of the community, with repeat clients and many friendships. The move had been a purposeful one, and it had worked out well. She might not ever be able to escape the pain of her father's suicide, but at least she no longer had to look into the pitying expressions of those around her. She'd kept that part of her life to herself, confiding only in Crystal after one of her awful mother's phone calls.

As the shops faded in her rearview mirror, her thoughts returned to Truman, and a thrill raced through her. Oh yeah, the guy had definitely piqued her interest in all the best ways.

She drove past Whiskey Bro's, a shady-looking bar with motorcycles parked out front she hadn't given much thought to until now. Was Truman a biker? A mile or two down the road she saw the Whiskey Automotive sign, and she turned down the long driveway, heading toward the building in the distance. The closer she got, the more nervous she became. What if he was just being nice and didn't really expect her to take him up on the offer to fix her car?

What if he offered his services as a way to see me again?

Butterflies took flight in her stomach.

She parked in front of the long building. Three of the four bays were closed. Light flooded the fourth. The right side of the building served as the office, with glass windows and signs for tires, mufflers, and other automobile supplies. She hadn't looked at their hours, and she was glad to see that someone was still there. She hoped it was Truman.

She grabbed the goody bag she'd brought for Kennedy, stepped out of the car and followed the sound of music coming from the bay, where she saw Truman with Lincoln nestled in his arms and Kennedy hanging on to his pants leg. Kennedy wore one of the pretty dresses they'd picked out last night. Gemma saw the playpen and wondered if the kids had spent the day there while he worked.

Truman reached for a backpack on the floor and turned as he hoisted it over his shoulder. Their eyes connected. *Connected* wasn't nearly strong enough of a word to describe the force of his powerful gaze as it locked on hers, drawing her forward along an electric river. Lightning seared through her veins, sizzling and burning with every step. His lips curved up in a genuine smile and his sharp blue eyes raked slowly down her body, and she remembered she was still wearing the short princess dress. His grin turned lustful, and she thought she might melt right there on the spot.

"You came," he said with what sounded like relief.

"Is that okay?" She felt her insecurities rising and thrust them down deep, refusing to overthink any part of tonight. She hadn't felt this turned on in...*ever*.

Kennedy peered out from around his leg and lifted her hand beside her face in a slow, shy wave.

Gemma waved back, watching Truman lift her into his arms like she was light as a feather. The little girl put her head on his shoulder, and his smile turned slightly apologetic as he closed the distance between them. "We were just heading upstairs."

She glanced at the door he'd motioned to.

"My apartment." He shifted his eyes to Lincoln, who was fast asleep in his other arm.

"Oh. I'm sorry I came so late. I can bring the car by tomorrow, or..." She should have come earlier, since she was sure he hadn't asked her to come by so he could see her again.

"Are you in a hurry?" he asked a little gruffly.

"No, but I don't want to—"

He smirked. "Sure you do. Come on up."

She followed him through a door and up a set of stairs, worrying about the *Sure you do.* Was her interest that obvious? "I can come back another time. I should have called to see what time you closed."

"You're here now," he pointed out. At the top of the stairs, he managed to turn the doorknob while holding both kids, then pushed the door open with his foot.

She followed him into a loft-style apartment. Wide-planked wood floors ran beneath a comfortable-looking brown couch with deep cushions. She wanted to crawl onto it with a book and disappear for hours. No, she wanted to crawl onto it with Truman and...She forced her eyes away from the sex-pit sofa, taking in a number of sketch pads and the *Parenting* magazine he'd bought last night littering the coffee table. Across the room glass doors led to a deck, and to the right of them, a large alcove housed several tall metal tool chests and a wooden workbench with a variety of tools hanging on the wall above it. Beside that stood a beautiful big arched window. To her left was an open kitchen with the bottles, jars of baby food, and other things they'd bought the night before. She glanced up at the exposed rafters in the ceiling. The tidy apartment was masculine and rough, like Truman. She felt like she should lower her voice an octave or ten before speaking.

"Can I at least help you somehow? Want me to take Kennedy while you lay Lincoln down?"

He eyed the little girl. "I've got her." He lifted his lips in a half smile and kissed Kennedy's forehead. "I'll be right back."

He disappeared through the hallway to their right, and she took a few steps into the apartment, listening intently as Truman's low voice filtered in from the other room. She knew it was rude to eavesdrop, but he sounded so calm and sweet, she couldn't help herself. She heard the water turn on as he talked Kennedy through brushing her teeth. Then it became quiet again, just his steady footsteps moving across the floor.

She couldn't make out his low, soothing murmurs. Curious, she stepped to the edge of the hallway, and his voice became clear.

"And Tinker Bell met Snow White in the forest, where they made applesauce." *Oh boy.* He'd mixed up his fairy tales. She smiled, listening intently as he continued his tale. "And the biker boys carried Tinker Bell in a special carriage to a beautiful field where Winnie the Pooh was waiting with a big jar of honey…"

She couldn't suppress her smile at the silly story, and tiptoed away, setting the bag of goodies she'd brought on the end table. She sat down on the couch to wait and picked up one of the sketch pads that was lying open, gingerly leafing through the first few pages, then slowing to take a better look. Graffiti-style sketches of people and animals filled every page, mesmerizing her with their fluidity and tortured expressions. A kaleidoscope of blacks and grays created eyes, angry mouths with viperlike fangs, contorted, tormented faces, dragons, and more. Their depths and emotions clawed off the page, bringing rise to goose bumps on her arms.

A large tattooed hand came down over the edge of the sketchbook, and she looked up into Truman's hard expression.

"I'M SORRY. I was just..." Gemma's brows knitted, her eyes pleaded, and then a devastatingly sexy smile spread across her lips. She splayed her hands in the air and shrugged, looking so fucking adorable it was hard to remain irritated at the intrusion of his privacy. "I was being nosy. I can't help it. It's who I am, and those drawings are amazing. Are they yours?"

Truman tossed his sketchbook on the table, trying to wrap his head around the web of emotions that were twisting and tangling inside him. In the past twenty-four hours his life had careened in every direction, and he felt like he was trying to balance on two wheels instead of four.

"They're nothing."

"Nothing?" Her voice arced up with surprise. "They're bold and dramatic, and so different from anything I've ever seen." She went for the sketch pad.

"Please don't." His stern tone stopped her midreach.

Her eyes darted to him, challenging and confused. She leaned back on the couch and her dress hiked up temptingly high on her thighs.

Shifting his eyes away from that enticing sight, he said, "They're really just mindless doodles."

"You're one hell of a talented artist if those are mindless doodles. I could feature you in one of the community newsletters I write for my boutique. I bet you'd get some interest in commission work."

He crossed the room to the kitchen to try to cool down from the heat stroking through his core. He didn't usually like pushy women, but her confidence, and the look in her eyes, made him long to take her in his arms and possess that sassy mouth of hers. "Can I get you a drink?"

"Nice change of subject." She popped off the couch and joined him, like a sinfully sexy ray of sunshine. Now that he wasn't in the midst of last night's nightmare, he saw Gemma more clearly. She was even more beautiful than he remembered. In her flat-heeled sandals she was about a foot shorter than him, and the dress she was wearing was like icing on the Gemma Wright cake—and he was ravenous. The bright color, the way it hugged her lush curves, and the thick gold belt gave her an edgy look, which contrasted sharply with the demure outfit she'd worn last night.

He needed to get a grip, because not only was an ex-con with two babies not high on any woman's hot list, but he had other priorities. Not to mention that he had no free time *or* a bedroom, making even the thought of taking her a ridiculous one.

"I have to confess, in addition to looking at your drawings, I heard a little of the fairy tale you were telling Kennedy, but um…I think you mixed up a few of the stories."

"I can't tell her the real stories. She's seen enough bad stuff in her life. So I made up a night-night story for her." God, he sounded like a pussy.

Her eyes warmed.

Maybe it's good to sound like a pussy. Jesus, he had more important things to worry about.

"You made up a *night-night* story just for her?"

He ground his teeth together. "Yeah. I'm surprised you didn't sneak a look at *that* sketch pad, too. I'm drawing it out so she can see pictures. It's not a big deal. Can we please talk about something else?"

"Yes, but making Kennedy her own fairy tale book is the sweetest thing I've ever heard. And I have to say it one more time. Seriously, Truman, your drawings are incredible. Why don't you want me to see them?"

Because they come directly from my soul. "It's not personal. I don't show them to anyone."

"Well, you should. They're really good." She looked at him like she wanted to push him for more answers as she had last night, but then she glanced over at the jars of baby food on the counter, and her expression changed. "I feel bad about showing up so late. Please don't feel like you have to entertain me. You were getting ready to come upstairs when I got here, and you probably have a million things to do while the kids are asleep. I was only supposed to drop off my car. I can go."

"It's fine," he said, cringing at his sharp tone. It wasn't her fault she'd come along at a time when his life was crazier than a three-eyed buffalo, and he didn't mean to make her feel like she was an imposition when he'd spent the day hoping she'd show up.

Softening his tone came easier than expected. "I'm glad you're here." He liked the way her expression brightened at that. "My life is not usually this fragmented. Hell, *I'm* not usually this fragmented. If you had come by at this time any other day, you'd have found me working on a car. But now…I'm managing schedules for three, and I don't even *know* their schedules yet." *If they even have schedules.* He opened the refrigerator, which was full of the groceries they'd chosen last night. "How about that drink?"

"I'm not a big drinker," she said. "Do you have anything nonalcoholic? I like wine. It's not that I don't drink, I'm just not in the mood."

"Unless iced tea, apple juice, or water have alcohol, I think we're good."

"Iced tea is great, thanks." She watched him intently as he poured the drinks. "Can't you ask your mom about the kids' schedules?"

He bristled, though he should have anticipated the question. It was a reasonable one. He handed her a glass and nodded toward the living room, then opened the doors leading to the deck to let fresh air in before he suffocated.

"She's not around," he said as he sank down to the couch beside her. He felt guilty leaving their mother's cremation for Quincy to handle, but he had more important things to deal with—two very small people with very big issues.

"Well, can't you call her? Or email?"

"She's…" He had to get used to saying it. Might as well start now. "She passed away unexpectedly."

"Oh gosh." She laid her delicate fingers on his forearm, and he liked it far more than he should. "I'm so sorry."

"Trust me. They're better off without her."

She drew back as if she'd been burned. "Why?"

He mulled over the question and took another drink of his

iced tea, wishing he had something stronger. He wasn't a big drinker and usually just had a beer or two when he was hanging out with the guys. But the babies didn't need a drunk guy taking care of them. He needed to be clearheaded and present, now more than ever. He set his drink on the table and ran a hand over his chin, remembering he hadn't shaved in forever. At least Dixie had watched the kids long enough for him to shower earlier in the day. Not having time for a shower, helping Kennedy brush her teeth, changing diapers… He'd become a parent overnight, and just as quickly he'd come to love the little babies sleeping in the other room.

His mind returned to their mother, bringing a wave of bile to his throat, and his mind back to her question. "Some people aren't cut out to be mothers."

She nodded as if she agreed and set her drink beside his. "Even so, I'm sorry you lost her. Regardless of whether she was a good or bad mother, she was still your family. The kids' family."

"Right," he said under his breath. She had the right idea, holding family in high regard. Unfortunately, Kennedy and Lincoln were born to a mother who deserved no such respect. "Well, I hope they don't remember a second of their life before last night."

"Last night? Is that when…?"

"Yes." He wondered why in the hell he was sharing this with her, but it felt good to get it out. It wasn't like *he* was the drug addict. He had nothing to hide—except six years of his life spent paying for a crime he didn't commit.

She touched his arm again. It was a gentle, soothing touch, the kind of touch you might share with a friend or relative. There was nothing sexual about it, but it sure felt good.

"Is that why you needed to buy so much for them? Was there a house fire or something? Did they lose all their stuff?"

"No. They never had any stuff."

"I don't understand. How could they have nothing?" She cocked her head to the side.

Who was he kidding? Of course she couldn't understand. She probably came from a normal family with normal problems, like where to go on vacation or which car to take to the store. He might as well cut this conversation short. He came from an effed-up family, and the minute she heard where he'd spent the last six years, she'd run like the wind.

"You know what? Maybe this wasn't such a good idea. Why don't you leave me your keys? I'll give you a loaner and call you when your car's done." He pushed to his feet.

She rose beside him. "Why?"

He arched a brow.

"You just told me that you were glad I was here."

"I am, but you don't need to hear this."

Those catlike eyes narrowed. "I wouldn't ask if I didn't want to hear it."

"Are you always like this?"

"Like what?" She cocked her head again and smiled innocently.

His eyes dropped to her fingers resting on her jutted-out hip. "Oh yeah. You're always like this." He couldn't suppress the smile tugging at his lips.

"You mean, friendly? Curious about a guy who offers to fix my car for free and makes me a little nervous?" The innocence in her smile smoldered right before his eyes.

"You don't act like I make you nervous." He stepped closer, and she held her ground. The air between them sparked like it had when she'd first arrived, before he'd gotten sidetracked with the kids.

"Why are you afraid to talk to me?" She lifted her chin, schooling her expression. But she couldn't mask her quickening breaths.

"Why do you *want* to talk to me?"

She pursed her lips. "Because you're so in love with your brother and sister it practically drips off of you, and I like that in a person. Love and loyalty aren't easy to find, especially in siblings. And you're protective of them, which is pretty telling, you're incredibly artistic, and you're obviously generous. You did offer to fix my car for free. You're a little mysterious." Her eyes dragged down his chest, making his cock take notice. When she met his gaze, she smirked. "And you're *mildly* attractive."

He stepped closer, their thighs brushing. "*Mildly* attractive?"

She rolled her eyes. "You could use a shave."

Damn, he liked her spunkiness. "In case you haven't noticed, my life is pretty messed up at the moment. Not much time for shaving."

"Messed up? No. I hadn't noticed that. But I have heard that you recently acquired responsibility for two very cute children, and I happen to be very good with children. If you talk to me, I might be willing to share some secrets about finding time to shave and *other things*."

With the exception of the Whiskey family, he'd never had help from a single person. The thought reminded him that he needed to back away from beautiful Gemma. "I don't need help."

She searched his face again. "Everyone needs help."

"You have no idea who I am."

"No, but generally that's why people talk. To get to know each other." She swallowed hard. "My friend reminded me that I've been overly cautious where men are concerned. I don't want to be overly cautious. I'd like to get to know you."

He could see how difficult that was for her to admit, and yet she'd not only admitted it, but she'd also followed it up with a very confident statement. A statement that made his heart take notice. Truman was no stranger to being hit on. Women pursued him often when he was out at Whiskey Bro's or shooting pool. When he was with tougher crowds, where things like prison time weren't a deterrent but a badge of honor. Women who brought their cars into the shop, both married and single, also hit on him, women who thought fucking a tattooed bad boy would be a thrill. But he never took them up on it. He had enough darkness in his past; he didn't need to bring it into his future and wonder whose wife he'd slept with.

But Gemma…Gemma was smart and savvy, and the more they talked, the more he liked her, which was exactly why he needed to end this conversation. He wasn't a glutton for punishment, and he didn't want to lead her on knowing his past would push her away.

Before forcing himself to take a step back, he couldn't resist stroking her cheek. She was stunning, and smart, and funny. She deserved a guy without a past hanging like a noose around his neck.

"I think in this case, Gemma Wright, you should be a little cautious. Let's get you that loaner car."

CHAPTER SIX

TRUMAN GRITT WAS not fooling Gemma, not for one second. He was a man who wore his emotions on his sleeve. *Raw* emotions. *Real* emotions, made clear in the way he looked at her, like a hungry wolf ready to devour his next meal. She'd seen the restraint it had taken to keep himself in check. She'd felt it in the lightning streak of that single caress. And when he talked about his mother, in those few short sentences she'd heard his disgust for her. Now she wanted to understand why, and to understand why he'd sent her away when he had so clearly wanted her to stay. That was precisely why she was standing on his back deck at six thirty the next morning with two to-go cups of strong coffee from Jazzy Joe's, her favorite coffee shop. She was armed and ready to interrogate, if that's what it took.

She smoothed her hand over her shirt, straightened her spine, and knocked on the glass just as the sound of Lincoln crying rang out. She knocked again, and the curtains swished on the other side of the door. Kennedy's face peered up at her. She was wearing the pink pajamas with little ice-cream cones printed on them that Gemma had chosen. She yawned, her little eyes squeezing closed with the effort.

Gemma crouched before her and waved through the glass.

Kennedy twisted from side to side. Her chin tilted up as Truman's big, shirtless—*breathe, breathe, breathe*—body appeared behind her. Gemma rose slowly, taking in every inch as she went. Dark blue sleeping pants hung dangerously low on his hips, beneath impossibly ripped and insanely lickable abs. Her tongue swept over her lips as she rose higher, her eyes playing over the brawny arm cradling Lincoln, ribbons of blue ink decorating his broad chest, sinking between thickly muscled pecs, over powerful shoulders, and up the right side of his neck. A knock on the glass above her head brought her eyes up to his again, and she felt her cheeks flame at his grin. His hair was tousled, his eyes sleepy and…*curious*? She really liked that sleepy look on him. It made him look like a gentle giant. His grin turned to a straight line as he tugged the door open. *Uh-oh*. She might have misconstrued curiosity for annoyed.

"Do you gawk and stalk all *mildly* attractive men?"

Kennedy wrapped her arms around his thigh, tugging his pants down lower. *That's it, Kennedy, tug a little harder.*

Oh, that was bad! She shouldn't want him to lose his drawers in front of the kids. Wow, who knew muscles had the ability to lower her IQ?

Thinking much faster than she believed herself capable with all the lust swirling through her, she said, "I'm not stalking. You need a shave, which means you need a shower, which is nearly impossible with two little ones underfoot. I came to help."

He rested his hand on Kennedy's cheek, and that tender touch made Gemma's heart open a little more to the guarded man.

"You don't listen very well, do you? I thought I said I didn't need help." He stepped to the side, a small smile forming on his lips.

"You did, but your eyes told me something different." She stepped into the apartment feeling a little victorious, and she noticed blankets and pillows on the couch, empty bottles on the counter, and the *Parenting* magazine lying open on the floor beside the couch. The bag she'd brought yesterday was still on the end table.

"Hard morning?" she asked.

"I'm not sure I know when night ended and morning began." He stifled a yawn. "Lincoln got a few shots yesterday and he's been running a low fever. I called the doctor and she said it's a normal reaction. I gave him medicine already to bring down his fever, and he seems okay now, but she said he'll probably need it again in four hours."

"Aw, poor little guy. You took them to the doctor already?" She set the to-go cups on the kitchen counter.

"She came here yesterday as a favor for my buddy."

"That was nice of her. I didn't know doctors made house calls anymore." Gemma reached for the baby. "Give me Linc, and you can down that coffee and grab a shower—and a shave."

He ran his eyes over her scoop-neck shirt and skinny jeans. "No princess dress today?"

"I save them for special occasions, like being told to leave."

He kissed Lincoln's head and handed him to her, his gaze falling to her mouth and lingering there so long her pulse quickened. When his eyes slid slowly down the length of her body, she felt the heat of it searing through her clothes.

"For what it's worth," he said in a low, seductive voice, "I like that outfit just as much as I liked the dress." He lifted Kennedy into his arms and kissed her cheek.

"Good to know. Just don't tell me to leave."

The edge of his mouth quirked up and he turned Kennedy's

face toward him. "Will you be okay with Gemma for a few minutes while I shower, princess?"

Kennedy looked at Gemma.

"We'll be fine," Gemma assured him, loving the way he worried over them. "It's good for her to have some girl time. Besides, I have some goodies for her."

"Coffee?"

"Yes, strong coffee, because that's what every child needs. What do you take me for? Everyone knows kids like Frappuccinos, not coffee."

Concern washed over his handsome face, and his hand splayed over Kennedy's back, like a lion protecting his cubs. Maybe he had a little Neanderthal in him after all. She liked that a whole lot.

"I'm kidding. I brought a few things last night." She pointed to the bag on the end table. "Stop worrying and go shower. And for goodness' sake, cover up all those mildly attractive, distracting muscles."

A gratified grin lifted his lips, and just as quickly his face went serious again. "You brought her gifts last night?"

She shrugged and reached for the little girl's hand as he set Kennedy down. Kennedy blinked up at Truman, who nodded, and she took Gemma's hand.

"Just a few things I thought she'd enjoy. Is it okay if I get them breakfast if they get hungry?"

"Sure, thanks." He crossed the floor, every purposeful step a visual reminder of his power and control. Even the way he lifted the backpack lying by the front door was determined, as if in his head he ticked off every move. He dug a hand into the opening and withdrew a handful of papers. "I fed Kennedy eggs yesterday morning and she seemed to like them. The doctor gave me these menu ideas, schedules, things like that."

She'd thought about how quickly his life must have changed only two days ago. Losing his mother, acquiring care of these two little ones. No wonder he acted like a guard dog. And here he was, staying up all night with a feverish baby and *still* needing to be pushed into accepting help. She knew mothers who would beg for help with toddlers just so they could get their nails done.

She looked down at her sleeve to see if her heart had slid out from her chest. This man did not need to change. He was perfect just the way he was.

"You know what, Tru? Don't shave if you don't want to. A little distraction is a good thing."

HOW WAS HE supposed to shower when Gemma was just a few feet down the hall taking care of *his* kids? Not his fucked-up mother's children, not the freaking government's, who would steal the only real family he had left. He had to figure that part out, but he *would* make it happen. Somehow. That was one worry he couldn't deal with yet. First he had to get through Lincoln's fever and figure out schedules, sleeping arrangements, and how the hell he was going to deal with them in the shop all day. There was too much to figure out in one ten-minute shower, and damn this shower felt good. He closed his eyes and tipped his face up to the warm water, his mind drifting back to Gemma. Smart, beautiful, pushy-as-all-hell *Gemma*. Gemma in the short, sexy blue dress, her long legs and creamy thighs on display, tempting him in ways he hadn't been tempted for a very long time. The swell of her breasts peeking out of the neckline. His hand slid down to his throbbing cock, fisting around it and giving it a slow tug. He pictured Gemma's slim fingers beneath his, that seductive look in her garden-green eyes. *Stroke. Stroke.* Her tongue sweeping over those crimson lips as she dropped to her knees. *Stroke. Stroke.* He pressed his palm to the wall, swept up in his erotic fantasy, thrusting through his fist as the image of Gemma sucking him off took hold. He stroked faster, sliding his rough palm over the head, then streaking down faster, tighter. In his fantasy, Gemma's eyes watched him from below as she took him deeper, sucked him hard, coaxing him closer to the edge. Lust pooled at the base of his spine, and he thrust faster, groaning—"Gemma"—as his release crashed over him, through him, into him. He stumbled back, slamming into the tile wall and panting for air. *Holy fuck.*

"Truman?" Gemma said through the door.

His cock twitched with renewed anticipation. What the hell? It was like Pavlov's dog now? That wouldn't be cool.

"Yeah?" he ground out.

"I made you breakfast if you want it."

He dragged a hand down his face, feeling guilty. She'd made him breakfast and he'd just come down her fictional throat. "Thanks. Be right out."

He quickly scrubbed the evidence of his fantasy from his skin, brushed his teeth and hair, and wrapped a towel around his waist. Hurrying, he crossed the hall to the master bedroom, tripping over Gemma, who was crouched beside Kennedy, helping her dress.

Gemma gasped, lurching forward, both hands reaching for Kennedy to keep her from falling as Truman found his footing. She looked up with an *oh-shit* turned *oh-my* look in her eyes. Her red lips and hungry eyes were cock height, and his fantasy came rolling back in as she stared at the rising bulge behind his towel. Her cheeks flamed, but she didn't turn away. She calmly lifted those seductive eyes to his, licked her lips, and made a twirling motion with her finger, her head nodding toward Kennedy.

Aw hell. Kennedy. He turned away, silently cursing his traitorous cock for sucking the life out of his brain.

"Best not to overreact," she said quietly. "I thought you had clothes in the bathroom. Sorry." She lifted Kennedy into her arms, taking one last, long eyeful over her shoulder before saying, "Come on, sweetie. Let's go check on your sleeping baby brother and let your *big* brother get dressed."

As she disappeared through the door, he looked down at his rigid cock, knowing there weren't enough cold showers in the world to calm the flames raging inside him.

CHAPTER SEVEN

FOR THE HUNDREDTH time in as many minutes, Truman glanced at Gemma leaning against the doorframe of the side bay door in her skintight jeans and cream-colored top. She was smiling down at Kennedy, who was sitting a foot away in the grass happily playing with a princess doll Gemma had brought her and wearing the plastic tiara she'd also given her. The doll had a matching tiara. Kennedy was so taken with the gifts, she'd been playing with them all morning. Lincoln was asleep in the playpen a few feet away. Gemma had draped a blanket over the top of the playpen to keep the sun from making him too warm. She made taking care of kids look so easy, while he stressed over every little thing. The serenity of the scene conflicted with the chaotic night he'd had—the chaotic couple of days he'd had—and yet she made it seem attainable for more than a few minutes. But if anyone knew how quickly life could change, it was Truman.

Like this morning.

The scene in the bedroom played out before him once again—her calm, interested gaze, the way she'd licked her lips, like she wanted to remove his towel and taste him as badly as he wanted to devour her. While neither had said anything about their encounter, the heat between them had amped up to inferno levels. Every time their hands grazed, sparks ignited. Every glance smoldered. As a result, he'd been sporting a hard-on at half-mast all morning. Luckily, Dixie and Bear weren't coming in today, so there was no one else to witness his ridiculous half-cocked barrel.

"Anyway," Gemma said, bringing him back to their conversation. She was telling him about her princess shop.

Truman listened as she described the differences between a two-year-old's birthday party and a seven-year-old's, which apparently included a walk down a red carpet with lights and music and lots of fanfare.

"We do manicures and pedicures, hair and makeup, but that's not the best part. The best part is watching the kids pick out their outfits without their parents telling them what to wear. Some of the primmest girls pick leather and lace, while some of the tomboys pick frilly dresses." Her eyes lit up, and she looked past him, as if she were watching a scene unfold in the distance. "And then there's this moment when it all comes together and these little girls suddenly *become* different people. That's even better than watching them pick out the clothes, actually. That moment of revelation and freedom when they realize they can become anyone they want to be. I love that."

For the first time in as long as he could remember, he began seeing something other than dark images taking shape in his mind, and his fingers itched to create without being driven by frustration. Gemma was artistry in motion. As she told him about her shop, he imagined painting her. He envisioned ribbons of yellow, pinks, and orange interspersed with blues and purples for her hair. He imagined painting her face in a flurry of swirls and feathery strokes of pastels with bold streaks of navy and black for those seductive glimmers that shined through.

And her body? All those luscious curves and strength could only be painted as a mix of flawless beauty and sweet rebellion, with golds, pale greens, yellows, and hot pink.

"Now that you know my passion, will you tell me about your drawings?"

He shook his head to clear his thoughts. "You've seen them. Tell me more about you." He wanted to know everything, even if he wasn't ready to reciprocate. "Why princesses?"

She narrowed her sharp eyes in that serious but playful way she had. "Why drawings?"

He shifted his attention back to her car to avoid the question.

"You'll let me barge into your apartment at the crack of dawn, but you won't talk to me about your drawings?"

He smiled and glanced at her again. "Pretty much."

She rolled her eyes. She did that a lot instead of pushing him, which he liked. It gave him time to think. But truth be told, no one ever pushed him, and he kind of liked it when she did. He liked knowing she was interested in him even though he knew when she really got to know him, she'd walk the other way.

"If you won't talk to me about your drawings, and you won't share any more details about your mother, then tell me how it is that I've lived in Peaceful Harbor for a few years now and I've never seen you around."

She'd peppered him with questions over breakfast, while he did the dishes, and when he'd thrown a load of laundry into the washer. She'd asked the same questions in ten different ways. She was adorably persistent.

"Do you frequent this end of town?" he asked, knowing the answer. There wasn't much down by the bridge, save for

Whiskey Bro's.

"Well, no, but you must come into town sometimes."

He concentrated on working the dent from her door. "Sure, when I need something. I pretty much keep to myself, and I only moved here a few months ago."

"Where did you live before that?"

Behind bars. He wasn't about to go there. He kept his eyes trained on the interior of the door. "Where did you live before moving here?"

"I grew up two hours from here."

He chanced a glance. She was winding a lock of hair around her finger, looking so at ease, with a casual and beautiful smile that reached her eyes. Man, she killed him with that smile.

"Was it anything like Peaceful Harbor?"

She shook her head. "No. I grew up in a very different environment. I wasn't allowed to play in the grass with a doll for hours. I lived a rigid life in a gated community with music lessons, etiquette classes, private language tutors..." She wrinkled her nose.

"Why'd you come here?" Her lifestyle was a world away from his, which was another reason he should keep his pants zipped.

"Let's see." She released her hair and met his steady gaze. "Gated community, music lessons, private tutors."

He laughed softly at her candor. "Most people would give anything to have those things."

"Most people have no idea how awful those things are. All I ever wanted to do was flit around with fairy wings, dress up in ten-dollar costumes, and build a tent out of sheets. I had this dream of running through meadows without a nanny watching over me, you know? Just being a kid, maybe having a tea party with those plastic little cups and fake tea. Just once it would have been nice to have homemade vanilla cupcakes instead of a three-tiered ganache birthday cake. It would have been so easy for my parents to give me any of those things, too. And *time*," she said dreamily. "A few minutes of their time without any sort of agenda would have been the best gift of all. I wouldn't have cared what we did. We could have sat in an empty room and talked for all I cared."

She drew in a deep breath and looked away. "According to my parents, I wanted to 'live the life of a pauper instead of a princess,' and maybe they were right, because I didn't care about any of the things they did. I never wanted to play the piano or learn French." She shook her head. "I'm sorry. It's not a nice word. 'Pauper,' was theirs, not mine."

He glanced at Kennedy and realized pauper was a step up from the conditions in which she'd lived. "It's not offensive."

She nodded, her expression relieved. "All I wanted was *time*. Time with them, my own time to run and play and be a kid. I would rather have had nothing and been loved like I was everything than have everything and feel like a commodity for them to show off."

At first glance, he didn't think they'd have anything in common, and he wondered how he could be so attracted to someone who came from such a different world. But the more he learned about her, the more he realized they did have things in common. Important things that he'd never expected.

"So, why princesses? It seems like you would want to go in the opposite direction."

"Because Princess for a Day isn't about just being a frilly little princess who's given anything she wants. It's about being whoever the *children* dream of being. We have rocker princesses, academic princesses, construction worker princesses. You name it, we offer it. Goth, frills, leather, lace, tomboy, twisted…I wanted to call it You for a Day, but the marketing specialists I spoke to said no one would know what it was or who it was for." She shrugged. "So I went with *princess*. What was your childhood like?"

He turned his attention back to the car, grinding his teeth together. "How many times can you ask the same questions?"

"How many times can you avoid them?"

"Pretty damn many." He lifted his gaze and she was smiling again. "What?"

"You're cute when you're trying to be all macho and evasive."

He laughed. "Cute? Lincoln's cute. Kennedy's cute. I make you nervous, remember?"

"Yeah." She pushed from the doorframe. "I've rethought that particular adjective. I think 'feverish' is a better term." She turned away and joined Kennedy in the yard.

How was he supposed to concentrate with that knowledge bouncing around in his head? He tried to focus on repairing the dent, but his mind kept looping back to Gemma. He'd thought about her a lot last night as he was pacing the apartment in an effort to coax and soothe Lincoln back to sleep. When he'd heard the knock on the door this morning, he was sure the other shoe was dropping and feared the worst, like the police coming to tell him they'd found his brother lying dead somewhere, or the authorities coming to take the kids away. When he'd seen Gemma through the glass, not only had he been relieved, but he'd been excited. He liked being around her, despite her incessant questions. In fact, her curiosity was part of her appeal.

The gentle cadence of Gemma's voice carried him through the meticulous and time-consuming work. A little while later, she carried Lincoln into the garage and another wave of happiness swept through him. He rose to take Lincoln, feeling slightly off-kilter by the rush of emotions.

"It's okay. I can feed him," she said.

"I must be holding you up from something. You've been here for hours."

She flashed a sweet, careful smile. "Sick of me already?"

"Not even close," he said, stepping closer. "But you're not a babysitter, and you've been here since dawn."

"I don't feel like a babysitter. I like getting to know you and the kids."

He brushed his fingers over Lincoln's forehead, glad it felt cooler. Holding her gaze, he let his hand drop to her arm. Electricity spiked along his skin, but it was the way her lips parted and the dreamy sigh that slipped out that had his heart beating faster.

"Wouldn't you rather be someplace else?"

Without a word, she shook her head. The urge to take her beautiful face between his hands and claim the kiss he'd been dying for was so strong his hands began to twitch. One kiss, one taste, he told himself. It had been forever since he'd kissed a woman out of passion rather than as a means to an end.

"But I was thinking," she said, breaking his train of thought, "I'd really like to take Kennedy to my shop and let her play there."

Kennedy slipped her hand in his. He wasn't ready to let her out of his sight yet. "How about if we all go after I finish up here?"

"Like a date?" Her eyes shimmered with mischief.

He slid his hand from her arm to her waist, and man did that small touch feel incredible. She was soft and feminine, and the breeze carried the faint scent of vanilla from her hair. He wanted to smell that scent on her skin, to taste it in her sweat when she was in the throes of passion. They looked at each other for a long moment, a sensuous thread weaving between them. This was dangerous territory. She deserved a man without a torrid past, but he wanted *her*.

He wore the skin of a killer and bore the heart of a lover. That was the tangled web of lies he'd created to protect those he loved, and it would forever more be the cloak that shrouded him. Once he revealed his past, she'd never look at him like this again.

He leaned forward, intent on taking that kiss in case this was all there would ever be.

"Tooman," Kennedy's voice chirped, severing his tunnel vision.

They both looked down at the innocent-eyed little princess with the crooked tiara. That was the first time Kennedy had said his name, shaking up his whirling emotions even more.

He scooped his little sister into his arms and glanced at Gemma, who was blinking rapidly, as if she were trying to settle the wild wind they'd stirred, too.

"Yes, princess?" he asked Kennedy.

"Hungy."

Returning his gaze to Gemma so there was no escaping the desire or the intent in his voice, he said, "Me too, princess. I'm *ravenous*."

BREATHING WAS SUPPOSED to come easily and naturally, not hitched and ragged. And thinking? Gemma had always been a fast thinker, but after spending most of the day with Truman and the kids, she'd come into the boutique to get things ready for their arrival, and her thoughts kept scattering, circling back to the voracious look in Truman's eyes before lunch and the way his hands had lingered on her skin at different points throughout the afternoon. And when he'd tripped over her wearing nothing but a towel? Her entire body heated up with the memory of how aroused they'd *both* been. She'd never felt this type of all-consuming lust, and it was wreaking havoc with her body and her brain.

She sat down to strap on her gold Mary Janes. She always dressed up for the kids' parties. Tonight she was dressing up for Truman as much as she was for Kennedy. She'd taken forever deciding which outfit to wear, wanting to look sexy, but not like she was trying too hard. She'd finally settled on wearing one of her favorite costumes—Passion Princess. It was a sexy little number with puffy sleeves adorned with white bows that fit around her upper arms, leaving her shoulders bare. The dress was baby-blue satin with gold trim, an iridescent paisley print, and tiny gems lining the sweetheart neckline. It laced up the back and tied off with a large white bow. The golden overlay skirt hung low in the back, leaving her thigh-high stockings on display in the front. The midthigh-length skirt had the same golden paisley print with white lace trim on the bottom, and a white tulle underskirt gave the outfit a flirtatious bounce.

She pushed the blue satin headband into her hair, drawing the sides away from her face while leaving a few long tendrils hanging free. She pulled on white gloves that covered her finger to elbow and fastened the steel-blue choker with a blue gem that reminded her of Truman's eyes dangling from the center around her neck. Her stomach was doing somersaults at the prospect of Truman seeing her dressed like this.

Taking a quick look in the mirror, she couldn't stop smiling. She loved this outfit. It truly was her favorite. It was the right amount of sexy to make it appropriate for an adult and still fairy tale enough to alight all those magical feelings fairy tales were known for. She'd spent so many years dreaming of being someone else and making up stories in her head to escape her lonely, dull life that it made dressing up in costumes even more fun. She lived out all of the fantasies she'd never had a chance to as a little girl, which made coming to work even more enjoyable.

She went into the play area to put all the final preparations into place, setting out the baskets and racks of clothes for Kennedy and the cute little activity gym she'd picked up on the way over for Lincoln.

Her phone vibrated with a text, and Crystal's face appeared on the screen. It was nearly six o'clock. She was surprised Crystal had waited so long to prod her for details about her day. They'd talked late last night and Gemma had filled her in on her plans to see Truman this morning.

She opened and read the text. *Does he have any ink below his belt?* Winky and smiley face emoticons had never cut it for Crystal. She was more visual than that. Hence the next thread of images lighting up her phone—a string of tattooed penises.

"Ouch," Gemma mumbled as she typed her response. *I don't know, but that looks painful, so I hope not. We haven't even kissed yet. I'm not sure I'll survive a kiss!*

Crystal's response was immediate. *Won't survive a kiss? Oh, man. I think I might have to crash my car.*

Gemma scowled. *Oh no you won't! Hands off! Gotta run. He's going to be here any minute. Kennedy's playing princess tonight.*

The next text came seconds later. *And you're playing hide the sausage?*

Another text. *Wizard of O?*

Her phone vibrated like it was on steroids as her friend's texts rolled in. *Princess Swallows? Prince Cunnilingus? Hokey Pokey? Are you going to help him LET IT GO?!*

Gemma laughed as the bells on the front door chimed the boutique's special magical tune and Truman came in holding Kennedy's hand and carrying Lincoln in his car seat. She put her phone on the counter and he set those beguiling blue eyes on her and swallowed hard as she approached, making her melt like a Popsicle. Her stomach spun into knots. She loved knowing she was breaking through that gruff barrier he tried so hard to keep up. Although when he'd come out of the bathroom in that very thin towel, it was hard not to notice just how much she affected him.

"Hey there." Averting her eyes from his piercing stare, she noticed that he'd changed into a pair of low-slung jeans that hugged him in all the best places. Great, now she was staring at his junk—and trying not to wonder if it was tattooed. *Damn it, Crystal!*

"That's a…" He licked his lips, his eyes drifting slowly down her body, lingering on her thigh-high stockings. "That's a great outfit. We might need more princess days in our lives."

She wanted to wrap that compliment around her like a velvet cape, but the way he was visually devouring her made her skin tingle with anticipation of a touch she hoped might come. She needed to get herself under control and focus on the kids or she was going to turn into a noodle-legged, swooning mess.

Shifting her eyes away *again*, she locked the door behind them and said, "I'm glad you found it, and I see you took my advice about Lincoln's car seat."

"Your directions were perfect, and whoever thought this up was brilliant." He lifted the baby carrier, his wolfish grin morphing into an adoring brotherly smile aimed at the happy baby.

How did he do that when she was still mentally untying the knots that hungry grin had given her? She crouched beside Kennedy, feeling the heat of Truman's gaze return. The wolf was back! Maybe she should have worn her Little Red Riding Hood outfit.

CHAPTER EIGHT

"TRU, HOLD STILL. You're almost done." Gemma worked the top buttons on Truman's white poplin jacket—the fifth or sixth outfit she and Kennedy had picked out for him. "I'll have you know, this Prince Charming outfit is very much in demand."

"With you working the buttons, I bet it is," he said under his breath.

She stood before him in those white thigh-high stockings he was dying to take off—*with his teeth*—nibbling on her lower lip. Her eyes were set in pure concentration as she shifted and smoothed, running her hands all over his chest and shoulders and sending titillating explosions directly to his core. From his vantage point, he had an enticing view of the swell of her breasts. Her sexy princess outfit pushed them up adeptly, creating cleavage so deep he wanted to bury himself in it and never come out. She was the epitome of sultry innocence, and he was nothing short of a gawking, lecherous dude who was quickly losing the struggle to keep his hands to himself.

"Do you dress like this for all the events?" He fisted his hands to keep from touching her. Jealousy clawed its way up his spine at the thought of other men leering at her.

She shrugged, squinting as she fiddled with his gold cuffs

and then the black velvet epaulets on his jacket. "Depends on my mood. Sometimes I wear long satin gowns like the one Kennedy is wearing."

He glanced at Kennedy, playing with a basket of tiaras, and imagined Gemma in a long shiny gown, her slim shoulders bared for all to enjoy, like they were now, beckoning his mouth to taste her smooth, tempting skin. The green-eyed monster dug its claws in deeper.

"Sometimes I wear lacier outfits with more frills," she added. "Or shorter outfits. If I'm feeling really daring, I wear the leather biker princess outfit. That's always a hit with the parties. Oh, and the fairy princess with the wings like Kennedy tried on earlier. I love that one, too. It makes me feel light and fun."

He imagined fathers bringing their daughters in for events solely to get an eyeful of Gemma. He struggled to push the jealousy down deep, but it was a losing battle.

"Do the parents dress up?" he asked tightly.

She smiled, her eyes widened with joy, and she nodded. "Sometimes." She ran her hands along the length of his arm, then from his chest to his waist, smoothing his jacket. "Oops, hold on." She knelt before him to fix the hem of his pants.

Holy fucking hell, it was his fantasy all over again. His temperature didn't just spike, it exploded, flaming beneath his skin, searing outward from his chest, racing down his spine, to the very depth of his bones—and his jealousy burned along the same path.

"Do you help the men dress?" She wasn't his to be jealous over and he knew he was a jerk for asking, but he was powerless to rein in the ugly emotions gnawing at him.

"Mm-hm." She popped up to her feet and stepped back, openly admiring him. "You look..." She sighed longingly and patted his cheek. "Like the baddest Prince Charming I've ever seen."

That touch. That voice. That sigh—*this woman.* His arm circled her waist like a bullet, tugging her against him so hard she let out a sexy little *squeak*.

"Bad as in not good?" he growled—an effect of his raging desire.

She pressed a dainty gloved hand to his cheek, her entrancing green eyes holding him captive as she spoke in a sultry tone befitting of a vixen rather than a princess. "Baddest, as in badass, coolest, *hottest* Prince Charming this princess has ever seen."

He felt her heart hammering against his, tasted her breath as it swept upward toward his mouth, and when her hand came to rest on his back, he warmed beneath her touch. He brushed his lips over her cheek, inhaling the vanilla scent of her shampoo, then pressed his face to her neck, filling his senses with another feminine scent—the scent of desire. Her fingers curled tighter against him, and his hand pressed more firmly to her back. He drew away, gazing into her eyes, which had gone dark and trusting.

"Three days ago, princesses weren't even on my radar," he whispered over her lips. "Now I'll never be able to hear that word without remembering you wearing this killer outfit, helping my kids, touching me."

"*Your* kids," she said with a shaky voice.

"Brother and sister," he corrected, then thought better of it. "But they're babies. They feel like they're my kids even though they're my siblings."

She nodded. "I know. I see that."

He looked at Lincoln, so tiny and innocent, finally eating as he should, sleeping safe and warm in a proper crib with someone to love and watch over him. And Kennedy, happily playing, smiling at herself in the mirror with her hair freshly combed and washed, her tummy full, and her heart…Well, he was working on filling that up, too.

"They're my kids, Gemma," he repeated. "Have been from the day I found them."

She rested her palm on his chest and her breath left her lungs, her fingers curling, *claiming*, her gaze serious and so full of emotions he couldn't even try to wade through them.

"I know," she said.

He felt Kennedy's hand on his leg as she tried to wiggle between them. He and Gemma both smiled, easing apart to let her in. Silent longing filled the space between them as Kennedy held her arms up toward Gemma. He felt a fissure form in his heart, a small tear at the sight of his little girl reaching for the only woman to make him feel something for the first time in years—maybe even in his life. The warmth in Gemma's eyes nearly did him in as she lifted Kennedy into her arms and Kennedy rested her head on Gemma's shoulder.

Truman swallowed past the new and unexpected emotions clogging his throat and pressed a kiss to Kennedy's cheek. "Time to go home, princess." He was speaking to Kennedy, though his eyes were still trained on Gemma.

He knew he should let whatever this was between them go, to allow her to find a more suitable guy, someone whose past wouldn't always hold him down and need explaining. But he'd spent his life doing things to protect others and putting himself last. Just this once, he wanted to feed the lover's heart he possessed, regardless of the killer's skin he wore.

"Come home with me," he said hopefully.

GEMMA LAID LINCOLN in his crib as Truman settled Kennedy in the bed. Gemma hadn't realized he'd given up his bed. Now the blankets on the couch made more sense.

Truman lay with Kennedy, tenderly whispering to her as she dozed off. "Sweet dreams, little princess. You're safe. You're loved. I'm right here."

A lump formed in Gemma's throat. After changing out of their prince and princess outfits, they'd returned to his apartment in separate cars, giving her just enough time to get nervous about where they were heading. Now all those nerves floated away, and in their place was something magical, something so overwhelmingly powerful, Gemma didn't even try to question it.

Truman Gritt was hard, he was tattooed, and he looked like he hadn't shaved in weeks. He was all the things she never thought she'd want, and in two days he'd shown her that none of those things mattered. And, she realized with an inward cringe, she'd initially judged him the same way her mother might have. She hated that and vowed to never do it again. Beneath all that rough armor was the kindest, gentlest, most loyal man she could ever imagine. He wasn't Prince Charming, and he wasn't the type of man her mother would ever approve of. But he was real, and he was good, and at this very second, as he unfolded his massive, masculine frame and maneuvered around the bedrails he must have bought over the last day for Kennedy's bed, he looked at Gemma like he'd just left a chunk of his heart on the mattress. She felt herself falling for him. It was impossible to fall for a man she barely knew, but as he took her hand in his and reached for the baby monitor with the other—*when did he buy that?*—impossible no longer mattered.

CHAPTER NINE

ALL IT TOOK was a glance, and Truman and Gemma were all over each other, kissing wildly as they pushed open the door to the deck and stumbled outside. Truman couldn't yank the door closed and set down the monitor fast enough. Even a second away from Gemma's sweet lips was too long. He'd never been so thankful for an outdoor sofa in his life as he was at this very moment as he and Gemma tumbled down in a fiery, passionate tangle of groping hands and hungry kisses. Her hands clawed and explored, finding their way beneath his shirt, eliciting a primal groan that felt as though it was ripped from his lungs. God, he wanted her. *All* of her. Her kisses, her hands, her fuckable mouth, her giving heart. Cupping her ass with one hand, her cheek with the other, he took the kiss deeper, their hips grinding and thrusting to the same frantic pace. She moaned into the kiss, sending lust sizzling through his core.

"Fuck, Gemma," he ground out, glad the kids were safely asleep behind closed doors and couldn't hear them.

Her eyes widened and just as quickly narrowed.

"I love your mouth—"

She grabbed his head, suffocating his words in another fierce kiss, a kiss that told him she was right there with him, so ready, so willing. His hand left her ass, seeking *more*, moving hard and fast over her hip, her ribs, to her full breasts, earning another needy moan. He drew back, pushed her shirt up, and his whole body shuddered at the sight of her creamy skin and taut, dark nipples straining against a pink lace bra with dainty satin bows at the edge of each strap.

"Christ," he uttered.

She smiled up at him and ran a finger along the edge of his cheek.

"Sorry," he said. "I just...You're just..."

There were no words to describe the way her beauty slayed him, and he didn't waste seconds trying. He unhooked the clasp and pushed the cups aside, taking one luscious nipple in his mouth and filling his hand with her other breast. She arched beneath him, fisted her hands in his hair, moaning and writhing, holding him in place.

"Oh *God.* That feels *so* good."

He teased and sucked, grazing his teeth over the sensitive tip. She inhaled a sharp breath, and he smiled as he did it again, loving this wild side of her. He drew back, using the tip of his tongue to tease slow circles around the hard peak. Rolling her other nipple between his finger and thumb and squeezing just hard enough to earn another wanton moan, he continued the torturous pleasure. Her hands moved over his shoulders, along his biceps, clutching him tight as one of her legs wrapped around his, her foot resting on the back of his calf. Damn, he liked the feel of her tangled up in him. He wanted to learn all the things that drove her crazy. Did she like to be fingered, licked, sucked, taken hard and fast or slow and sensual? He shifted, taking her breast in his mouth again as his hand moved over her hip and dipped between her legs.

Holy fuck. Her jeans were hot and, if he wasn't mistaken,

damp. His cock throbbed behind his zipper. He kissed his way down her belly, which rose with each quick breath. Seeing his tattooed hand against her soft femininity made him harder, pushed him further. He imagined burying himself deep inside her, imagined seeing those perfect breasts bouncing as she rode his cock.

He lowered his teeth to the button on her jeans, ready to throw caution to the wind and let their wild desires lead them. But putting the kids to bed had kicked open the door to his past. Truman wanted to be selfish, to take everything she was willing to give and deal with the ramifications later, but as he thought about pushing his hands beneath that denim and seeking the wet heat he so desperately wanted, his conscience kicked in. He drew back, gritting his teeth, telling that fucking voice in his head to shut the hell up, but no matter how much he tried to convince himself otherwise, he wasn't that type of man. And more than that, this—whatever *this* was—was totally different from anything he'd ever experienced. Gemma wasn't a poolroom chick looking for a fast fuck who didn't care about his past because she wanted nothing more than to get off. He needed to slow this runaway train long enough to let her in, at least enough for her to make the decision to go further with clarity.

Another mind-blowing realization. He'd never let a woman into his life before. His chest constricted at the prospect.

He reluctantly released that tiny flap of denim and pressed his mouth to the sensitive skin just below her belly button, slicking his tongue over it as if his mouth were nestled between her legs. He couldn't resist sliding his tongue beneath the waist of her jeans. She arched her hips. He was *this close* to kicking his conscience to the curb, but when he lifted his eyes and saw her blissful, trusting expression, another organ constricted.

His heart.

His heart brought his mouth to her belly in an apologetic kiss. His heart made him move up her body and refasten her bra despite her resistance, right her shirt, and gather her in his arms. He pressed his cheek to hers and breathed her in—her lust, her sweetness, her disappointment—memorizing all of it. All of her, because once he said what he had to say, she'd be gone.

"I want to make you feel more than you've ever felt in your life," he said in her ear, unable to look into her eyes just yet. "I want to eat you for breakfast, hold your hand and fuck you until you feel me the next day."

"Then do it," she said breathlessly.

"I don't want to hurt you." He forced himself to draw back and meet her confused gaze. He felt the rigid edge of a knife slicing down his chest, a hand reaching inside the broken walls, clutching that organ that was driving him.

Her lips curved up, but she trapped the lower one in her teeth and ran a tender finger along his hairline. "Are you *that* big?"

He laughed and dropped his forehead to her shoulder for a brief moment of sheer and utter euphoria.

When he met her gaze again, she was smiling.

"Yes, but that's the least of my worries."

She mouthed, *Wow*, her smile growing wider.

He returned her smile, but reality pushed its ugly head in, stifling the happy moment. Hating to spoil this, *her*, *them,* he gazed into her eyes and said, "I want you, Gemma. I've never wanted anyone so badly in my life, but if we cross that line, it has to be with honesty from the very start."

He drew in a deep breath as the dark lie he lived under

shadowed all hints of a smile, of hope, of anything good he'd felt seconds earlier, and the painful, horrible truth came out.

"I'm not the man you think I am."

GEMMA LAY BENEATH Truman in a cloud of confusion. Her body was still thrumming from his touch, his kisses, and the emotions that seemed to seep from him and slither beneath her skin. But he was pushing away, sitting up and helping her do the same, and the torment in his eyes brought shivers of worry, scattering those decadent feelings.

"I don't…" She swallowed hard. "I don't understand."

He leaned his elbows on his knees and gazed into the darkness. Tension radiated off of him, fighting against something else, something much sadder, further confusing her.

He shook his head, his chin dropping to his chest, those intense blue eyes closing briefly, shutting her out. She felt his retreat, could almost *see* his walls cinching into place as his eyes opened. His jaw lifted, tightened, and he stared intently into the night. A deep inhalation expanded his chest. His shoulders squared as he turned to face her with a colder, guarded expression, like she'd seen the first night they'd met. In the space of a breath she saw sadness brimming in his eyes, and then, as if he'd pulled a curtain, his gaze shuttered again.

"What I have to tell you will make you question everything you thought you knew about me. It will probably infuriate you, and it might even make you wonder if you can trust your own instincts."

"You're scaring me," she admitted warily.

He nodded, his jaw working over whatever was in his head.

"I know. I'm sorry. But I can't touch you like we both want me to with this hanging over my head."

A nervous laugh escaped her lips. "You make it sound like you're some kind of awful person."

He shook his head, his mouth curving down in a frown. "I don't even know what I am anymore, but I know I'm not the guy who can take anything more from you without being honest."

"Truman, what does that mean, 'you don't know what you are anymore'?" She shifted, putting a few inches between them.

He scrubbed a hand over his face. His scruff jumped as the muscles beneath clenched. "You asked about my childhood. It was nothing like yours, which I assume you've realized by now. The only reason we had a roof over our heads was because my grandmother left my mother her house in her will. At some point she must have sold it, or abandoned it. God only knows. My mother was like cancer. She destroyed everything she touched."

"She didn't destroy you," she said softly, unable to keep from caressing his arm.

His eyes dropped to where her fingers lay, and then they blinked slowly, remaining closed for a beat before fluttering open again.

"Yes, she did." He paused, his struggle written in the lines mapping his face, the darkness burrowing into his gaze. "It's a miracle I survived childhood, but by the time I realized she had a problem…I was a kid. I had no idea. I don't even know when she began using drugs. She was fourteen when she had me. My grandmother was still alive and we lived with her, but she was a mess, too. Who knows? Maybe I was the reason she started using. Lord knows I'm learning how hard it is to raise an infant, and the way she treated me, it's an easy assumption to make."

He paused, and she could barely breathe. Her fingers tightened around his arm. She wanted to hold him until his painful past disappeared, but she sensed his walls and knew that the small touch he was allowing her was as much as he was going to accept right now.

"My memories aren't clear enough to know much about when I was young, but what I do know is that after my grandmother passed away, things got bad. And when Quincy was born, things got even worse."

"Quincy?"

"My brother," he said softly. "I basically raised him until…for many years."

"I didn't know you had another brother. Do you have other siblings?"

He shook his head. "The night I found the kids was the first time I'd seen Quincy in months. The last time was when I pulled him out of a crack house and tried to get him help. He wanted no part of me or my help. As far I know, I don't have any more siblings."

His voice cracked, and he cleared his throat, shifting his body so her hand slipped off his arm. He stared into the darkness again.

"I told him to stay away from the kids until he gets clean. I don't even know their birthdays." His eyes glazed over, and he cocked his head to the side, looking at her with a solemn expression. "The doctor thinks Kennedy is around two and a half and Lincoln is around five months." He pressed his finger and thumb to the bridge of his nose, as if he were in pain, and turned away again.

Thank God those babies had him. Tears welled in her eyes,

and when she touched his back, he bristled and lifted his eyes toward the sky, blinking repetitively.

"Yes, you do," she said softly. "You know their birthdays. Thursday the fifteenth of September. The day you rescued them."

He turned with tears in his eyes and a blatant lack of embarrassment that cut straight to her heart. He didn't say a word, simply leaned forward and wrapped her in his arms, holding her so tight it was hard to breathe. He held her for a long time, and after he'd been so honest with her, it felt right to be in his arms. When he drew back, the tears were gone, the hard set of his jaw in place once again, and her stomach sank, realizing there was more.

How much more could one man endure?

He set a serious, and once again apologetic, gaze on her. She wanted to tell him there was no apology necessary, that they didn't get to choose their parents. But that would mean speaking, and her throat was too thick with emotion to manage a single word.

"After Quincy was born, a string of men came in and out of our lives. Never for long, and not good men. Users, pushers, collectors, in for a day, a night, a week. My mother would come home bruised and high. She'd disappear into the bedroom with a guy and tell me to watch Quincy, which was a joke. That woman never paid him any attention. She'd shove a bottle in his mouth to shut him up, but that's about as far as it went. I won't bore you with the details of my shithole life, but I moved out when I was eighteen and tried to take Quincy with me. She sicced one of her crackheads on me. He had a gun and pretty much told me to stay the fuck away from the house. I didn't listen."

"Jesus. Your own mother did that to you?" She couldn't hide her disbelief.

He nodded. "Bear Whiskey, a guy I'd met, took me under his wing and taught me to work on cars. When I moved out, he rented me this apartment. His family became my family. He and Dixie, his sister, run Whiskey Automotive, and they run the bar with their other brothers, Bones and Bullet." He must have caught her curious expression, because he said, "Biker names. Anyway, I grew up across the bridge, and I was afraid of causing trouble for Quincy, so we worked out a schedule of sorts. Our mother would go out for hours, supposedly for work, but..."

He drew in a deep breath and blew it out slowly. "Anyway, for a few years we saw each other every other day or so. I gave him money for food, bought him clothes, whatever he needed. And then one day I showed up and heard screaming coming from inside the house."

Truman covered his mouth and closed his eyes, as if whatever he was going to say made him physically ill. His hand dropped to his thigh, and he turned so his whole body faced her.

"My only thought was *Quincy* when I barged through the front door." His voice was low and contemptuous. He pushed to his feet, pacing the deck, rubbing his hands on his jeans, wringing them together, and raking them through his hair, every determined step heightening the tension rolling off him.

"Quincy was huddled on the floor with a gash on his cheek and blood on his shirt, shaking uncontrollably." He gritted his teeth as he spoke, the veins in his neck bulging, his hands fisting so hard his knuckles blanched. "A man I'd never seen before was violently raping our mother. I tried to pull him off and he swung back, knocking me away. There was a knife on the table…"

GEMMA GASPED, TEARS streaming down her cheeks as Truman leaned his palms on the railing and his head dropped between his shoulders. Memories slammed into him, momentarily sucking the wind right out of him. He wanted to tell her he didn't do it. That the knife was already bloody, the deed was already done when he'd walked in the door, but the words wouldn't come—and he knew they never would. His brother might be fucked up, but Truman couldn't give up hope that one day Quincy would find his way back to a cleaner, better life. And Truman would not be the man who fucked that up for him. He'd keep their secret until he breathed his last breath, no matter what the cost.

Lifting unseeing eyes toward the dark abyss before him, he said, "I wasn't supposed to go to prison. The guy was involved in some big-time drug ring. The public defender called it a 'heat of passion' murder. But my mother lied in court. She said she wasn't in any danger. For twenty-two fucking years she couldn't clean up her act enough to be a proper parent, and she somehow managed to get clean for long enough to send her son to prison."

CHAPTER TEN

GEMMA THOUGHT HER father's suicide was the worst thing she'd ever have to face. She thought the worst thing a person could do was *choose* to leave their loved ones behind. But *this*? Truman being thrust into such tragic surroundings, having no choice but to rescue his mother and brother from the horrific situation she brought into their home? And his mother not only turning her back on the son who put his own life in jeopardy to save her, but also sending him to prison? She couldn't wrap her mind around such a dreadful scenario, much less what his upbringing must have been like. She was trembling all over, breathing hard, tears raining down her cheeks, and when she finally found the courage to look at him, Truman was still standing with his back to her. His shoulders rounded forward, as if all the air had deflated from his chest.

A chill spread through her as she tried to grasp what he'd told her. He had killed a man.

Killed.

He had taken a knife and ended a man's life.

To save his family.

How does a person process that information? She had a million questions—and about as many fears. Would he do it again? Was he unstable? Was he telling her the truth?

Breathe in. Breathe out. That was about as much as she could handle.

Lincoln's whimpers came through the baby monitor. Truman turned slowly. His gaze never came near her as he walked into the house, as if on autopilot, and disappeared into the bedroom.

She exhaled a long breath and gripped the edge of her seat, trying to make sense of the overwhelming pieces of his past he'd just revealed.

When Truman returned to the deck, she stood on wobbly legs, trying to reconcile the man she'd come to know with the person he'd just admitted to being. It was all too much, his painful expression, the ache in her heart, the weight of his confession.

"I didn't expect you to still be here," he said solemnly.

Her eyes filled with more tears and her hand flew to her mouth, untrusting of what might come out. Emotions bubbled up inside her as her thoughts swam—his bravery, his loyalty, *his crime*. Hearing his confession didn't wipe away what she felt for him. The words weren't delete buttons; they were painful, heavy truths, each one landing like lead on the good she saw in him, weighing it down, driving it deeper into a sea of unknowns. At the same time, all the goodness that had drawn her to him since the get-go and magnified with every moment they spent together refused to sink. They flailed beneath the negative weight, trying to win, trying to rise above the darkness, leaving her gasping for air.

He nodded silently, a look of resigned acceptance in his eyes. He picked up the baby monitor and turned to go inside.

"Truman—" His name flew desperately from her lips, and when he turned, her heart cracked open. She knew what devastation looked like. She'd seen it in her mother's eyes after her father took his life, and she'd seen it in her own reflection in the mirror in the weeks that followed, when their world crumbled down around them and her mother became even colder, losing herself in anything *but* caring for her daughter.

"I don't…I can't…" Too overcome with emotions, she took a step back and pressed her hand to the railing to stabilize herself from the spinning world around her.

"It's okay, Gemma," he reassured her. "That's why I stopped us from going any further."

You stopped us. Even amid all that passion, you were thinking of me. She didn't think as she touched his hand, needing the connection despite her confused state. His fingers were shaking as much as hers were. "It's…" She gulped a breath to try to calm her nerves. "It's a lot to take in."

He nodded solemnly. "I couldn't mislead you."

"Did you…? How long were you…?" She couldn't even say the words. Saying them made it even more real.

"I served six years of an eight-year sentence for voluntary manslaughter, and I've been out for six months. Every Thursday morning I call and check in with the parole office, and I'll continue to do that until the full term of my sentence is complete. Not a day goes by that I don't think about that man. I wanted to save my mother and protect Quincy, but no part of me wanted to *kill* him. I wanted to *stop* him. I *needed* to stop him."

He was breathing hard, like everything he had rode on those words. What was it like for him, living with that on his shoulders, made worse by the complete and total loss of his mother's love? How many times had he been forced to explain his past? *Voluntary manslaughter. Six years in prison.*

Prison. The word echoed in her mind.

"Gemma, I swear to you, I've never used drugs a day in my life, and—"

She held up her hand, unable to listen to more. Not now. It was too painful after feeling so much so fast. Too scary to think his past had actually happened to him. To *anyone*. Too overwhelming to think he'd witnessed and been through all that he had. She needed space, time. *Air*.

She needed to breathe.

"I'm sorry," she said as she pushed past him and made her escape.

TRUMAN STOOD ON the deck long after he heard Gemma drive away. He'd spent six long years honing his ability to turn off his emotions, and tonight, as pain coursed through his veins and anger gnawed at his gut for all the parts of his life he hadn't chosen—and the parts he had—he realized he'd been repressing his emotions for a hell of a lot longer than that.

When his mother had irreparably screwed him over, he'd felt like she'd stabbed him in the chest. When he'd found out Quincy was using, that knife had jammed in deeper. When he'd tried to help Quincy and his brother had turned him away with hatred in his eyes, it was like he'd yanked on the knife, slicing him open from naval to sternum. And when he'd found out he had two siblings who had been living a life no child should ever have to, he felt like someone had grabbed each side of that gaping wound and torn it open, allowing his guts to pour out.

Gemma walking away should feel like a pinprick. He hadn't known her long enough to validate the way she sucked the air out of his lungs.

His next move took no thought. He had to move on, to push past the fucking self-loathing for the choices he'd made. Only he didn't think he'd made the wrong decisions, because he would do it all over again to protect Quincy. But this time he'd be smart enough to turn his mother in to the police and get Quincy into a stable home, instead of leaving him there without anyone to protect him from his mother's dirty habits. She'd always left Quincy alone. She'd left Quincy to *him*. And then she'd put him in jail.

At the threshold to his bedroom, he crammed all those awful memories aside, forcing himself to leave them outside. He couldn't allow any of those noxious emotions to touch the kids. Closing his eyes, he breathed deeply, using all the mental techniques Bear had taught him to clear his mind. The techniques that had carried him through his adult life. Only then did he enter the bedroom and turn on the radio very softly, making sure he could hear it through the monitor. Bear had given him the long-distance video monitoring system as a gift when he'd come by earlier. He'd also watched the kids so Truman could shower before seeing Gemma. Bear was as taken with the babies as Truman was. When Truman had gone to jail, he had offered to try to fight for custody of Quincy, but Bear's past wasn't exactly *clean*, and Truman worried that the truth would come out. He wasn't willing to chance his brother being tried as an adult, and he wasn't about to implicate Bear in the crime by telling him the truth about what had happened.

He brushed a kiss to Kennedy's forehead. "Love you, princess." Leaning into the crib, he touched his lips to Lincoln's forehead and was relieved to feel his fever had relented. "Love you, buddy."

His heart swelled within his chest. He didn't know if he'd ever see Gemma again, but he knew there was no way in hell he'd ever look at these babies again and *not* think of her.

With the monitor in hand, he locked the front door, turned on the porch light, and headed out back. He carried the metal box from the deck and made his way down the steps and through the wooden gate to the junkyard. The weight of his painting supplies was familiar *and* unsettling. He stopped inside the gate, checked the video reception on the monitor, and turned up the volume. Hearing the radio loud and clear, he made his way to one of the cars he *hadn't* yet released his demons on, set up the monitor, and unpacked his supplies.

Eleven shades of black, including his favorites, raven, spider, obsidian, grease, and soot. Seven shades of gray. Gauntlet and meteor shower were his go-to grays. Images of Gemma suddenly burst into his mind—Gemma admiring his drawings, holding Lincoln, looking up at him after he stumbled into her in the bedroom, and finally, with tears in her eyes as she pushed past him, fleeing from his apartment. He trudged up to the shop, monitor in hand, and retrieved another box of paints. Truman didn't plan his artwork. He didn't think about style or design or much of anything. His art was an extension of him, born of wars, old and new. As the familiar sound of aerosol soothed his ravaged soul, he disappeared into the zone.

When Lincoln whimpered, he was surprised to see three hours had passed. He gathered his things and headed up to the apartment—never once looking back. He never looked back. It was the only way to leave the demons behind—and still they slithered after him, sneaking under the crevice of doorways, through cracks in his armor, and sticking to him like glue.

CHAPTER ELEVEN

SUNDAY EVENING GEMMA threw open her apartment door, set her hand on her hip, and glared at Crystal. "How many times do you need to hear 'I'm fine' before you believe me?"

Crystal rolled her eyes and *clomped* into the house.

"I'm sure my downstairs neighbors appreciate your combat boots."

"You think so?" Crystal stomped her foot three times. "I hope they like my torn jeans and skull shirt, too. If not, I'll send my boot right up their ass." She stalked into the living room and looked around, lifting the couch cushions, checking behind the curtains and under the table.

"What are you looking for?" She was *not* in the mood to play games. She'd spent the day trying to get lost in one of her women's fiction novels to escape thoughts of Truman and ended up re-creating the characters of every story in her head, imagining how the story would change if the hero was an ex-con who had killed a man.

"My bestie, Gemma Wright. Maybe you know her? She's your doppelgänger, but she *calls* me when shit goes down in her life. She doesn't hole up in her apartment and give me some line of crap about being *fine*." Crystal plowed forward, invading

Gemma's personal space. "Gemma doesn't say she's *fine* when she *is* fine. She says girly words like 'fantabulous' or 'peachy.' And she doesn't say 'fine' when she's not. She says she's 'pissed' or 'angry' or wishes she could smash something."

Gemma rolled her eyes. "I was graced with a call from Mommy Dearest earlier. I hit my limit and couldn't fathom another discussion." Her mother would probably have a heart attack on the spot if she knew Gemma was dating a man who had been in prison. *Why does that give me a slight ripple of joy?*

"What happened? Did her servants forget to serve her tea and she wanted you to run your ass two hours to her place to fetch it?"

"I didn't answer it. Her message said"—she drew her shoulders back and used a high-pitched proper tone—"*Gemaline, darling. Don't forget the fundraiser is only two months away. Be sure to wear your pearls. All proper girls wear pearls, blah, blah, blah.*"

"Oh, Mommy Wright, you are a little minx, aren't you?" Crystal waggled her brows. "A pearl necklace is a killer idea, but it might get a little sticky." She motioned with her hand like she was jerking off a guy.

They both cracked up, and boy did Gemma need that laugh.

"Why does she bother calling you? She knows you'll show up for your annual daughterly commitment, and she knows you'll do all the right things. Wear your pretty pearls. The shiny kind, not sticky heat-of-passion cumdrops. Don a new fabulous gown, and you'll leave right after dinner."

"I've got a better one for you," Gemma said flatly. "Why did she bother having me at all?" Gemma trudged over to the couch and flopped down.

Crystal followed her to the couch but remained standing. "Because everyone knows rich people need children to fit in with the Joneses. God forbid anyone should have something they don't. After all, money can buy anything, right? Even nannies to fill in for absent parents." She set her hand on her hip and stared at Gemma. "I just came from the shop."

"So?"

"So…your badass tattoo man left a message. Do you care to explain why he's leaving you a message at the shop and not texting you?"

Gemma's stomach tumbled. She was happy he had reached out but sad at the same time. Still too overwhelmed to think straight, she fidgeted with the edge of the cushion. "We never exchanged numbers."

Crystal plunked down beside her and studied her face. "Mm-hm. What happened last night?"

"What did his message say?"

"Tit for tat?" Crystal lifted her chin.

Gemma's emotions were all over the map. She'd been reining in her sadness all day, and every time she thought she had it under control, anger pushed in, followed by heartache again. It was a race to the finish line and she was climbing over each unwanted emotion and falling on her ass time and time again.

"Titty for tatty?" Crystal arched a brow, and they both laughed.

"Yes, he got tit and…I like his tats?" Gemma choked out between laughs.

"Or, he got tit and gave you a tat? The tat on his big, fat—" Crystal fell forward laughing. "Finally those girls of yours got some action."

It felt so good to get out of her own chaotic head, Gemma

had tears in her eyes.

Crystal picked up one of the paperbacks from the coffee table, her laughter quieting. "Four women's fiction books is *not* a good sign. Come on." She pushed to her feet and pulled Gemma up with her. She grabbed Gemma's keys and dragged her out the front door.

"Where are we going?" Gemma asked, trying to keep up as Crystal pulled her down the stairs.

"Luscious Licks. One way or another I'm going to find out why Truman said you could pick up your car and leave the keys to the loaner on the seat so you wouldn't have to see him."

Gemma stopped at the sidewalk. "He said that?"

Crystal looped her arm through Gemma's and tugged her toward the corner ice-cream store. "He did," she said softly. "He said he knew you wouldn't want to see him, but that he'd finished fixing your car and he'd leave the keys on the front seat and for you to do the same with the loaner. Gem, what happened?"

She still couldn't get herself to verbalize what he'd done. "I'll tell you. I just need a few minutes." *Or a lifetime.*

They walked in silence to Luscious Licks, the scent of sugary goodness bringing an air of happiness Gemma wasn't ready to accept.

"Hey, girlfriends," Penny, the perky woman who owned Luscious Licks, looked up from the freezer. She had hair the color of walnuts, and it was pinned up in a funky twist, held in place with a big clip. Her bright smile dropped into a firm line. "Uh-oh, what's going on?"

Crystal put an arm around Gemma and said, "We're not having a great day."

"Then we'd better get some ice cream on tap. *Stat!*" Penny

waved to the flavor board. "Want me to mix you up a Go Away Gloomy Day special? Or is this a man problem? I could whip you up a He's a No-Good Pile of Poop sundae. Lots of chocolate with mashed-up Oreos and gumdrops."

Gemma stared at the flavor board. "I don't think I could stomach either, but thanks, Pen."

"Oh, one of *those* days." Penny turned and filled a cup with ice cream, then she went to what she called the *hard-knocks cabinet*, where Gemma knew she kept tiny bottles of liquor, and poured something over the top. She handed it to Gemma. "Eat this. Brown sugar and brandy. A little delish dish to take the edge off."

"Thanks, Penny." Even the thought of eating made Gemma's stomach churn, but she couldn't refuse Penny's offer. Gemma had spent countless hours chowing down on her ice cream while writing her community newsletters. Penny had been the subject of her first article when she'd moved to the Harbor, and she always felt inspired when she was here. But tonight all she felt was the desire to head down to the other end of town and see Truman.

Crystal ordered a four-flavor soft-serve cone, and practically drooled when Penny handed it to her. The colorful layers of mango, pistachio, blueberry, and lemon were Crystal's favorites. The combination made Gemma feel sick.

Penny came around the counter and hugged Gemma. "This one's on the house for my two favorite princesses."

A group of teenagers came through the front door laughing and joking around.

Penny lowered her voice and said, "The little redhead has a thing for the guy with the trendy haircut." Then, louder, she said, "Good luck with whatever's gloomin' on you today. I hope the ice cream helps, and if not, there's a liquor store around the corner." She winked and went to tend to the customers.

As Crystal reached for a chair, Gemma headed for the door. "Let's sit down by the water instead."

They ate their ice creams in silence as they made their way down to the beach. She loved that Crystal knew her well enough not to prod her for information. She also loved that her friend knew her well enough to drag her out of her apartment. It was just what she needed to try to refocus and figure things out.

They took off their shoes and walked down to the edge of the water to sit in the sand. Being near water never failed to put Gemma in a good mood, but today it barely dulled the ache.

"When I didn't hear from you last night, I thought…You seemed so into Truman."

"I was into him. I *am* into him." The admission rocked inside her like a paddleboat in a storm.

"So? What's the issue?" She watched Gemma mix the remaining ice cream in her cup into mush. "I've never seen you like this. Usually if you've had a bad day, you gobble your way through as much ice cream as you can handle. What happened?"

Gemma set the cup in the sand and glanced at the people on the beach and the waves rolling up the shore, trying to put words to what she felt, as she'd tried throughout the day—and failed. Epically.

She shook her head, her voice failing her.

"It's okay. I've got all night. When you're ready to pour your heart out, I'm here. Or I could, you know, go beat the shit out of him."

Gemma laughed and patted Crystal's leg. She was wearing what Gemma called her skeleton jeans, which were black with horizontal slashes all the way up each leg. "He could squash you with one hand tied behind his back." She thought about what she'd said and added, "But he never would."

Crystal finished her cone and changed the subject to the shop, giving Gemma a little reprieve, until the conversation circled back to last night.

"I saw the new baby gym was still at the shop and wondered what was up."

"You should have seen him when we were playing around at the shop. Kennedy picked out all these outfits for him to wear. The dark prince, the flower prince, which was hilarious, and of course, Prince Charming. He didn't fight it like some of the guys do. He looked at that little girl's face and told her he'd be whatever she wanted him to be."

"Sounds like he loves those kids," Crystal said.

"He does. *So* much, Crys. He wants them to feel safe and loved, and I have no doubt he'll do whatever it takes to make sure they are." Just like he did for his mother and brother. The ache in her heart intensified with the thought. "I fell really hard for him last night."

"Then why did he sound like he'd lost his best friend on the machine, and why are you alone instead of spending the day with him?"

Gemma looked out at the water. She'd debated going over and talking to him all afternoon. She had so many questions, but every time she thought about voicing them, sadness consumed her.

"Have you ever wanted a guy so much that the thought of not having him made you feel like you wanted to cry, only you couldn't pinpoint the reasons why—you just felt it in your bones?" she asked tentatively.

"Yeah. Remember Thirteen-Inch Theo, the guy I told you about from high school?"

"So many escapades, so little time," Gemma said. "I'm serious."

"Then the answer is no, because I've never met any man who could deal with who I am and not think I'm a freak for one reason or another."

Gemma looked at her gorgeous raven-haired friend. She had several piercings in one ear and dressed like a punk rocker from the eighties most of the time. But she was funny and kind and generous. She was loyal and honest and the best friend a person could have. So what if she was an adrenaline junkie who would probably walk a tightrope across the New York skyline if someone dared her to?

"I don't think you're a freak," Gemma said.

"That's because you *like* my freakiness. And because you're the least judgmental person I know."

"I thought I was, but now I'm not so sure." She drew in a deep breath and told Crystal about her conversation with Truman. By the time she let it all out, she was as teary-eyed and flustered as she'd been last night.

"Holy. Shit." Crystal dug her feet into the sand.

"I know."

"His own mother put him in prison after he saved her ass?" Crystal said angrily. "Who does that?"

"A drug abuser, I guess. That's the thing that stood out most to you?"

"Well, no," Crystal said. "The whole story is crazy, but he walked in on some asshole raping his mother, and you said he tried to pull the guy off. He did what he had to do. He wasn't just protecting his mother. You said his younger brother was there, too. I could see doing that," she said easily. "If someone were raping my mother, there's nothing I wouldn't do to stop them. I don't think it would take any thought, either. *Mom. Raped. Kill the fucker.*"

Just hearing her say it like that made Gemma's heart race. It was hard for her to think like that about her mother. Truth be told, it was hard for her to think about her mother at all. And the really messed-up thing was that part of her wondered how she'd tell her mother she was dating a man who had been in prison for voluntary manslaughter.

"That also explains much about what you've said about him. No wonder he's so protective."

It did. She knew it did. "But…he *killed* a man."

"A drug-dealing rapist," Crystal pointed out. "Not exactly a pillar of society."

"How does a person move past that?"

"How does a person, or how do you?" Crystal asked. "Because it sounds like he's been moving past it for months, and the way you talk about him, it sounds like he's got his shit together better than most of the guys I know."

Gemma lay back on the sand staring up at the graying sky as the sun began to set. Crystal lay down beside her.

"If you didn't feel anything for him, or if you thought he posed a danger to you or those kids, you would have already called someone—Social Services to protect the kids, or me to protect you. Are you afraid of him?" Crystal asked.

Gemma shook her head. "No," she said honestly. "Not even a little."

"What *are* you afraid of? That your gold-digging mother will have a conniption, or that he's as uncaring or unstable as your father was?"

Gemma turned to face her. Even though those things were true about her parents, she hated hearing them said aloud. "No. I mean, we know my mother would probably lock me up in a tower and throw away the key if she found out, but that would mean she'd have to leave her throne. We both know that's not happening. And Truman is more than caring, and I don't think he's unstable. If he were, I would see it, right? They wouldn't have let him out of prison early. Besides, an unstable person doesn't make his younger brother a priority after he moves out, or stay away from drugs because he knows what they do to a person. An unstable person would take the easy way out and do drugs to escape their life."

"That's what I was thinking, but what do I know?"

"You know me, and you've known people who were in prison before. Your brother, for one." Crystal hated talking about her brother, Jed, but she knew her friend wouldn't mind, given what she was going through.

"He was a thief. *Is* a thief." Crystal stared up at the darkening sky. "From what Jed told me, if you are a certain type of person, no amount of time in prison will change you. He was arrested two months after being released—and that was only because he got caught. He told me that he was stealing days after he got released. So based on that, if Truman were the type of man who could kill without remorse, he'd probably have flown off the handle lots of times, not just one time when his mother was being raped."

"He grew up with her bringing men in and out, and from what he told me, he never lashed out. Even after he moved out, a guy threatened him with a gun to keep him away from the house, but he didn't retaliate. He just kept on going back and watching out for Quincy. But I don't know how you accept that type of thing. He *killed* a man. It doesn't even feel real. When I looked at him after he told me, I didn't see a killer. I saw the man who didn't think twice about raising siblings he never knew existed. The man who was ready to refuse my help because he thought I might want to harm them. But he *did* kill a man, and he was in prison. *Prison*, Crystal."

"Yes," she said sternly. "He killed a man to protect his shitty-ass mother and his younger brother. He went to prison because he was protecting his family, but in a sense, you've both spent time behind bars. You grew up in a gated community you rarely left, you were guarded twenty-four seven and forced to do things you despised. Which is worse? Being imprisoned in a life you hate by your parents, or being imprisoned because you stopped a man from possibly killing the only parent and brother you had?"

"It's not the same," Gemma said lamely.

Crystal drew in a deep breath, and her eyes turned serious, the way they did when there was no room for kidding in their conversation. "No. Nothing is the same as being the person who drove a knife into the man who was raping your mother. Imagine living with that for the rest of your life."

Tears filled Gemma's eyes.

"Now," Crystal said softly, "imagine raising the babies of the woman who sent you to prison."

A tear slid down her cheek. "Is it wrong that I like him so much? It feels like he's so good. He stopped us from fooling around to tell me what he'd done. He could have slept with me and told me later. Or not at all. But he said he wanted us to be honest about everything."

Crystal turned onto her side and faced her. "That tells you so much about him, doesn't it? It's not wrong that you like him so much. You see in him what you've never seen in anyone else. Something worthy of that big heart of yours. In all the years I've known you, I've never seen you shed a tear over any man."

TRUMAN LAID LINCOLN in the playpen and sat down in the lawn chair beside it. He glanced at Kennedy, sitting on Bear's lap with her head on his shoulder. Bear had come to the shop earlier in the afternoon to get some work done on a motorcycle and had stuck around for dinner. They'd grilled burgers and had been shooting the shit ever since.

"I just wish Gemma would get here." Truman ran a hand through his hair and leaned back in his chair.

Kennedy lifted her head. "Gemma?" The fire's glow cast dancing shadows across her sweet face.

"No, princess," Truman answered.

Bear kissed her cheek and gently guided her head back down to his shoulder. "She's not coming, man. It's a lot to deal with. You might not ever see her again."

"She's got to pick up her car at some point." Truman had hoped to catch a glimpse of her when she arrived. "I just want to know she's okay."

"She's *not* okay. How can she be? The dude she likes just admitted to being in prison for killing a man. Regardless of the chivalric reasons, to a girl like Gemma, you're the Big Bad Wolf."

Truman leaned his elbows on his thighs. "Tell me something I don't know."

Bear rubbed Kennedy's back as her eyelids grew heavy.

Truman's hands felt too empty, like the rest of him. "You

ever think about having a family? Before these two, the thought never entered my mind, and honestly, before Gemma, I never wanted a woman in my life, either. But now I can't imagine a day without them." *And I miss the hell out of her.*

"It has entered mine plenty." Bear looked thoughtfully at Kennedy. "Someday I want what you stumbled into. I love kids. I love family. But I also love *variety*. You know me."

"Yeah, I do." He chuckled at the term *variety*, but he knew how loyal Bear was. "You saved me, man. Too many times to count."

"No I didn't. No one can save anyone else. You know that. You saved yourself. You dragged your ass on that bus and got yourself here, and you dragged your brother here. Man," Bear said, "even as a teenager you worked harder than half the men I know."

Truman smiled, remembering the thrill he'd gotten from learning and accomplishing whatever task he'd been given. "You gave me a chance to get out of that hellhole I grew up in. You taught me what it was to have a sense of pride." He got up and paced as headlights beamed down the driveway. His pulse sped up.

"That her?" Bear asked.

"Who else would come around this late? I'll be right back." He'd put a note in Gemma's car for her, but he wanted to see her face when she read it.

"Dude," Bear called after him. "You told her she wouldn't have to see you."

Truman stopped walking, and an unfamiliar car pulled into the parking lot. The passenger door swung open and a tall figure stepped out, staggering slightly.

"That's not her." He glanced back at Bear. "Stay with them

for me?"

"You know it." Bear rose to his feet and stood between the parking lot and the playpen.

Truman's eyes froze on Quincy's long, lean frame moving slowly toward him. His brother's hair hung in front of his eyes. His body swayed like a tree in the wind as he stumbled forward.

"That's far enough," Truman commanded, trying to catch a glimpse of who was driving the old boxy sedan, but it was too dark.

"Hey, man," Quincy slurred.

Truman crossed his arms. "Who's in the car?"

"No one." Quincy put a hand in his front pocket, then took it out, then slid it in again.

"I take it you're not here for help to get clean."

Quincy looked away, and Truman stepped forward, taking a long hard look at his brother's glassy, heavily lidded eyes.

"I used my food money on Mom's cremation." His words ran together. "I was hoping you could help me out."

"Bullshit. I gave you money for that."

His brother looked away again, then back at the car. "If I don't pay..."

Headlights turned off the main road onto the long driveway. *Gemma.* Truman's gut fisted. He didn't want Quincy or his cohorts anywhere near her or the babies. He stepped closer, smelling the rancid stench of not enough showers and too many drugs. The world he'd grown up in and fought against. The world he'd tried to save his brother from.

The world that had fucked up his entire life.

He couldn't even lie to himself. *He'd* made the choice to save his brother's ass, but that didn't stop the anger and frustration from pouring out.

"I told you to stay in school. I told you to stay straight. Where did you lose your way?" Acutely aware of Gemma's car approaching, Truman's patience snapped. "You made this fucking mess of a life you're living in. Unless you want to get out of it, don't show your face around here again. Mom is dead. Do you get that, or are you too fucked up to care?"

Gemma slowed as she drove around the running vehicle. Truman waved her on, not wanting anyone to get a look at her. She continued driving to the far end of the parking lot where her car was parked, and pulled in beside it.

"Get the fuck out of here. And don't bring this shit around my family again."

Quincy looked past Truman toward Gemma, who was climbing into her car. Truman stepped into his line of sight.

"You wanna know when I lost my way?" Quincy said with a voice full of hate. "The day you went to prison. Mom offered me a hit of crack, and there was no one holding me back anymore."

Truman grabbed him by the collar and slammed his back against the car. "Don't you ever blame me for your shitty choices. I was there for you every fucking day." He gritted his teeth and lowered his voice. "I rotted in a fucking cell so you wouldn't have to."

"And I rotted in mine." Quincy wrenched out of Truman's grasp and climbed into the car. The car sped around Truman and drove away, leaving a spray of dust in its wake.

Truman looked across the parking lot at Gemma, who was wide-eyed, having witnessed the whole ugly scene. In her hand was the note he'd left in her car, flapping in the breeze. His feet were rooted in place. He wanted to go to her, to apologize for his whole fucking life. To convince her to give him a chance.

Their eyes held, and that electric burn he'd come to expect seared a path between them despite everything—his confession, the ugly scene with Quincy.

He didn't deserve the conviction that had forever changed his life.

But as she climbed into her car, severing their connection, he knew she didn't deserve it either.

CHAPTER TWELVE

MUSIC ECHOED OFF the boutique walls as seven little princesses took their final strut down the catwalk Tuesday afternoon. Strobe lights flashed like magical stars as Crystal moved like a professional photographer, snapping one shot after another. With her long black hair, and wearing layers of gray and silver taffeta, she was the perfect ghostly princess and a talented photographer. Gemma was lucky to have her on board. After the catwalk, Gemma would make a big deal of presenting the birthday girl with a special jeweled tiara. Then the group would have their photographs taken with Crystal and Gemma. And finally, Crystal would photograph the girls with their parents—the ones who actually stayed for the event. Today there were only two parents. One more than usual. Parents were quick to escape for a few hours of freedom. That had always bothered her. Shouldn't parents want to see their children in a state of sheer happiness? It surprised her that they were totally fine with leaving the children in the hands of strangers, even though she knew she and Crystal were perfectly safe.

Gemma checked the goody bags one last time. The leafy skirt on her Princess Gardenia outfit *swished* noisily with each step. She reached across the table, lifting the colorful blooms and ivy that snaked around her arms to keep them from tangling in the bows on the bags. Then she *swished* her way to the registration desk to get the special tiara for the birthday girl and couldn't resist sneaking another peek at the drawing Truman had left in an envelope taped to the front door of the boutique this morning. Her eyes swept over the image of the dragon she'd first seen in his sketch pad and the note he'd left with it. Her heart lurched, as it had the first three times she'd read it. He'd left a picture on the door yesterday morning, too. Another dark and telling drawing from his sacred sketch pad. Shades of angry blacks and grays, without a spec of color on the page. Pictures he'd made clear he didn't share with anyone. And yet he'd left *two* for her here at the shop even after she'd run out of his apartment without a word of explanation. The first picture he'd left taped to the door had been the face pushing through a tight opening, contorted in a scream, teeth bared, with two hands trying to force the tight space open wider. The note he'd written on that one had been straightforward and heartrending—*You know my story. I have nothing else to hide.* She imagined the picture was Truman's self-portrait of life behind bars, or maybe it was him trying to break free from the life he'd been born into. She didn't know if she was right or if she was on the wrong path altogether, but she *wanted* to know.

Her mind traveled back to the note he'd left in her car the night she'd picked it up at the shop, when she'd seen him slamming some guy against a car. That note had been heartfelt and simple, though she knew it had probably been terribly difficult for him to write—*I'm sorry for my past, and I understand why you wouldn't want any part of me or my life, but I promise you, I'm not a bad guy. The kids and I miss you. Tru.* She had no explanation for what she'd seen, and strangely, that didn't scare her. For Truman to treat a person like that, she imagined they deserved it. She wasn't sure why she had such faith in him, especially after hearing about his past, but something inside her told her she should. And no matter how many times she told herself she shouldn't, she ignored the advice.

Each note had revealed a little more of the man he was. But the note he left today with the picture of the dragon contained a piece of his soul—*Chasing the dragon is slang for inhaling the vapor from heated morphine, heroine, oxycodone, and other drugs. For as long as I can remember, I've wanted to slay the dragon that lured my mother into death and swallowed my brother whole. We miss you. Tru.*

She stared at the note. *I miss you, too. All three of you.*

"Princess Gardenia," Crystal called from across the room, startling Gemma out of her stupor. "It's time for the birthday girl's crown."

She snagged the tiara, pasted on the practiced smile that had gotten her through her youth, and went to give the performance of a lifetime.

"DO YOU THINK I need to hire a babysitter?" Truman asked Dixie as he fed Lincoln. The shop had been closed for an hour, but he and Bear were working late, and Dixie had stuck around to play with the kids.

"Absolutely not," Dixie said, lifting Kennedy into her arms. "These are Whiskey babies as much as they're Gritt babies now."

"She's right, you know. We might need someone to come in and help when the little guy starts to crawl, but right now we can handle it." Bear reached for Kennedy and Dixie turned her shoulder so he couldn't take her away. She nuzzled Kennedy's neck, causing an eruption of giggles.

"I was hoping you'd say that." Truman had been thinking the same thing. He hated the idea of having someone else watch the kids. He couldn't imagine not having them with him twenty-four seven. He thought all he wanted was for the kids to be safe and happy, but he realized that wasn't enough. He and Kennedy both missed Gemma. And although Lincoln couldn't ask for her, like Kennedy could, he had a feeling he missed her, too. Truman missed everything about her. Her smiles, her sassy repertoire, and even her annoyingly invasive questions. But most of all, he missed the way she looked at him, the way she touched him—a hand here, a finger down his cheek—and he missed the love she showed the children every minute of the day. Longing filled him every time Kennedy said her name.

He hoped by sharing the parts of himself he'd never shared with anyone else, Gemma would eventually come around and give him a chance to prove to her who he really was. Part of him wanted to tell her the truth, that it had been Quincy who had killed the man, but he'd never throw his brother under the bus. Not even for Gemma. He'd spent six long years in prison. He knew how to bide his time. Bear had reminded him too many times to count in the past forty-eight hours that he might never see her again, but that didn't mean he was going to give up. No way in hell would he ever give up on her.

Truman handed Lincoln to his forlorn buddy, Bear. The smile his friend flashed when he nestled the baby in his arms brought warmth to Truman's heart. He knew without a shadow of a doubt, if something happened to him, the Whiskeys would care for the babies. At some point he'd have to deal with the legalities of all of that, but there was no way he'd gain legal custody of the kids with a felony conviction, and he wasn't ready to figure that out yet.

"I was thinking," Truman said. "We have the old office that we use for storage, and we have acres of yard. If I pay for it, what do you think about fencing in a play area right outside the door and fixing up the office for the kids, like a playroom? It's already got carpet, so all we'd need is to clean it up and paint it. It's got two nice windows to let fresh air in. And I was thinking we could replace the lower half of the wall with Plexiglas so we can keep an eye on them."

Dixie and Bear exchanged an approving smile.

"Crow can get us deals on everything," Dixie said excitedly.

Bear scowled. "If he thinks he can get in your pants."

Dixie rubbed noses with Kennedy and said, "Do you hear how silly Uncle Bear is? He's a goof, isn't he?"

Kennedy giggled, and Truman arched a brow at Bear.

"You know him as Lance Burke, the guy who owns Mid-Harbor Housing Supplies. Crow's his biker name and he's had a thing for Dixie since we were kids."

"And the plot thickens," Truman teased. "What's wrong with Lance? He's not a good guy?"

Dixie rolled her eyes. "Is any man good enough for me in the eyes of my big brothers?" She sighed dramatically and set Kennedy down to play in the playpen. Crossing her arms, she glowered at Bear. "He'll give us a good price." She dropped her eyes to Lincoln, his little hands going for Bear's chin. "Are you going to turn that away because you think he'll ask for something in return? Because if you are"—she swung her wild red hair over her shoulder with a confident smirk—"then you clearly have no idea how well y'all have raised me."

Bear's eyes dropped to Lincoln. He lowered his face, letting the baby stick his fingers into his mouth. "Okay, but *I'll* call Crow. Not you."

"You're impossible," Dixie groaned. "But fine. Anything for these little muffins."

They talked out their ideas, and once they agreed on the layout, they began putting a game plan together to start renovations. Bear and Dixie insisted on sharing in the costs of supplies, since the renovations would have an impact on the value of the business.

Later, Truman fed and bathed the kids. He was getting the hang of things, thanks to his refusal to let them down. The baby bath Gemma had suggested he buy at Walmart certainly helped where Lincoln was concerned. And as long as he added bubbles to Kennedy's bath (another big thank-you to Gemma), she was willing to take one alone. After getting the kids to sleep, he went to the tool chest and pulled out the bottom drawer. Adrenaline spiked through him at the piles of sketch pads before him. He also had boxes of them stored in the master bedroom closet. He fingered through them, knowing what each contained without ever having gone back to look at the pictures after drawing them. He could hide them in the closet, leave them out back in the pitch-dark, or shove them away in drawers, but the images never left him.

Lifting out the sketch pad he was searching for, he fingered through the pages and found the picture he wanted to leave for Gemma tomorrow morning. He carefully removed it from the sketch pad, wrote a note in the margin, and tucked it into an envelope. Gemma's beautiful face sailed into his mind as he wrote her name on the envelope. He set it on the coffee table, gathered his painting supplies and the baby monitor, locked the front door, and pulled open the glass door to the deck—and his world careened at the sight of Gemma standing before him, her hand stopped in midair, as if she were getting ready to knock.

CHAPTER THIRTEEN

"GEMMA?" TRUMAN SAID in a husky whisper, losing his grip on the metal box and catching it before it dropped to the deck.

Gemma had gone over this moment in her head so many times she thought she had her emotions under control, but nothing could have prepared her for the pulsing knot clogging her throat, or the currents of heat drawing her closer to him. She lifted the baby gym she'd brought from the boutique. Her excuse to come over. A lame one, but it had gotten her there. Weak-kneed and more nervous than she'd ever been, but *there* nonetheless.

"I. Um." *Needed to see you.* "I brought this for Lincoln."

He looked at the baby toy, his brows knitted, disappointment weighing down his features. He set the box down, then pulled the door closed behind him. Ignoring the toy, he stepped closer, like he couldn't stand the distance between them either. Like nothing mattered but closing the gap.

"Gemma," he whispered. His blue eyes were warm and grateful and so full of longing she could feel it wrapping around her and carrying her another step forward. "I've missed you."

He lifted his hand, as if he was going to touch her cheek, and she sucked in a sharp breath, the familiar buzz of electricity searing through her. When he lowered his hand without touching her, she wanted to kick herself for that breath.

"I…" She set the baby toy down on the deck. "Can we talk?"

He nodded, waving to the sofa they'd been sitting on when he'd revealed his past to her. Her heart raced as he sat beside her. She didn't know where to start or what to say. She had so many questions, but now that she was here with him, all those questions seemed to have taken flight, pushed away by the desire to be in his arms again. She wasn't afraid of him, not one little bit. She'd seen too much of who he was before knowing the truth of his past to change all that goodness into malice.

She blinked several times, trying to clear her mind, but the way he was looking at her, like he needed her just as badly as she needed him, wanted her just as desperately as she wanted him, shattered her thoughts.

It turned out she didn't need to think. The truth spilled out. "I can't stop thinking about you and the kids."

A half smile lifted his lips, tugging at her heart.

"I have so many questions, but they seem rude or selfish, like how you moved on afterward and what it feels like to have done what you did. But that's morbid curiosity, because of course you were devastated and horrified. You told me as much the other night. I just…I'm still putting it all together." Her words came so fast she couldn't stop them. "I never imagined myself getting involved with someone who had been in prison or had done what you did. But I doubt you imagined your life turning out the way it has either."

She lifted one shoulder and said, "But I don't want to walk away because you tried to protect your family. I've seen you with the babies, and I've spent enough time with you to know you're not violent. But I need to understand it. All of it, until you're sick of explaining. I won't blame you if you get fed up with my questions, because you know how I can be."

"It's natural to want to know, and I like how you are, so don't worry. I won't get sick of explaining. We're past that. I was afraid to tell you, but now that I have, I'll answer whatever you want or need to know." He paused long enough to try to gather his thoughts. "You asked about how I moved on. Every morning I wake up and see that scene—my mother, my brother, the blood, that rapist. And I have to consciously remind myself how it happened, because it doesn't feel like I'm the one who actually did it. I'm not a violent person, despite my incarceration. Once I remember the scene, moving on starts to happen. I can't explain it, but there's no choice. I just keep going, and the remorse never goes away, even though he was raping my mother. I wish…I wish things had been different."

She pressed her finger to his lips, the emotion in his voice too raw to listen to anymore. "I don't want to make you relive it. I want you to know, I'm not afraid of you. But I may have more questions over time, and I have to know you'll be okay with that."

"Gemma." He closed his eyes for a beat, breathing deeply. When he opened them, he moved his fingers over hers. "Those pictures I sent you might seem like nothing, but they're everything to me. I have nothing to hide anymore. You've heard the worst of it."

"I know how much they mean to you," she said softly. "Thank you for sharing them." She looked down at his hand, all that blue ink covering his skin. She wanted to know more. Were his tattoos like his drawings? Did they represent the horrors of his past? "What do they mean?"

"The pictures?"

She shook her head, wanting to know everything there was to know about him. "Your tattoos." She lifted her gaze to his. Her fingers curled around his. "Is that okay?"

His lips pressed into a straight line. He was breathing so hard his chest inflated with each inhalation, and then he turned his hand under hers and laced their fingers together, holding her tight.

"Everything you do is okay. I'm just so glad you're here, and you're speaking to me, and you're not afraid of me."

"I'm not afraid of you," she repeated.

Without a word, he brought her hand to his mouth and kissed it. His scruff tickled her skin, but it was the look in his eyes that made her glad she was already sitting down, because the emotions she saw slayed her.

He guided her fingers over his tattoos, explaining them one by one. "Ace of spades, the death card. A reminder. I got it after I was released from prison." He moved her finger over the image on his left hand. "The symbol of the Whiskeys' motorcycle club. They saved me in so many ways. I owe them a lot."

As he worked his way down one arm and up the other, moving her fingers along his skin, explaining each tattoo, more of his life unfolded before her. Tattoos symbolizing strength to remind him that even at the worst of times he was strong. Hundreds of tiny dots formed an explosion on one hand, coming outward from a camera, depicting the shattering of his world as he'd known it, and a thickly inked tattoo of a net to catch the pieces, because he wasn't ready to let it all go. These marks she'd initially seen as visual warnings meant to keep people at a distance were a detailed map of the man before her. His ability to overcome his heartache and pain proved his strength. His loyalty to his family and friends spoke to all the lonely parts Gemma had tried to hide, even from herself, for so many years they felt like they'd never fill up.

The emotion in his voice made her heart beat faster, her body grow hotter.

He released her hand and she realized she was shaking. His face was solemn as he reached for the hem of his shirt.

He looked at her with a question in his eyes, and she nodded, wanting to see them all. He lifted off his shirt slowly, as if he wasn't sure she was really ready to see what she'd asked to, revealing the ink she'd seen the other morning but had failed to notice in detail. She focused on the tattoo across the broad expanse of his chest of the angry, vicious dragon he'd drawn, its spine arched high, its neck stretched low, craned forward, breathing fire—blue, like the rest of his tattoos—onto a gnarled, keening tree, bare of all leaves. On the opposite side of the tree was a man, his arrestingly familiar tattooed arms outstretched, his hands pressed against the tree, straining to hold it up. One leg stretched behind him, the other bent at the knee, his feet curved at the toes as he fought against the dragon.

His pain ran so deep. Tears welled in Gemma's eyes.

"Don't feel sorry for me," he said roughly.

She shook her head. "Not sorry for you. Overwhelmed at all you've survived. Amazed that you turned out to be the man you are."

He held her gaze, breathing harder again. "Do you want to see the rest?"

She nodded. "Every one of them."

His face was solemn as he went for the button on his jeans. She suddenly thought of the pictures Crystal had sent her and added, "Unless you have a tattooed, um…" She glanced at his crotch.

He let out a raspy laugh that made them both smile. "Sorry, but some things aren't meant to be near needles."

"Thank God." She let out a relieved sigh.

He released his hold on his jeans. "Gemma, you know how I react to you. If my pants come off..." He was breathing hard. She was hardly breathing at all. His hand pushed beneath her hair, embracing the nape of her neck. "Gemma," he said roughly, something primal brimming in his eyes.

She slid her hand from his chest to his cheek and felt tension pooling there and restraint in his muscles as she tried to pull him closer.

"Gemma." The warning in his voice was clear. His gaze smoldered, traveling over her face, searching for what, she wasn't sure. "If I could change my past, I would," he said heatedly.

His nearness was like a drug, luring her in. She wanted to crawl beneath his skin and feel what he felt, to experience his strength and ease his pain.

"I'm not going to run." She'd had no idea the promise was coming, but she was driven by a sense of urgency, a carnal need to be closer to him. She leaned in, unable to find any more words.

He pulled her to him, claiming her in a hot, hard kiss that sent her senses reeling, and then they were kissing wildly, pawing and clutching, unable to get their fill. He took the kiss deeper, held her tighter, and it felt exquisite. During their days apart, she'd dissected his past until there was nothing left, and still it hadn't touched this avalanche of need bowling her over. She clung to his neck as they kissed and nipped and made maddening sounds of desire. He shifted his weight, and she lowered herself down on her back, bringing him with her. His hips rocked against hers in a greedy, hypnotizing rhythm, and he slowed the kiss, sweetly draining any remaining doubts.

"Gemma," he said against her mouth. "I think we've been here before."

She smiled. "Not where we're headed, we haven't."

His wolfish grin returned, and his eyes filled with wicked desires. "Stop me now if you're going to stop me, because I've thought about making love to you, I've thought about fucking you, and I've thought about begging for your forgiveness—and once our clothes are off, you're getting all of me. I won't be able to stop."

"Don't stop," was all she could manage.

His mouth slanted over hers, hard and hungry. Gemma clawed at his back. His hands moved up and down her sides, over her breasts, down her hips, like he couldn't believe she was lying beneath him. She was right there with him, stroking his skin, reveling in the feel of his weight bearing down on her. The kiss was soft and rough at once, easing, then flaming, bringing waves of ecstasy with each thrust of his hips and sparking white-hot tremors that burned through her, clawing at her core. He tore her shirt over her head, and her bra followed as his talented mouth claimed her breast. She clutched his head, a stream of noises escaping her lungs. She didn't care. Her impatience grew with every slick of his tongue, with the feel of his lips soft and then hard, and then his mouth was on hers again. His rough whiskers scratched her cheeks and his hands—*Lord, those hands*—moved over her body with confidence and control—adeptly melting everything in their wake, and it was all she could do to keep breathing.

DRIVEN BY TOO many emotions to think about, and one he couldn't ignore, Truman rose above Gemma, looking down at the gorgeous, trusting woman beneath him. "I want you in my bed."

She smiled up at him, a bright flare of desire beaming in her eyes as she pulled him back down to her. "You don't have a bed anymore."

"I'm buying a bed tomorrow."

He crashed his mouth to hers again, both of them laughing, but those smiles quickly turned to ravenous pleas of passion. Heat stroked down the length of him. He loved the feel of her bare breasts against his chest, her heart beating fast and furious for him. He wanted to possess every inch of her, to claim her as his own. He was so used to fast, meaningless sex, where he got in, got off, and got out. This desire was new and so fucking real. He didn't want to just fuck her—he wanted to make love to her, with her, for her. He was powerless to temper his greed as he kissed and sucked his way down her body and yanked open her jeans.

He glanced up, needing her approval one final time before he took his first taste. She lifted her hips, pushing her jeans down and giving him the green light he sought. Her jeans fell to the floor, and his breath rushed from his lungs in a guttural groan. He forced himself to take a moment to feel her luscious hips fill his palms, to press kisses to her inner thighs as she writhed beneath him, his throbbing cock begging to be set free. He slicked his tongue over the cleft of her sex, and she moaned into the night. *Good fucking hell*, she tasted divine, and the scent of her arousal beckoned him like metal to magnet. She was so damn sexy he uttered a curse, gritting his teeth. He should go slow, to pleasure her in every way possible, but slow would have to wait. He needed her *now.* Lifting her legs, he guided them over his shoulders and covered her sex with his mouth. He sucked and licked and thrust his tongue in so deep her inner muscles clenched around it, spurring him to take more. She rocked and moaned and clawed at his shoulders as he took his fill. Bringing his fingers to her center, he thrust them in and sucked her clit between his teeth. Her hips bolted up, her thighs pressed against his face, and she cried out his name in a heated whisper. He knew she was being quiet for the kids, and that made his heart swell even more.

"Tru—"

So fucking sexy, so damn *real.* He stayed with her, fucking her with his fingers, loving her with his mouth, until she began coming down from the peak. Then he flattened his palms on her inner thighs and slicked his tongue over her sensitive flesh in a slow, repetitive motion. Her nails dug into his skin, her breathing shallowed, and her body quivered and shook.

"More, Tru, *please.*"

He continued teasing, loving her slowly, drawing out her pleasure, until she was clutching the cushions, pleading for more. Only then did he seal his mouth over her sex and give her what she wanted, taking her up, up, *up*, until she shattered in a river of turbulent explosions.

When the last shudder rolled through her, he kissed a path along her belly, tasting her arousal with each press of his lips, and gathered her in his arms. Her eyes fluttered open, the sated smile of a gratified lover on her lips.

"More," she pleaded, and *holy hell*, did he want more.

He kissed her again, softer this time, wanting to be even

closer. Her taste stayed with him as their tongues tangled, and it was so damn hot that she didn't fight it. He brought his hand between her legs again, taking her right to the peak of another climax, and swallowed her cries of pleasure. Christ, he could do this all night long. Feeling her come was ten times better than he dreamed, but he needed to be inside her more than he needed his next breath. He stripped off his jeans, careful to keep his weight off of her, and stopped cold.

"Condom," he ground out. "In the bedroom."

He kissed her again, long and slow, not wanting to part for even a few seconds. When he moved to stand, she held on to him.

"Not yet," she whispered, and drew him into another kiss.

Her hand moved through his hair; the other moved down his side and flattened on his back, holding him tight. When their lips parted, she kept him close, nuzzling against his neck and placing light kisses from his collar to his jaw.

"I like the way you smell." Her breath whispered over his skin. "And the way your body fits with mine." Her fingers moved over his back in feathery touches like she had all night to lay with him. Touching him lovingly, like no other woman ever had, she awakened other needs in him. Needs he hadn't realized he had. Despite how much he ached to feel her wrapped around him from the inside out, right now, *this* was what he wanted: her touch, her kisses, hearing her soft sighs of a different type of pleasure.

"I like how big you are," she whispered. "And protective. You make me feel safe."

"Despite my past?" He couldn't stop the question before it left his lips.

She gazed up at him with a smile so sweet all his defenses

peeled away. "Maybe *because* of your past."

He kissed the corner of her lips, feeling like he'd been given the biggest gift of his life, and gathered her close again, shifting them onto their sides. He slid one knee between her legs and the other over her hip, so their bodies were completely intertwined.

"Mm. See? We fit perfectly," she murmured against his neck, her fingers still trailing along his back in a slow, gentle pattern. "You're our Tru Blue, the most loyal sentinel of all."

"Our?"

She yawned and rested her hand on his cheek. "Me and the kids."

He wondered if she could hear the way his heart tumbled as he fell even harder for this remarkable woman. He kissed her softly, reveling in the feel of her nestled safely in his arms and replaying her words like a rerun he never wanted to end.

"Gemma." His throat thickened, stifling his words. *Holding you. Feeling you touch me. This is everything I want.* He was hard as steel, his cock resting against her damp curls and the warm skin above, but as she snuggled against him and her breathing fell into the easy cadence of sleep, everything inside him settled into place, and finally—*God, finally*—his life didn't feel so out of control.

CHAPTER FOURTEEN

GEMMA AWOKE ALONE on the couch on Truman's back deck, her naked body covered with a soft, warm blanket. The sun was just beginning to peek over the horizon, and Truman's voice came through the baby monitor. Wrapping the blanket around herself, she didn't feel panicked or embarrassed by her lack of clothing. She warmed all over at the sight of him on the video monitor pacing the bedroom with Lincoln on his shoulder. He was shirtless, wearing only a pair of dark briefs. His big hand moved over the baby's back in slow circles. Gemma couldn't see the baby's face, but by the way his hands hung limply by his sides, she assumed he'd already fallen back to sleep.

She found her clothes folded on the deck, smiling at Truman's thoughtfulness as she pulled on her shirt and panties and moved to the railing to watch the sun come up. Listening to Truman's loving voice through the monitor, she knew she'd made the right decision coming to see him last night. He was not a man to be feared.

And last night…

She sighed.

Just thinking about the way he'd held her and the way he'd stripped away his walls and let her in made her feel light and dreamy. The electricity between them was undeniably magnetic and explosive, but their intimate connection went so much deeper. When she was lying in his arms last night, they'd been in perfect sync, and the way he breathed easier when they were close filled her with unexpected happiness. She hadn't meant to fall asleep, but she couldn't help it after all those intense orgasms and being held tight and warm and safe in Truman's arms. As much as she longed to wake up in his arms, waking to him loving up Lincoln was even better. He gave those babies all the love she'd wished for growing up, and she knew better than anyone that nothing could ever replace that. Those kids had found a home in his heart, and they were lucky to have him.

The magnitude of her feelings engulfed her, like a tangible thing she could feel and taste and see. She gazed over a sea of mangled and forgotten cars in the distance and heard Truman step outside. When his hands circled her waist and his warm lips touched her cheek, she smiled and turned in his arms, smelling the scent of minty toothpaste and soap.

"Sorry to leave you alone," he said in a gravelly, sleepy voice.

She felt feminine and petite against his enormous frame. *My gentle giant. My Tru Blue.* She had no doubt that her gentle giant would turn into a hulklike creature if the situation called for it. Her heart squeezed at the sight of the ink on his chest, seeing it clearly for only the second time. She traced the angry dragon's neck with her finger and pressed her lips to the flames. She couldn't change his past, and as terrible as his past was, it made him the man he was, just as her parents' lack of attention and love, and her father's suicide, made her who she was. When she met his gaze, she was surprised to see a look of wariness staring back at her.

"You look worried. Is Lincoln's fever back?"

"No," he said seriously. "Just trying to read you. Any regrets with the dawn of the new day?"

She shook her head and smiled up at him. "Only that you've bared your soul to me and I haven't shared nearly as much with you."

Relief washed over his face. "You've shared more than you know." He leaned down and kissed her, and she kept her lips tightly closed. He laughed, cradling her face in his hands. "I *would* like you to share a better kiss with me, though."

She covered her mouth to spare him her morning breath. "I haven't brushed my teeth."

He laughed and lowered her hand. "I had my mouth buried between your legs last night. Do you really think I care if you've brushed your teeth?"

Something was different. Maybe everything was different; she couldn't be sure. His words came easier, his smiles came more naturally, and that rumbly laugh she really, *really* liked tumbled out without hesitation. He was letting her in even more, trusting her with more than just his confession. She saw it in his eyes. Relief and something much more powerful. Something that told her he had needed to hear her say that she had no regrets in order to believe it.

When his mouth came down over hers, she felt the difference in his kiss, too. He kissed her more intimately, cradling her jaw in one hand, his other holding her around her waist, bringing their bodies together. It was an intoxicating and territorial kiss. A kiss that said, *You are mine and I am yours.*

It was the kiss she hadn't realized she'd been waiting for her whole life.

When their lips parted, his fingers slid over her cheek, brushing lightly over her lower lip, and he kissed her again, soft and tender. Oh, how she liked *soft* and *tender*!

"You taste perfect in the morning," he said with a haughty grin.

She wrinkled her nose.

As if to prove his point, he kissed her again and licked his lips.

She laughed, loving this new Truman. "Sorry I fell asleep on you last night."

"I'm not."

"But you…" *Made me come several times.* "And I didn't reciprocate."

"I've gone my whole life not being touched the way you touched me last night." His words were laced with deep emotions. "I want to make love to you, but what I want more than that is to be close to you and to feel everything that's brewing between us. To see your sleepy smile as you touch me and hear all those things you said to me last night. I never thought…I never imagined…"

He embraced her, his cheek resting against the side of her head. "I never thought I needed anyone, but I'm starting to think I was just waiting for you."

TRUMAN WHISTLED AS he stood in the back of his pickup truck, maneuvering the mattress he'd just bought to the tailgate, where Bear was waiting to help him carry it upstairs. It was seven o'clock in the evening and Dixie was watching the kids. He'd been in the best mood all day. He'd been peed on twice while changing Lincoln's diaper, and even that hadn't put a damper on his mood.

"Someone got laid last night." Bear gripped the mattress.

"Nope." Truman jumped from the tailgate and shifted the mattress so he could get a grip on it.

They carried the mattress around the shop to the steps leading up to the deck. Gemma had a late birthday party at the boutique, and she wouldn't be off work until nine, which gave Truman just enough time to get things ready and put the kids to sleep.

"Then why are you in such a good mood?" Bear asked as they hefted the mattress up the stairs.

"Because she came back, man. And she makes everything better."

"Gemma? She came back?"

Truman couldn't suppress his grin. "Yup."

"And she's cool with your past and the kids and *Quincy*?" At the top of the stairs Bear rested the mattress on the railing. "Get the door. I've got this."

Truman pulled open the door and they carried the mattress inside. "I think she's okay with it, maybe not totally cool with it, but I wouldn't expect her to be." He nodded to the couch. "Let's lean it against the back of the couch."

"Cool enough to warrant a mattress." Bear smirked. "Which means you will be getting laid soon enough."

"It's not like that. I mean, it is. Don't get me wrong; she's hot as fuck, and I can't wait to get closer to her, but it's not like that's all there is."

"Good, man. I'm happy for you. Not many women would be okay with all the shit going down in your life. You hear any more from Quincy?" Bear asked.

"No. I left him a message offering to get him help…*again*."

"No one can say you're not a loyal son of a bitch."

Despite his heartache over Quincy, he smiled at Bear's words, thinking of Gemma. *Tru Blue.*

"He's family. I may not want him around the kids when he's fucked up, but that doesn't mean I'll give up on him for good." Needing to change the subject, Truman crossed the room to the alcove where he kept his tools. Quincy was the one person who could ruin his mood. "Help me out. I want to get all this stuff downstairs."

"All of it?" Bear cocked a brow. "The workbench, too?"

"Yup. I'm making this one-bedroom apartment into a two-bedroom. Eventually we're building a wall here." He waved to the front of the alcove.

"We are? Isn't this my place?"

"Oh, right. You mind?" Truman began taking the tools off the wall and putting them into a box.

"Nah. 'Course not." Bear was busy texting.

"Hot date?"

"Yeah, with my brothers." He glanced at Truman and shook his head, then turned back to his vibrating phone. "Bullet and Bones are on their way over to help." He shoved his phone in his pocket.

An hour and a half later, Truman, Bear, Bullet, and Bones had relocated all of the shop paraphernalia downstairs and brought up the box spring, pillows, sheets, rug, and other things Truman had bought.

Truman swept the alcove, and they rolled out the shag area rug and set up the bed.

"No bed frame?" Bones asked.

Truman shrugged. "What do I know about bed frames?"

Bullet ran a hand over his beard and took a swig of his beer. At six five, he had a good two inches on Truman and his brothers. Colorful tattoos snaked along his arms, and Truman knew he had tats on nearly every inch of his chest and back, too. "This little gal's got your nuts in a knot, huh?"

Truman smiled. "You could say that. It's nice to be with someone who actually cares."

"I believe our little boy is growing up," Bones teased. He'd come from work, still dressed in his white button-down and slacks. No one would guess that beneath that professional attire were tatted-up shoulders and a badass biker.

"Hey," Bear said. "We care."

"Yeah, but he doesn't want you sucking his dick," Bullet said gruffly, then more amused, "Or do you?" He waggled his brows.

Truman laughed. "Man, I don't want you bringing that nasty beard anywhere near my junk. You might have mice living in it for all I know."

"Hey, sweethearts love my beard." Bullet stroked his beard. "Tickles their thighs."

As Bullet's brothers gave him shit about shaving his beard off when he was asleep, Truman pondered the rest of his surprise for Gemma. "Y'all know anything about sheet forts?" The saleslady had told him to buy *sheers*. He'd had no idea what the hell a sheer was, but once she showed him, he knew he had to buy them along with the sheets. The sheers were more feminine, which reminded him of Gemma, so he bought extras to use as curtains.

The three brothers exchanged a look of confusion.

Truman pulled out his cell phone and texted Dixie. A few minutes later she came through the door with Kennedy at her side and Lincoln in her arms.

"Oh my gosh! This place looks so different without all the

shop stuff up here." Her high-heeled boots tapped across the hardwood floor.

"Tooman?" Kennedy said, lifting her arms for him to pick her up. "Gemma coming over?" She'd been talking more each day, and it warmed his heart to know that she was settling in okay. Gemma had stayed for breakfast, and Kennedy had been over the moon about seeing her.

"Yes, princess. But you might be asleep when she gets here. Want me to send her in to give you a kiss?" He lifted her into his arms and she nodded forcefully. "You've got it." He kissed her cheek and showed her his bed, which was now draped in layers of earth-toned sheets and blankets. "What do you think of my new bed?"

"Pwetty," she said.

"With a little paint, curtains, and a few plants, you'll have a romantic little nook." Dixie sat on the mattress and ran her hand over the blanket. "That's really soft."

He didn't have time for paint, but one day…

"'A romantic little nook.' I think that's my cue to take off." Bullet lifted Kennedy from Truman's arms and kissed her cheek, rubbing his beard over her chin. She giggled, and he handed her back to Truman. "Even Kennedy likes my beard. See ya, squirt." He gave Truman a one-armed hug, then leaned down to kiss Lincoln, who was still in Dixie's arms.

"Me too. I've got a date. Let me know if you need anything." Bones slapped Truman on the back, kissed the top of Kennedy's head, and gave Lincoln's foot a shake.

"See you guys. Thanks for the help." Seeing his buddies love up the children made Truman's heart feel full. He set Kennedy down and Bear scooped her up.

"Be-ah." Kennedy giggled.

"Don't Be-ah me." He rubbed noses with her, making her giggle again. "Are you going to be good tonight?"

She nodded.

"Good, because if you're not, you know what happens." He wiggled his fingers in front of her belly.

"Tickle monstah!" she squealed. "Tooman!" She leaned toward Truman and he lifted her into his arms.

"Good luck tonight, buddy." Bear patted him on the shoulder.

"Thanks for your help."

"No sweat. Oh, and I talked to Crow. He's having the fencing delivered tomorrow, and the rest is on order."

"You rock, man. Thanks." It was hard to believe how much his life had changed over the past few days, but they were good changes. He was happier than he could ever remember being.

He sank down to the mattress beside Dixie, and Kennedy crawled to the middle of the bed and lay down.

"You're doing a really good job with these little guys," Dixie said, handing him Lincoln.

He cradled the baby in one arm, pressing a kiss to his forehead. "Thanks. I don't want to screw them up, you know? They're so little."

"Truman, you couldn't screw them up. You only know how to do right by people." She put her arm around him and sighed. "Before we get into the nuances of sheet forts, which I happen to be very good at building, do you want to unload? To talk about Gemma or the kids?"

His smile came naturally. Just thinking about Gemma—or the kids—made him happy. "What's there to say? One day I was surviving, and the next I was living. It's chaotic with the schedules and never-ending caregiving from morning until night, but…"

"You're giving them all the things you never had."

"Yeah. I hope so. And Gemma? I don't even know what to say, Dix. She's…*everything*."

"I assumed so, when I got your text." She glanced at Kennedy, who was lying on her side almost asleep. "Want help putting the kids down? Then we can get to work. It'll be years before I have kids, so this is fun for me."

"Hey, you never know. Look at my life."

His phone vibrated with a text, and he dug it out of his pocket, smiling when a picture of Gemma appeared on his screen. He'd taken it this morning in the parking lot before she went home. She had that dreamy look in her eyes she sometimes got. The one that made his heart turn over in his chest.

He clicked open and read the message. *Running late. One of the kids puked all over. I probably can't get there until closer to ten. Still want me to come by?*

He typed a quick response as Dixie carried Lincoln to the bedroom. *Definitely. Can't wait to see you.*

Her response came immediately. *Whew. I was afraid I'd have Tru Blue withdrawals.*

He lifted Kennedy into his arms, carried her to the bedroom, and grabbed her night-night storybook from the dresser, wondering what he'd done with his evenings before he'd found them—all *three* of them.

CHAPTER FIFTEEN

GEMMA CLUNG TO the railing as she ascended the steps to Truman's apartment. She could barely lift her legs in her tight, short leather skirt and four-inch spike-heeled boots. She felt like the Leaning Tower of Pisa, but tonight's party had been all about rocker princesses. Nine thirteen-year-old girls dressing up in black velvet and leather dresses with strict orders from the birthday girl of *no lace*. They'd had a blast, temporarily dying their hair pink and purple, with gaudy makeup and appropriate attitudes to match.

The door to the deck slid open—and Gemma's knees weakened at the sight of Truman, clean-shaven, wearing a white button-down shirt, the sleeves rolled up to his elbows, a pair of dark jeans, and his badass black boots.

"Holy cow." She couldn't take her eyes off of him or his wickedly seductive smile.

He slid a hand to her hip, his eyes taking their own slow stroll down Leather Lane. "Hi, sweetheart."

Sweetheart. She trapped her lower lip between her teeth as he tugged her against him, causing her to stumble on her heels. She grabbed on to him to keep from falling. He smelled spicy and delicious, and she leaned in closer, filling her senses with his scent. A husky laugh rumbled up from his lungs, stealing more of her brain cells.

"My girl's gone hot biker chick on me." He nuzzled her neck. "Please tell me you didn't let other guys see you in this, because if you did, their wives are in for a surprise tonight."

Her body hummed with his praise. "I guess you like it?"

"I'd have to be gay not to, and even then, I have no doubt that you could turn me." He lifted her chin and kissed her long and deep, making her already wobbly knees pure liquid. He tightened his hold on her, smiling into the kiss. "God, I love that."

"Knowing you have complete power over my limbs?"

"Absolutely." He captured her mouth again, his hands moving over her ass, pressing her against his hard body. "I love when you get so worked up you need to hang on to me."

He kissed her neck, and his scent wound around her again, lulling her into a euphoric state. "Tru…" She wrapped her hand around his neck, pulling his face closer. She pressed her cheek to his whiskerless face and her body shivered with the new, exciting feel of his hot, smooth skin.

"And I love when you say my name breathlessly. Every. Damn. Time." He sucked her earlobe into his mouth, and she curled her fingers over his shoulders. "And when you touch me like that."

Every kiss, every raspy word, every touch made her senses reel. Ever since they'd come back together, her heart had become an open door for him, and she couldn't see it ever closing. She rubbed her cheek over his again. It was sensuously soft and titillatingly strong at once. Gazing into the eyes she'd begun seeing in her dreams, she said, "I loved your scruff. It grew on me and became as much a part of *you* as everything else about you. You didn't have to shave for me."

He shrugged humbly, but his smile told her how much he appreciated her words.

"I thought you might think it was more appropriate in case I come by your shop when you have customers."

"Oh, Tru." She pulled him into another kiss, deeply touched by his consideration. "I like you as you are—scruffy, clean-shaven, none of that matters. Seeing you like this totally blows me away, but I honestly don't care what anyone else thinks." She had a pang of guilt, because no matter how much she tried to ignore it, she knew her mother would give her hell, but she wasn't about to let that impact her relationship with Truman.

"I'm glad you survived your pukey night. Was the little girl who got sick okay?"

"We won't talk about that in detail, but yes. She's fine. Too much punch and too many twirls on the red carpet did not sit well with the birthday girl, Princess Patty." She touched his cheek again, marveling at his chiseled jawline, and noticed a fine white scar running parallel to his jaw. She kissed it and he bristled. Despite his reaction, she traced it with her fingertip, wanting him to know that whatever it was from wouldn't scare her or make her run. "How...?"

"Prison," he said softly.

Her heart ached at the thought of him being behind bars, and even worse at him being hurt while he was there, but she didn't want to make him relive whatever caused that scar. He had much deeper scars. The kind that would never be visible. And she had faith that when he was ready, *if* he was ever ready to discuss those years, he would let her know. She pressed another kiss to the scar and then to his lips.

"I didn't realize it was possible to miss a person as much as I missed you today," she admitted as he led her toward the door.

He stopped short of going inside and slid his hands beneath her hair, cradling her face. "Me too. I was afraid to tell you how much I missed you. Afraid of being too much—"

"Tru." *Breathless. Always breathless*. "I've never had enough. Please be too much. I need too much. I need *you*."

They kissed with the greed of two people who have never had *enough*—and who were ready to give it all to each other.

They walked inside as they kissed. A floral scent hit her at the same time her eyes adjusted to the darkness. Candles danced on the countertops and coffee table. In the middle of the living room long gauzy sheets of colored fabric hung loosely from the rafters to the floor like an Arabian tent. Tiny white holiday lights sparkled along each panel, intertwined with ribbons of leafy green ivy. Her hand flew over her rapidly beating heart as he guided her forward, to the space where the gauzy panels parted. Beneath all that spectacular beauty, a red and white checked picnic blanket covered the floor. A children's tea set, prepared with service for two, was spread out with candles and a single red rose alongside a carafe of wine and two wineglasses.

"Truman," she whispered shakily.

"I wasn't sure if you wanted tea or preferred wine, so I went with both. And I hope the *sheer* fort is okay instead of a *sheet* fort."

"It's perfect. You're perfect."

The denial in his eyes pierced through her, but that was okay, because he was right—no one was truly perfect.

"In a perfect world," she said softly. "We both would have had loving parents, and you never would have faced what you did. We didn't grow up in a perfect world, but you're *my* perfect."

He pulled her tight against him again and pressed his lips to hers. His heart was beating fast, so sure and steady it spoke louder than words ever could.

He held her close as they walked around the magical tent.

"Ohmygosh. Truman." She wasn't even sure if the words left her lips, she was so awestruck. The alcove that had once housed tools, big metal tool chests, ladders, and other gritty paraphernalia had been transformed into the most luxurious bedroom she'd ever seen. And it had nothing to do with expensive furnishings, because there were none. She could hardly believe Truman had gone to all this trouble for her. Gold sheers hung from floor to ceiling surrounding a thick mattress, which sat atop a beige shag rug. A fluffy cream-colored comforter, several pillows, and soft-looking knit throws in earthy hues were strewn across the foot of the bed. Sheers were also draped over the window, allowing the dusky, romantic moonlight to shimmer through. On the floor beside the bed was a hubcap, with a wide candle in the center. She loved that hubcap best of all, because she loved his world. This life he'd created for the kids—and for them. He'd gone to such lengths to give her something beautiful and meaningful, when all she needed was him.

She turned to face the man who had obviously listened at a time when he'd been busy with her car and overwhelmed by his upended life, and had cared enough to do something so big and meaningful when he had so little.

"I think my heart just exploded." She blinked up at him with damp eyes. "How did you…? With the kids to take care of and your job?"

"I had a little help from my friends."

She threw her arms around him and kissed him. The fact

that he'd asked his friends to help do all of this for her made it even more special, because Truman never asked for help.

"I think I need to make a whole new prince outfit for my shop. *Prince Truman*, because no prince, fictional or real, could ever hold a candle to you."

TRUMAN REFILLED THEIR wineglasses, Gemma's toes playing over his. Gemma had gone in to kiss the kids good night as Truman had promised Kennedy, and they'd long ago cast aside their boots and polished off a few glasses of wine. They were lying in the tent playing a game, weaving each other into their pasts as if they'd known one another forever. It was a game of pretend, something they'd both missed out on as kids—although he'd spent his whole childhood pretending his life was something it wasn't—and playing this game made him feel even closer to Gemma.

"Do you remember the night I scaled the gates around your house and snuck into your bedroom when you were sixteen?" He ran his finger along the length of her arm, loving the way she shivered under his touch.

She leaned forward, fiddling with the buttons on his shirt, her fingers nimbly unbuttoning, then touching his chest. "How could I forget the night of our first kiss?"

"That was a night of many firsts." He set their wineglasses off to the side and lowered her gently to the floor, perching above her. She gazed up at him with lustful eyes. He traced a path from her chin, down the graceful column of her neck, along her cleavage, to the first button of her black leather vest, slowly unfastening it.

"That was the first night you let me touch you." He pressed a kiss to the swell of each breast. "Remember?" He wished the things they were making up were true and liked imagining having known Gemma back then.

"That was the first night you tried," she countered, arching up beneath him.

He rained kisses over her shoulder, the curve of her neck, and the dip at the center of her collarbone. "Was it the first time I tried?"

Her eyes narrowed, but she was breathing harder now. "No, but I had to play hard to get. You had all those other girls after you, and everyone knows guys want what they can't have."

Her fingers traced a tattoo down his arm to the space between his finger and thumb, where she caressed little circles that sent pinpricks of heat straight to his core. "Do you remember that time I came to your house and found you sitting on the back porch with Quincy?"

His stomach clenched at the mention of his brother, but this was part of the game, and he knew this was her way of showing him that she didn't hold his past, or his family, against him.

"Yes. You wore those sexy little shorts that made me crazy." He pushed a hand beneath her skirt and she sucked in a breath.

"On purpose." She took his hand and moved it higher up her hip. His fingers grazed lace. A sinful smile spread her lips, her green eyes glimmering with seduction. "Remember what you said to me?"

He moved his fingers along the edge of her panties. Her eyes fluttered closed, and her lips parted on a sigh. Leaning closer, he ran his tongue along the bow of her upper lip. "Tell me, sweet girl, what did I say to you?"

Her eyes opened. "You said..." Her words came out breathy and low.

She leaned up and he claimed her in a kiss so hot it could smolder metal, and then took it deeper, feeling her heart beat faster, her hands clutch him tighter, and her body—God, her glorious body—arch into him from knees to chest.

When their lips parted, she panted out a few breaths and said, "You told me something bad was going to happen and to wait for you. And I promised I would."

"Gemma." Her name came out like a plea.

She placed her finger over his lips, silencing him. "Do you remember what else you said to me?"

Biting back the emotions threatening to tear from his chest, he shook his head. She stroked his cheek, and he leaned into her palm, wanting to soak in every bit of her—from her sweet words to the adoring look in her eyes.

"You said, 'Don't worry, sweet girl. It's going to take a little time, but together we'll do all the things we missed out on.'"

He searched her serious expression, seeing vulnerability and longing looking back at him. "I wish we were together when we were younger. Having you in my life would have made every day infinitely better. I would have given you all the memories you wish you had. Meadows and fairy wings and strong arms around you when you were lonely or scared."

"I know," she said. "And I would have been there for you, through all of it."

The pain of wishing for something they'd never have was staggering. "You're really good at playing pretend."

"I wasn't pretending just now."

"You're killing me, sweetheart. Tearing me down one word at a time."

She touched his cheek again, and his insides melted. She had the power to wreck him and the power to make him feel so very loved. He was totally, utterly *hers*, and he couldn't wait another second to make her *his*.

He took her mouth with savage intensity, crushing her to him, and she was right there with him. They ate at each other's mouths, grinding and groping through their clothing, pleading moans escaping their lips. Shoving her skirt up around her waist, he tore off her panties with one hard yank, shredding the lacy material. She grabbed his hair, tugging to the point of scintillating pain, sending electric shocks pulsing through him. Her hips rose off the floor and he thrust his fingers inside her, crooking them up, seeking the spot that would make her go wild. She moaned into his mouth, writhing as she rode his hand, guiding him until she cried out into their kiss. He tore his mouth away with the need to see her face in the throes of ecstasy. In the space of a breath he drank in her flushed skin, her swollen, pink lips, and the needy whispers escaping them. He had to have her, had to feel all that passion wrapped around him. His mouth came down over hers hard and insistent as he gathered her in his arms. Her arms circled his neck, never breaking the kiss while he carried her through the sheers and over to the bed, reaching behind him to pull the gold sheets across the opening. Kennedy hadn't attempted to crawl out of bed yet, but just in case, he thought it best to have a barrier until he could build a proper wall.

"We need to be quiet," he said.

"I know," she whispered, and reached for him.

He resisted with a slow shake of his head.

"Nothing is going to come between us this time." He stripped off his clothes, and her eyes locked on his eager cock.

She licked her lips.

"You have no idea what I have planned for that sinful mouth of yours." He saw a shadow of worry wash over her, and his heart sank at what he knew she was worried about. "I'm clean. I've been tested. And I'm sure you're wondering, so…There was no ass fucking in prison. Not for me anyway, and I have never had sex without a condom. Hell, sweetheart, I haven't gone down on a girl since before prison. Not until you. I want all of you, Gemma, but you don't have to do anything you aren't comfortable with. Not now, not ever when you're with me."

She breathed a sigh of relief. "Thank you for telling me," she said shyly. "I was a little nervous about it."

"I know, and it's okay. You have to be able to tell me what worries you." He smiled. "Not that you hold back very often."

She returned his smile. "I am kinda pushy."

"*Be* pushy. Don't hold back with me. Don't hold back your worries, your desires, or anything."

Without a word, she lifted her hips off the bed, unzipped her skirt, then wiggled free, her way of showing him she was done holding back. When she went for the buttons on her vest, he took her hand and brought her up to her knees on the mattress. Her cheeks flushed, and she nibbled on the corner of her mouth. He sank to his knees, took her face in his hands, and kissed her like he never wanted to stop.

And then he kissed her again.

"I want to watch you."

With trembling hands, she began unbuttoning her vest, but he was too revved up to watch and not play. He gripped her hips, running his hands along her luscious curves as she unbuttoned one, two, and finally, the last button, parting the leather to reveal her beautiful breasts. The leather hitched on her nipples, keeping them hidden.

"You're so beautiful." His hands moved to her ass, cupping her cheeks as he trailed kisses over her shoulder and up her neck. When she inhaled a long, shaky breath, he sealed his mouth over the curve of her neck and sucked. She arched into him, moaning eagerly and clutching his biceps.

"More," she begged.

His hands moved down her ass and between her thighs, grazing over her wet heat. She rocked forward and back along the length of his fingers, coating them with her arousal as he took her in another fierce kiss. His tongue thrust to the far reaches of her mouth, claiming all of her as he teased her down below, and she continued rocking, panting, arching, and driving him out of his mind.

He drew back, gazing into her sultry eyes. He wanted to give her everything, not just in bed, but also the safety and security she needed and deserved for the faith she gave him so readily.

"Let me love you, sweetheart."

He shifted onto his back, guiding her until she was straddling his mouth. She pressed her palms to the wall with a low groan as he made love to her with his mouth, taking her deep with his tongue, until she rode it as if it were his cock. He gripped her hips and grazed his teeth over her most sensitive nerves. She whimpered and slapped her hand over her mouth seconds before her body bucked with the force of her climax. He rode the waves of her pleasure with her, loving her to the very end. Then he shifted her onto her back and reached for a condom, which he'd tucked beside the bed. His heart slammed against his ribs as he tore it open with his teeth and sheathed his hard length. He'd waited so long for this moment, had built it up to epic proportions in his mind, but nothing compared to seeing Gemma lying beneath him, her eyes so full of desire it poured off of her.

She leaned up and cupped his balls, teasing him with a wicked glint in her eyes.

He grabbed her hands and pinned them beside her head, nudging her legs open wider with his knee. It was a reflex, how he'd always had sex. He gazed down at Gemma, so willing to be whatever he needed, so trusting. In her eyes he saw all those things. He felt his heart open even more, unlatching the last of the locks he'd lived behind for so long. She was looking at him like he was all she ever wanted, and when a smile lifted her lips, it was too much.

She was too much. *Too sweet, too sexy, too real.*

He released her hands and she reached for him. In that split second, the truth poured out.

"I want to wrap you up in me until you can feel how much I want you. I want to make you feel as *wanted* as you make me feel, because I want you, Gemma—all of you. I've never felt like this before. I feel like this is my first time."

He kissed her, sinking into her slowly, wanting to remember every glorious second. The way her mouth tasted of want and need and something much deeper. The feel of her breasts crushed against his chest, her fingers pressing into his lower back. The smell of her arousal mixed with the sweet unique scent of *Gemma*. When he was buried so deep they felt like one being, he gazed into her eyes, struck mute by emotions.

Their mouths came together and they found their rhythm. In seconds they were a wild tumble of whispers and kisses, and giggles, and *Oh my God! Right theres*. She wrapped her legs around his waist, allowing him to sink further into her. When they hit that phenomenal peak where stars collided and the earth spun around them, they swallowed each other's explosive cries.

Slick with sweat, Truman didn't know where Gemma ended and he began. He was lost—in her, for her, *with* her. Passion brimmed in her eyes as she leaned up and he met her halfway in a warm and wonderful kiss, with all the depth and emotion of knowing that this was only the beginning.

CHAPTER SIXTEEN

GEMMA LEANED AGAINST the bedroom doorframe wearing one of Truman's shirts, which fell nearly to her knees, listening to him hum as he gave Lincoln a bottle. It was four thirty in the morning, and he was wearing a pair of dark briefs and a T-shirt. She couldn't wait to curl up in his arms again. They'd made love twice and had fallen asleep wrapped up in each other's arms, waking when Lincoln began to cry. Truman hadn't pushed from the bed with a begrudging groan or rued his missed sleep at all. He'd even told Gemma to get some sleep when she'd offered to feed Lincoln.

He set the bottle on the dresser, and Gemma draped a burp rag over her shoulder, motioning for him to give her the baby. She loved these moments with the kids, and she loved the smile on Truman's face as he settled Lincoln in her arms and rubbed his nose over hers in an Eskimo kiss.

"When I was little," she whispered, patting Lincoln gently on the back, "I came home from kindergarten and asked for Eskimo kisses. I had just learned what they were, and I felt like I'd missed out on something really fun. My parents could have given me one, right? Just rubbed their nose with mine for one second. Instead I got a lecture on how it's rude to call them *Eskimo* kisses and that little girls shouldn't ask for kisses."

Truman stepped closer and pressed a kiss to the back of Lincoln's head. Then he leaned in and rubbed noses with Gemma again. "From now on, not a day will pass without Eskimo kisses. I promise."

How could something so little mean so much?

She kissed him softly and Lincoln let out a burp. They both smiled. She placed the baby in his crib, stroked his little head, and then they returned to their makeshift bedroom.

"You're going to make an amazing mother someday," he said as they climbed into bed. He tucked her beneath his arm, her face resting on his chest, and kissed the top of her head.

"Maybe," she said a little forlornly.

He tightened his arm around her. "Definitely. Don't you want your own children? I just assumed..."

"My love for children is like God's cruel joke." She tried to play it off as such, but the familiar longing twisted inside her. In the past, she'd worried about telling men that she couldn't bear children, but she didn't have that fear with Truman. He'd been so open with her, she found herself wanting to share all of herself with him. Even the hardest parts.

"Why?"

She draped an arm over his middle, drawing strength from him like a leach drew blood. "To really understand the cruel joke part you kind of have to understand the rest of my life, and I don't want to bore you."

He tipped her chin up and kissed her lips. "Please bore me. I want to know everything about you."

She swallowed hard, mustering the courage to start at the beginning. "I've told you about how all I ever wanted was time from my parents, not material things. But it wasn't just their time and attention that I missed out on. I'm not sure they were capable of *really* loving anyone."

His fingers brushed soothingly through her hair and along her back. She closed her eyes, reveling in his ability to know exactly what she needed.

"You know about my constant nannies and ridiculously strict schedule, but when you love someone, truly love them, the way you love Kennedy and Lincoln, and the way I can see you love Quincy, regardless of his current situation, you don't turn your back on them." Her throat clogged with the sadness and anger she'd thought she'd dealt with years ago.

He lifted her higher, cradling her against him, and tucked a lock of hair behind her ear. She focused on the ink on his chest, reminding herself that her loss was nothing compared to his.

With a gentle finger beneath her chin, he brought her eyes up again. His thumb brushed over her cheek in silent support. It was that support that gave her the courage to continue speaking.

"When I was eight, my father's investment company went south. I was just a kid, so the things I noticed weren't necessarily telling, but I knew something was wrong. He was angry all the time. Nervous. My father was never nervous. He didn't do weakness. He used to tell me that weakness bred incompetence. It was such a big word, and I'm sure I didn't understand what it really meant, but I intimated, you know, like kids do. Then things started happening. He had a fleet of cars, and it dwindled. My mother was always cold, but she became colder, angrier, until they barely spoke even to each other. And one day one of my nannies came to get me at school and I'll never forget that day. I had so many nannies, and they changed from day to day sometimes, but that time they'd sent Ben. Ben was nicer than the others. Not warm, but if he saw I was sad, he'd sometimes touch my chin and say, 'Chin up, little lady. The sun's still shining.'"

Truman listened intently; his blue eyes welled with empathy.

"Ben was big, like you. He wore a black suit. They always wore black, the men and women who worked for my father, because of his crazy need for professionalism. 'Look strong, be strong.' I started to hate the word 'strong,' and I fought against wearing anything black, even shoes. I was a bit of a brat about it." Old anger brewed in her belly. "My father cared about what his staff wore, but he couldn't give me a fucking Eskimo kiss?"

Tears slid down her cheeks. She couldn't stop them if she wanted to. She was too deep in the memory, reliving it as if it were yesterday.

"I'll never forget Ben folding his big body down and kneeling beside me. He took both of my hands in his, and I knew something was wrong because none of the staff touched me like that." She spread her hand over Truman's ribs, remembering the feel of Ben's hands around hers.

"He held…" She sniffed back tears, forcing the words to come. "He held my hands and looked right into my eyes with this apologetic but also stern look, and he said, 'Your father has died. It's time to go home, little lady.' Like I needed to suck it up. As if that was something *any* little girl should ever have to hear."

Truman crushed her to him. "Sweetheart. I'm so sorry."

Her chest constricted, and her fingers dug into his skin. "My father, the man who preached strength, was too weak to face bankruptcy. So he *chose* to leave us. He chose to ignore the fact that I didn't care about his wealth or what we had. All I wanted was him. I wanted a father." Her last words were swallowed in sobs. She cried like she never had in all the years since her father's death, ridding her body of a river of anger, an ocean of pain and disappointment, until she had no more tears to cry. And Truman held her, safe and tight, murmuring support laced in love. He didn't have to say he loved her. She knew it, could feel it in his every breath.

Only then did she swallow her pain and tell him the rest of her truth.

"At a time when my mother and I should have been pulling together to support each other and trying to figure out how to move forward together, she set out to find her next sugar daddy. Instead of helping her grieving daughter, my mother disappeared. I saw even less of her. My nannies had dwindled down to two, and I was under their care every minute of the day. I ate with one of them standing beside the table like I was a prisoner—no offense—and I woke up to my clothes laid out for me and my mother God only knew where. She married five months after my father died. My new stepfather traveled a lot—and she went with him."

She pushed up to a sitting position so she could see Truman's face. She knew her eyes were probably red and puffy, and she was probably sporting a Rudolph nose, but he'd been brave enough to confess so much more. She owed him—and herself—the same honesty.

"I grew up swearing I'd shower my children in love, not *things*. That I'd never ignore them, not when they were cranky or when they wanted to tell me a silly story. Not ever."

"You shower my children in love, and it's like a gift to me and to them. Were you worried that you'd turn out like your mother?"

She shook her head, wishing it were that easy. "No. I feel

too much to ever be that cold. People like you and me? We can't turn off our emotions like that. The cruel joke is that when I was a teenager and all my friends got their periods, mine never came. It turns out, some dreams aren't meant to come true. I was born without a uterus and with a shortened…um." This part was much harder to admit, even though she'd dealt with it long ago. It wasn't exactly something any woman wanted to say to her boyfriend.

Truman was looking at her with so much empathy, it made it easier for her to admit the rest.

"A shortened vagina. It's called MRKH. It's not hereditary or genetic. It's a rare congenital birth defect. I don't mean to gross you out—this is way too much information—but I didn't want to give you half the story. I've never told anyone but my best friend about this."

She looked away, embarrassed. With a tender touch, he drew her face back toward his.

"Gross me out? This is your body, and there's nothing gross about it. Honestly, I didn't notice anything out of the ordinary…down there. Making love to you was the best experience of my life. Literally."

He kissed her so intensely she wanted to keep kissing instead of revealing the rest of the story, but she'd made up her mind, and she truly wanted him to know.

"That's because of the wonders of medicine. I had surgery when I was younger to fix *that part*, but I can never bear my own children." She placed her hand over her barren belly. "I'll never know what it feels like to have my baby inside me."

"Oh, sweetheart. I'm so sorry." His voice was thick with sorrow.

"Thank you, but I'm actually lucky. I was born with ovaries, so I can use a surrogate one day if I ever decide to go that route. *Someone* can still give birth to my babies."

"I can't pretend to know what it feels like to be a woman and know I couldn't carry my own children, but what I do know is that whether you give birth to your children or not, any child who grows up with you in their life will be damn lucky."

"Does it bother you that I can't get pregnant?" she asked carefully.

A sweet smile appeared on his handsome face and he shook his head, gathering her in his arms again, more gently this time, somehow knowing she no longer needed to steal his courage—he'd already given her enough.

"No, sweetheart. It doesn't bother me."

He pressed his lips to hers in a series of slow, intoxicating kisses, easing all her fears.

"If there's one thing I've realized with Kennedy and Lincoln," he said quietly, "it's that whether they're yours in the traditional sense or not doesn't matter. The heart doesn't care about bloodlines or birth parents. It just seems to know how to love in the same way our lungs know how to breathe."

CHAPTER SEVENTEEN

OVER THE NEXT week, Truman and Bear installed the fence around a play area in the side yard and began working on the office renovations. In the evenings, Bones and Bullet swung by to help, and Gemma and Dixie, who had become fast friends, took the kids on walks or hung out in the yard while Truman and the guys worked. More often than not, they all hung out and had dinner together, grilling out back and playing with the kids. They hadn't begun building the wall in his apartment yet, but they'd get there. With Lincoln's early-morning feedings, and working late into the evenings on the renovations, Truman's days were long and exhausting, but he didn't mind the hard work, and he loved working alongside his buddies.

He gazed out across the grass at Gemma, heading his way with his little boy in her arms. She looked sexy as sin in a pair of cutoffs, a white T-shirt, and a purple hoodie as she made her way through the knee-high grass with Kennedy, who looked adorable in a pair of pink leggings and hoodie he'd bought her the first night they'd met. It had been eight days since they'd first made love, and their sex life had gotten hotter and their love had grown deeper with every passing day. Regardless of how tired he was at the end of the day, all it took was one of Gemma's sweet smiles to rejuvenate him. Every night after the kids went to sleep, they fell into each other's arms in a ravenous tumble of hunger and need. And later, after they'd devoured each other, satiating their erotic greed, they made love. Two totally different experiences, both intimate and meaningful and both devastatingly satisfying. He was having trouble remembering a time when she hadn't been part of his life.

Gemma waved a hand in front of him, as if he'd been zoning out, which he totally had, and whispered, "If you keep looking at me like that, you're liable to burn my clothes off." She went up on her toes and kissed him.

"And that would be bad because…?"

She shifted Lincoln to her shoulder and patted Truman's butt. "Save it for after they're in bed, lover boy. If you burn my clothes off now, we'll never get to the beach."

He'd lived there for half a year and he had yet to go down to the harbor. The evening out was Gemma's idea. *The kids need to get to know their community. What better way than a stroll by the water and a cone at Luscious Licks?* She knew how to *be* a family. That was just another of a long list of things he adored about her. Although she spent most nights at his place, when she had stayed at her own apartment, he'd dropped off drawings for her at the boutique in the morning, as he had before. He'd feared sharing the ghosts of his past with anyone, but Gemma wasn't afraid of the demons that had driven him to create such darkness, and it was cathartic getting some of the poison that ate away at him out of his system. Their lives were coming together seamlessly, and Truman was beginning to feel like he had a real family. If only he could get a handle on Quincy, but he'd dropped off the grid again.

"Ice cweam," Kennedy chimed in.

Kennedy thrust a fistful of wildflowers toward him, reminding him of what Gemma had said about wishing she'd been allowed to run through a meadow and just be a kid when she was younger. It astonished him that she had no spite in her, despite her upbringing. The love she showed him and the kids was so genuine, sometimes he felt selfish for accepting it so readily.

"We're going, sweetie." Gemma smoothed a hand over Kennedy's hair, untangling a wayward lock from the pink barrette she'd put in it.

That was just one of the little things that Gemma took the time to do for the kids that made him think about her childhood. Who put barrettes in her hair when she was a little girl? Her nannies? Or was that another thing she'd missed out on?

They drove down to Luscious Licks. Another *first* for Truman. The pistachio-colored building had two giant sculptures of ice-cream cones out front. Truman lifted Kennedy up, and she pretended to hold one while Gemma took a picture. Taking kids out for ice cream was such a normal thing to do for most people. But Truman had been so busy trying to hold his and Quincy's lives together when they were growing up, ice-cream shops weren't even on his radar. Now his mind sped down the path of possibilities. Could life be like this? *Normal?* He wanted that so bad he could taste it.

Carrying Lincoln, he draped his free arm over Gemma's shoulder and leaned down for a kiss. "Thank you," he said quietly.

She looked up at him with a curious expression. "For?"

"This is another first for me, and if I hadn't met you I might have missed out on it altogether." She'd not only expanded his and his kids' worlds, but she'd changed him without even trying. He no longer felt as guarded as he always had.

He held open the door for Gemma to pass through, and a pretty woman popped up from behind the counter.

"Gemma!" She looked to be in her midtwenties. Her hair was pinned up in a messy bun and held in place with a…*straw*? Wiping her hands on a towel, she came around the counter with a bright smile. "Who have you brought for me to meet today?" She crouched in front of Kennedy.

Kennedy moved behind Gemma's leg and peered around it at the friendly woman. Gemma placed a hand on Kennedy's back, soothing her so sweetly and naturally Truman's heart gave a little tug.

"Hi, Pen. This is Kennedy." Gemma knelt beside Kennedy. "Kennedy, this is my friend Penny. She loves to give little girls ice-cream cones."

Kennedy blinked warily at Penny. She had come out of her shell at home, but she was still tentative around strangers.

"What's your favorite flavor?" Penny asked.

Gemma glanced up at Truman. "That's what we're here to find out." She lifted Kennedy into her arms and walked over to the freezer, allowing Kennedy to see all the vats of colorful ice cream. "I think we need to taste a few."

"A girl after my own heart," Penny said. She rose to her feet and smiled at Truman. "But first, who is this tattooed man with the baby following you around? A stalker?"

"I can't believe I didn't introduce you." Gemma touched Truman's hand, looking at him with that expression that made his stomach go funky. "This is my boyfriend, Truman. And this little guy"—she tickled Lincoln's cheek—"is his little boy. Kennedy's brother."

Those five words stole his focus.

My boyfriend and *his little boy*. Truman had never been a boyfriend before. Hearing Gemma claim him like that, so readily and with pride in her eyes, reinforced how important of a role it was. For both of them. Hearing her call Lincoln his little boy made him want to correct her, because they'd become so close, the kids felt like they were *theirs*, not solely his, but he held his tongue.

"Gemma's boyfriend? And you're a package deal with these two adorable kids? Where have you been hiding?" Penny went in for a hug. Then she squeezed his biceps and patted his stomach.

Truman looked over her head at Gemma, who laughed at his discomfort.

"Nice to meet you, too, but I'm not carrying any weapons if this is a pat down."

"Pat down? Ha! This is a feel up." Penny laughed and walked around the counter. "I gotta get my feels where I can."

"Once is all she gets," Gemma said.

Truman loved the territorial glint in Gemma's eyes.

Kennedy tasted a bunch of flavors, finally settling on birthday cake, and as they ordered, sadness swept through him. He was sure Kennedy had never had a birthday cake. He glanced at Gemma, who looked like she was thinking the same thing. They were so in sync, in the bedroom and out, and it never failed to surprise him.

By the time they said goodbye to Penny, Kennedy had come out of her shell. She waved with a sweet smile and a mouthful of ice cream as they headed outside.

"Let's take the stroller down to the beach. It's too nice of a night to drive." Gemma opened the trunk of her car, and Truman handed her Lincoln so he could set up the stroller.

She brought so much joy into his and the kids' lives, he

couldn't wait to show her how being with her had changed him. He'd taken advantage of the evenings when Gemma hosted events to finish the painting he'd begun what seemed like a lifetime ago. The demons that used to propel his every move had morphed to something altogether different, and it was reflected in his latest painting. For the first time since he was a teenager, when he'd first begun painting in the junkyard, he *wanted* to share it with the woman who brought light to his darkness.

"Isn't Penny great?" Gemma's voice pulled him from his thoughts.

"Yeah. Is Penny always like that?"

"Yes. She's a riot, isn't she?"

He lifted Kennedy into the stroller, then lowered the infant bed in the back and settled Lincoln in with his blanket. He gathered Gemma in his arms, heat blazing between them as their bodies connected. "I don't like other women touching me."

Gemma went up on her toes and pressed her lips to his in a delicious ice-cream kiss. "I think that might make you the perfect boyfriend."

"DON'T WE HAVE enough pictures?" Truman asked as he lifted Kennedy into his arms and brushed off her tiny bare feet.

Gemma smiled, knowing she'd take a million more. Truman had built a sand castle with Kennedy. They'd collected shells to put in a bowl at the apartment and had watched the sun set while Kennedy tried to outrun the waves creeping up the shore. Gemma had taken tons of pictures. She'd taken one of her favorites when Lincoln had gotten fussy. It was a beautiful picture with the moon rising in the background and Lincoln cradled against Truman's broad chest. Truman was looking down at Lincoln like he was the most spectacular sight he'd ever seen, and Lincoln's little hand reached for his cheek.

This had been the most perfect evening Gemma could remember.

"You're going to be happy you have these." She shoved her phone in her pocket and helped Truman settle Kennedy in the stroller. "We need to make photo albums so you can embarrass Lincoln with his first girlfriend and Kennedy with her prom date or before she gets married. Those are important rites of passage for a little girl."

"Did you go through those rites of passage?" He pushed the stroller onto the boardwalk and pulled Gemma against his side.

She looked up at his handsome face. He'd been working so hard lately, but he looked more relaxed than she'd ever seen him, and she realized she had been more relaxed lately, too. Truman was so attentive toward her, and every time he saw her he lit up, like he'd been thinking about her all day and he was happily surprised to see her, even if they'd made plans. It was an amazing feeling to be adored and cherished. They may have come from different sides of the tracks, but at some point those tracks merged, because he understood her like no one else ever had.

"No. All our pictures were posed," she admitted, remembering those awful times when she was told what to wear, how to stand, and even how wide to smile.

Way deep down inside, she'd wondered if she'd built up hope for finding someone unattainable, a man who would be happy with her and with life instead of making her feel like she was never enough, as her parents had. Truman erased that deep-seated fear. The only thing he wanted more of was *her*.

"Well, then, I'll need to take lots of pictures of you when you're not expecting them." He slid his hand around her neck and gazed into her eyes. "I'm falling so hard for you, Gemma. I want to right all the wrongs you've had done to you."

He was so thoughtful and caring and so much *deeper* than any man she'd ever known. Falling? She *leaped* over the edge. Goose bumps raced over her skin.

"I'm falling for you, too."

A group of guys walked by and Truman tightened his hold on her. She loved his possessiveness. She'd caught him watching the guys on the beach who noticed her, tossing out *back-off* stares like confetti. She'd also noticed him acting just as protective over the kids. As Kennedy ran from the waves, he did the same, looking like a giant beside the petite toddler. And when people glanced into the stroller to look at the pretty baby—and Lincoln was a very pretty baby, with his downy-soft reddish hair and creamy skin—Truman stood with one hand on his little boy, watching the friendly strangers like a hawk. But right now all that intensity was focused on her, and she'd never felt anything so luxurious or so hot.

"I'm one hell of a lucky bastard." He drew her into another delectable kiss.

The kids fell asleep on the way back to the car, and Gemma's head lingered in the clouds as they put the children to bed. Truman turned on the radio by the monitor, as he did every time they went out to the deck after putting the kids to sleep, and took her hand as they left the kids' room. As soon as he shut the door, he pinned her hands above her head, pressed his body into hers until her back hit the wall, and kissed her. The force of the kiss sent the pit of her stomach into a swirl of heat and lust. His hips ground into hers as he took the kiss deeper, moaning intensely, the vibrations obliterating her brain cells.

When their lips parted, he bit her lower lip and gave it a tug. "I have been dying to do that all night."

She slid her hands up the back of his head and pulled him in to another kiss. He smelled like sea and sand carried on the wings of desire, and she wanted to drown in him.

"Come with me," he said against her lips.

She'd go anywhere with him. Do anything with him.

If only her legs would move.

His mouth curved into a gratified grin. "God, I love when that happens to you." He wrapped an arm around her waist, his legs becoming hers. "Come on, sweet girl. I want to show you something."

He grabbed the baby monitor, locked the doors, and led her outside, kissing her again before heading down the back steps.

"Does the one-eyed python want to play in the grass tonight?" Getting down and dirty outside had been hot the first time, and the heat between them had only amped up since.

Crushing her to him, he pressed his mouth to hers again, showering her with the most exquisite kisses.

"My snake always wants to play in your grass." He rubbed noses with her and her heart soared. "But I want to show you something before I tear those clothes off and have my wicked way with you."

"Mm. I like that 'wicked way' idea." She followed him through the gate and into the junkyard, holding him a little tighter. She'd never been back there, and it was pitch-dark.

Truman dug his phone out of his pocket and turned on his flashlight app, illuminating the mass of rusted and mangled cars she'd seen from his deck.

"Stay close," he said, holding her against him.

"Why? Is something going to come out and bite me? Because it feels like there might be monsters down here." She clutched his arm, and he chuckled.

"No. Because I want you close to me." He grinned down at her, aiming the flashlight at the ground. Even in the darkness she saw the heat in his eyes. He kissed her again, long and mind-numbingly slow, successfully kissing away her worries.

He guided her around a van, and when he lifted the light, a sea of ghosts came to life. She clutched him tightly again as she took in the frightening images. Dark eyes shadowed with tortured dullness, claws and fangs and skeletons pushing out of doorways. Men's faces, gaunt and glassy-eyed, had swirls of smoke drifting upward from evil-looking, twisted mouths. Every car in sight had a different scene painted on it. And she knew they were ghosts of Truman's past. She moved on shaky legs, less from fear than from the harsh reality of the poisons of his past surrounding them. Horrific, incredibly detailed, and artistic images came to life on car doors, across hoods and side panels. Villains painted on the inside of the windows, clawing to get out. She'd never seen anything so alive with fear, hate, and vulnerabilities. Like his sketches, they were all done in shades of blacks and grays, the nuances so slight and yet so real, she could feel the pulse of breath coming from them.

"Tru." She must have let go of him without realizing it. His arms circled her waist, then shifted, tucking her safely against his side, and together they continued walking through the maze of Truman's life.

Faces with bushy brows and scraggly beards leered with unseeing eyes. She stopped behind a van, taking in the image of a little boy curled into a fetal position within what looked like a giant bird's nest. A bird with long, jagged talons swooped from a dark cloud above, so vivid and real Gemma sucked in a breath and stumbled backward into Truman. Holding her close, he stepped around the van to a long dark car with a missing hood. On the side panel was an unmistakable self-portrait of Truman, standing tall, wearing denim pants—not black. A ray of yellow sunlight shined down like an arm reaching from the upper edge of the trunk, forming a hand at his back, as if it were urging him forward. His legs were painted midstride. Gemma lost her breath at the torturous beauty before her. This was the only color painting amid a world of angry, haunted images. On the door panel was a picture of a baby, his arms and legs stretching upward, a smile on the baby's lips. His tuft of strawberry hair brought a lump to her throat. *Lincoln.* Crouched beside him was a little girl—*Kennedy*—wearing a pink dress, one tiny hand reaching for Lincoln, the other reaching across the seam of the front panel toward…*me.*

She could hardly breathe as she took in her image painted through Truman's eyes. She wore a bright green and yellow bodysuit. Two transparent, and beautifully depicted, wings sprouted from her back. Bright golds and whites glittered against the dark backdrop. One hand was outstretched toward the kids, the other reached higher, as did her gaze, toward Truman. As Gemma tried to bring air into her lungs, she looked more closely, following a sliver of sunlight that wound its way around Truman, beneath the kids, and bloomed into two open hands, cradling them. The light looped around Gemma's middle like a whip, making her one with the light and drawing them all together.

Truman lifted his phone higher, illuminating the car windows. Shadows hovered over an image of the man she'd seen at the shop the night she'd picked up her car. *Quincy.* Another sliver of sunlight stopped short of him. As if Truman would never stop reaching for his brother, but he knew only Quincy could take that final step. And in those dark clouds was the face of a woman. A woman she now recognized in the faces of her children. *Your mother.*

Gemma turned to face Truman and clutched his shirt, shaking from the impact of what he'd revealed. His face was a mask of sadness and hope, strength and determination. This man. This *incredible* man should be too damaged to know how to love. Too broken to want to embrace life. And yet here he stood, her pillar of strength, revealing all his weaknesses and fears, baring his tormented soul. He was the strongest man she'd ever known, and she wanted all of him.

Her arms circled his neck, splaying across his taut muscles as she drew his face toward hers. Conflicting emotions warred in his eyes, but she pulled harder, wanting to experience that battle with him. He'd known tragedy, desperation, and destitution. He was a survivor, a savior to his siblings and mother. He should be crumbling, but his painful past had etched composure and dignity into his handsome face. He set the monitor on the ground and gripped her arms with strong hands. She knew he could see how what he'd revealed had sparked so many emotions she felt like she'd gone up in flames. He had to see the raging inferno that made her skin burn and her sex throb. Had to feel her need to be closer. Emotions that powerful couldn't remain hidden.

"I wanted you to see how you've affected me," he said in a voice full of restraint and laced with unmistakable lust. "You make a normal, happy life seem possible, and I want that." He turned and gazed at the incredibly beautiful pictures he'd painted of Lincoln and Kennedy. "For them." He turned to face her again. "For us. I'm not afraid of sharing my past with you because you accept it. You accept me, and you help me deal with it and get it out of my system."

He pressed his body to hers and heat consumed her, searing between them like lightning. He clutched her hips, and their bodies took over, grinding together. The need to be closer grew inside her like a volcano ready to erupt. *Skin.* She needed to feel his skin. She tore at his shirt, lifting it up and bending to kiss his chest. She slicked her tongue over his nipple and he groaned, his fingers digging into her flesh. She did it again, spurred on by the heady noise, and he grabbed her face—hard—lifting it so she had no choice but to look into his serious, dark eyes.

"I came down here after telling you why I was in prison," he said strongly, almost angrily, though it was raw, primal passion blazing a path between them. "I thought rage would pour from my hands, but…" He clenched his jaw, holding her impossibly closer, and his breathing quickened. "There was only *you*, Gemma. Your face, your tears. Your touch on my skin. I could fucking *taste* your mouth on mine, and you wouldn't let that darkness in. You're my light, Gemma. You're everything I always thought life should be, and I know you can get any man you want, but I'm so damn happy you want me—"

She smothered his lips in an act of desperation. Her emotions whirled as he took control, and she succumbed to his forceful domination. The kiss was rough and urgent, messy and wet, and so damn hot the rest of the world disappeared. He tore at her pants, and she tore at his, each struggling for speed, unwilling to break their kiss as they fought their way free from their clothes.

"Condom." He grabbed his jeans, fishing for his wallet, and she clutched his wrist.

"Are you really clean? Tested?"

"I wouldn't lie."

"Take me, Truman. Just you, with nothing between us. I want to feel all of you."

He lifted her into his arms, guiding her legs around his waist, and she sank down onto his cock, feeling the broad head as it stroked over her sensitive nerves and every inch of his thick, hard shaft as he filled her.

"Oh *God. Truman.*"

She clung to him, angling his mouth so she could kiss him harder as his strong hands guided her hips in a fast rhythm, greedily fucking her. And she freaking loved it! He knew just how to move, taking her rough and hard, then easing to a torturously slow pace, until she was begging for more. An orgasm teased just out of reach, taunting her into a pleading mess of wanton desires.

She dug her nails into his shoulders, tearing her mouth from his. "Faster. Please, Truman. Come with me. I want to feel you lose control."

Her back met the side of a van, giving him leverage to pound into her with reckless abandon and deftly shattering any hope of cognitive thought. Her limbs tingled, her insides pulsed, and when he buried his face in the tangles of her hair and grunted out her name, she exploded in a firestorm of sensations. Aware of every pulse of his release, every beat of his heart, every frantic breath he took, she knew, without a shadow of a doubt, she wasn't falling for him. She'd already jumped.

CHAPTER EIGHTEEN

AUTUMN SWEPT THROUGH Peaceful Harbor like an artist's brush coloring everything in its path. Bursts of reds, oranges, yellows, and every hue in between flared from the trees and bushes along the streets, kissing the grass and sidewalks with promises of bare trees and even colder nights. Chilly mornings gave way to extra snuggles and led to steamy nights of endless lovemaking, and Gemma couldn't be happier. It was the weekend before Halloween, five life-changing weeks since she'd met Truman. She spent most nights at his place, and probably had as many clothes at his apartment as she did at her own.

Crystal held up a royal blue gown with faux diamonds lacing the sweetheart neckline. "How about this one?" She waggled her brows and waved her hand above the neckline. "Perfectly bare, which is ideal for your *pearl necklace*."

They were shopping for a gown for the fundraiser while Truman and the guys finished installing the door on the new bedroom wall. She'd offered to take the kids with her, but Truman had insisted that she needed time alone with Crystal. He was so thoughtful, always making sure she didn't slight herself because of him or the kids. She wondered when he'd realize that spending time with him and the kids was her most favorite thing of all.

Gemma laughed and shook her head. "I *really* don't want to go this year."

"Gee, I hadn't noticed. We've only spent the last three weeks looking at every dress store in Peaceful Harbor. I know we have plenty of time before the event, but at this rate…" Crystal hung the dress on the rack and glanced in the mirror, pulling her hair into an updo. "Maybe because you told your man not to go with you?"

"Are you kidding? I'd never punish him with the likes of my mother and her pretentious cohorts. Besides, he and I talked about it, and being around that many people would be too much for Kennedy."

Both Lincoln and Kennedy had progressed well over the past few weeks. Lincoln had tried baby food and had gone straight through it, preferring finger foods, and he was sleeping through the night, which was a big milestone. And even though Kennedy had become less wary around strangers, the people who attended the fundraising events weren't exactly warm and welcoming. She wasn't about to put those sweet children in a situation she didn't even want to be in. In addition to the kids, she had Truman to consider. He had his own worries and didn't need the stress of contending with her awful mother.

Crystal dropped her hair and it tumbled loosely over her shoulders as she spun around and set a narrow-eyed stare on Gemma. "You still haven't told your mother about him, have you?"

Gemma turned away, pretending to inspect another gown.

"Gemma Wright, what are you thinking? If you don't tell her, she'll fix you up with another one of those uptight pricks like she did last time, and I don't think Tru Blue is going to be cool with that."

Sighing, Gemma dropped her shoulders in defeat. "It's on my to-do list, but you know what conversations with my mother are like." She didn't even want to think about her mother. She was happy. Really, truly happy, and her mother had a way of squashing the happiness of everyone around her. Besides, she had enough on her mind. Truman still hadn't heard from Quincy, and even though he didn't talk about it, she knew he was worried about him.

"I know, and when she tells you you're dating him as part of your ongoing rebellion—like your business, and moving away, *yadda, yadda, yadda*—tell her to shove it up her ass. Because I've seen you with Truman, and you've never looked at a man that way."

She was glad Crystal saw how much she cared for Truman, and she had a point about her mother. She probably would accuse her of dating Truman to spite her. But the truth was, even though Gemma had thought about her mother's reaction, her mother's opinion did not factor into Gemma's decision to be with Truman. What Gemma saw in Truman were all the qualities her mother could never see even if he were a suit-wearing billionaire. How could her mother recognize intense loyalty that knew no boundaries, love that came directly from the heart, and a firm grasp on doing things for the right reasons, when she didn't possess those qualities herself?

Crystal looped her arm through Gemma's and dragged her out of the store. "Come on. We're going to Pleasant Hill." Pleasant Hill was about an hour away.

"What? Why?" She walked fast, keeping pace with Crystal as they crossed the parking lot.

"Because you *are* going to have to tell her, which means you'll have to listen to all of her socialite news about people you don't know or care about and probably a diatribe about dating a man from the wrong side of the tracks. She'll have you tearing your hair out in no time." She climbed into the car and slid a coy smile to Gemma. "If she can torture you, it's only fair to give her a little payback. We're going to Jillian's."

Jillian's was an upscale and slightly outlandish dress shop. "A *payback dress.* Oh, Crystal. You are brilliant."

Two hours later Gemma stood before a three-way mirror wearing a floor-length black leather gown with a plunging neckline that dipped almost to her navel.

Jillian Braden, the owner of the shop and designer of many of the gowns, moved in her four-inch heels as if she'd been born in them. She tucked her hair—a spectacular cross between burgundy and dark auburn—behind her ear and walked in a slow circle around Gemma. "You have a great figure, and your face is so refined and classic looking that it gives you an elegant and sweet vixenish quality that not many women can pull off. You're *killing* it." She adjusted the shoulder straps, then smoothed a wrinkle at Gemma's waist.

"She's right, Gem," Crystal agreed. "But don't let Truman see you in it, because it'll be shredded before you ever step foot outdoors."

Gemma's stomach quivered at the thought of Truman's hands all over her. She turned to the side, admiring the way the leather hugged her curves, making her feel sultry and alluring—and her stomach knotted. She wanted to be sultry and alluring for Truman, but the idea of wearing that dress out in public without him by her side made her feel uneasy. Plus, she might give her mother a heart attack if she showed up in it. As much as she disliked her mother, she didn't want to ruin her event.

"My mother would totally flip out if I showed up in leather."

"Isn't that the point?" Crystal smirked.

"I don't know. It's a fun idea, but the more I think about it, the more I worry that it'll end up backfiring and the night will be even more painful. I think I need less vixen and more refined rebellion."

Jillian guided Gemma by the arm toward the dressing room. "If there's one thing I'm certain of, it's that a woman should never wear a dress she's not totally comfortable in. No matter what the reason." She gave Gemma a little shove through the curtain. "Take that off. I've got *the* dress for you."

Gemma stripped, and a few minutes later Jillian's voice came through the curtains.

"Try this one. I think it strikes the perfect balance—*proper defiance*—and it's one of my favorites. My brother and I designed it together." Her hand parted the curtains, and all Gemma saw was a mass of shimmery black material and lace.

"Your brother designs clothes too?" She slipped the dress over her head. The luxurious material slid over her skin like silk, hugging her from shoulder to thigh, where a slit revealed her right leg.

"Mm-hm. My twin, actually. Jax. We've been designing together on and off for years, but his specialty is wedding gowns." Jillian zipped up the back of the dress and fidgeted with the shoulders and waist, then stood back and ran an assessing eye over Gemma. "Gorgeous. Go on out to the three-way and I'll grab heels."

As soon as Crystal spotted her following Jillian out of the dressing room, she jumped from a plush chair and squealed.

"Oh my gosh, Gemma! You look stunning."

"Really?" She turned to look in the mirror and her jaw

dropped. The neckline fell just below her collarbone. A pattern of black lace and silk created capped sleeves. A narrow path of lace ran down her sides, dipping in at the waist, to just below the curve of her hip. She glanced over her shoulder at the low back.

Jillian knelt by her feet. “These are comfortable *and* sexy. You don’t need to rock sky-high heels in this dress.” She stepped back, and her smile radiated with approval. “The fishtail accentuates your waist, and since you’re not showing any cleavage, the touch of lace looks elegant rather than racy. What do you think?”

“I think I want to marry this dress.” Feeling a spike of rebellion, she added, “And the neckline is perfect. No room for pearls.”

TRUMAN CLOSED THE new bedroom door to the unfinished room and eyed the gorgeous woman lying on the bed paging through a flyer of children’s Halloween costumes. She wore a pair of boy-short panties that barely covered her ass and a spaghetti-strap top. Her knees were bent, her feet dancing above her as she suggested costumes for Lincoln. Kennedy had already picked hers out. She was going to be the cutest Tinker Bell that ever lived.

“A pumpkin? There was a pumpkin in Cinderella.” Gemma pointed at a picture of an infant wearing a pumpkin costume.

Truman lay down beside her, ran his hand up her thigh, and squeezed her ass. “I like your pumpkin.”

She flashed a haughty smile. “I still think he should be Winnie the Pooh. That’s who Kennedy says he is in her night-

night book, and she should be allowed to choose his costume. As his older sister, it's her right."

He slid his leg over the back of her thighs and kissed her shoulder. "He's only a few months old and already women are ruling his life." He nuzzled her neck. "I think he should wear a boy's costume. He can be a prince, like I'm going to be."

She leaned in to him with a tease in her eyes. "Kiss me again and maybe I'll consider it."

He leaned toward her lips and she turned away and pointed to her shoulder. He chuckled and kissed her shoulder again.

"Shoulder kisses are the best," she said in the breathless voice that made his body ignite.

He continued kissing her shoulder, moving slowly down her breastbone. Still looking at the magazine, she reached over and lifted his chin so he was kissing her shoulder again. God, he loved everything she did.

"I think Kennedy wants you to be her only prince, and she was pretty clear about wanting Linc to be Pooh. But if you're so adamant about not letting him be a fuzzy bear, which for the record, I think he should be, then how about if he dresses up like one of the Lost Boys from her storybook?"

He gave her a light smack on the ass, earning a sexy giggle. "The Lost Boys are bikers in her book. You know how I feel about that."

"You love your biker friends." She turned on her side and pressed her body to his. "Just because we put him in a biker outfit doesn't mean he'll go all rebellious on you when he's older. Besides, *you* made the Lost Boys bikers. Isn't that hypocritical?" She pushed him onto his back and pressed her lips to his jaw, his neck, and continued kissing her way down the center of his body, making it hard for him to concentrate on anything but her incredible mouth.

"I'm filling their heads with the *good* the Lost Boys do. One day they'll learn the difference between motorcycle clubs and biker gangs. *Then* he can dress however he wants."

"I spent my entire childhood making up stories about being everything from a fairy princess to a biker girl, and I didn't turn out so bad."

She continued kissing him, and he was seriously reconsidering Winnie the Pooh. There was a fine line between a motorcycle club and a biker gang, and thinking about Lincoln growing up and heading down that path scared the hell out of Truman. Gemma was right, though. Lincoln was too young for Truman to worry about that type of thing—but Truman was enjoying the way she was trying to convince him to give in. He loved when her mouth was on him anywhere, but when she went down on him, he felt even closer to her. Not because of the thrum of erotic pleasures it brought, but because she seemed to *enjoy* pleasuring him and the control that came with it. Seeing Gemma enjoying anything made life a million times better. Seeing her enjoying *him* was pure bliss.

She grazed her teeth over his nipple, intensifying the lust coiling low in his core. "He'd be super cute with a bandana on his little head and a Harley shirt and jeans." She swirled her tongue over his abs, her hands playing over his ribs, trailing lower by the second.

"Gem…" He curled his fingers in the sheets to keep from pushing her lower.

"I have an idea. Let's make a deal." She ran her tongue around his belly button, and his cock twitched with anticipation. "How about you let me write an article about you and your artwork—*Local Creative Genius Unveiled*—and you can choose Linc's costume?"

She'd been urging him to let her write an article about his artwork for weeks. She was convinced that everyone in Peaceful Harbor would think he was far more talented than he believed himself to be. She even talked about him illustrating children's books that they would write together. She loved making up stories, too, and said that together their stories would have more interesting twists. What did he know about any of that? He wrote stories for his kids, but other kids might hate them.

"I don't want the attention," he said honestly. "Nobody knows about my conviction. I'd rather keep it that way."

She lowered the waist of his briefs slowly, revealing just the head of his cock, and slid her tongue over the tip. "Hm. What can I do to change your mind about *one* of those things?" She practically purred every word.

She pressed her hands against his hips, holding his briefs across the center of his cock, and ran her tongue over his sensitive, swollen glans, driving him out of his fucking mind. Using her teeth, she dragged his briefs down, then pulled them off and tossed them to the floor. He rose up, and she pushed him back down.

"Anxious, aren't we?" she teased.

"You make me crazy."

A mischievous smile split her lips as she wrapped her warm, slender fingers around his shaft, pulling a groan from his lungs. He greedily watched her slide that naughty tongue of hers over the bead at the tip and gloss it over her lips.

"Holy fuck, Gemma." He reached for her and she leaned out of his grasp.

"Mine," she whispered, smiling as she swallowed him to the back of her throat and began working her hand and mouth in quick succession.

His head fell back to the mattress, eyes shut. He rocked into her fist, deeper into her mouth. She kept him nice and slick, working him with a fast, tight grip.

"That's it, baby. *God*, your *mouth* is lethal."

She lifted her head, releasing his cock to the cooler air, and rolled her hand over the head, then stroked his shaft again. She used tight stokes, easing as she rolled her hot, wet palm over the head, then repeating the scintillating torture, bringing him right to the verge of release before easing again. He opened his eyes, and the daring look in hers told him she knew exactly what she was doing.

"Take your clothes off," he commanded.

She shook her head, her eyes narrowing, her hair billowing around her beautiful face. "Not yet."

She dragged her tongue from base to tip. Scooting lower, so she was lying between his legs, she licked his balls, still fisting his cock, working him into a frenzy. She knew how much he loved that, and if she didn't fuck him soon, he was going to come all over her.

He tangled his hands in her hair, holding her mouth to his balls and watching her love him. Her skin was flushed, her lips slightly swollen, and the challenge in her eyes made her even sexier. God, he loved her. He loved her so damn much he felt it in his bones. He grabbed the hem of her shirt and pulled it up over her head. She reared up on her knees, holding his gaze as she wiggled out of her panties. When she pushed his chest again, he went down willingly and reached between her legs.

She shook her head and brought his hand to her mouth, placing several openmouthed kisses to his palm, leaving it wet. Then she wrapped his hand around his cock and straddled his thighs. Before he could protest, she sucked two of her fingers into her mouth and brought them between her legs. *Holy shit.*

Truman didn't jerk off in front of women. *Ever.* He never let other women touch him the way he let her. He *fucked* them. Then again, everything he did with Gemma was different—and there was nothing he wouldn't do for her.

"My good girl has just become a dirty girl."

"Your good girl only wants to be *your* dirty girl."

She was a visual feast as she fingered her pussy and brought her other hand to her breast, stroking and caressing while staring daringly into his eyes. She licked her lips and dropped her eyes to his fist, watching as he worked his cock. When she brought her wet fingers to her clit, her head tipped back, and he nearly blew his load. He rose off the mattress, still fisting his cock, and tangled his hand in her hair, crashing their mouths together in a brutally ruthless kiss as her orgasm claimed her. Her tongue stilled. A long, pleasure-filled moan rumbled up from her lungs into his. *Heaven. Sheer heaven.* He held her trembling body tight, kissing her more tenderly as she came down from the peak, and swept her beneath him. She smiled up at him with that sweet, sinful look that hit him square in the center of his chest every damn time.

"You're mine, sweet girl. *Only mine.*"

"Always."

Her hands circled his neck as their bodies joined together, sealing their late-night promises with kisses and loving each other like tomorrow might never come.

They lay together for a long while afterward, their skin still moist from their lovemaking, their fingers intertwined. When Gemma got up to use the bathroom, Truman refused to let go.

"I need to pee," she said with a soft laugh.

"I've waited my whole life for you. I never want to let you go." He gathered her closer.

"God, I love you." She pressed her lips to his.

He drew back, searching her eyes to see if she realized what she'd said, but she was looking at him like he'd taken away her favorite lollipop.

"Tell me again," he said quickly.

Her brows knitted.

"You said you loved me," he reminded her, hoping she wasn't going to take it back.

She laughed and pressed both hands to his cheeks. "Haven't I said it before? Gosh, Tru. I feel like I've been saying it for weeks. I love you. I love you more than the sun and the moon and the stars. I love you more than chocolate ice cream and fairy wings. I love you and I love the kids so much I—"

He pressed his lips to hers, overwhelmed by how deeply and completely her love touched him. When he deepened the kiss, she melted into him.

"That's my favorite thing," he said, kissing her again. "I love when you go completely boneless, like my kisses wreck you."

"Mm." She kissed him again. "Your kisses complete me, but they never wreck me."

He liked that even more. After a few more kisses, she put on his T-shirt, another thing he adored, and went into the bathroom. Lincoln's whimper came through the monitor and Truman got up.

Gemma peeked into the bedroom and said, "I've got him."

Truman sat on the edge of the bed listening to her voice come through the monitor. "Hey, sweet boy. Ohmygod." Her voice escalated, and he jumped to his feet, stepping into his briefs as he hurried out the bedroom door.

"Trum—"

He was already beside her, both of them marveling at Lincoln, who was sitting up in his crib. *Sitting up*.

"He's sitting!" she whispered excitedly, and grabbed Truman's hand.

Seeing Lincoln sit up for the first time was overwhelming. How could something so little feel so big and mean so much? He put an arm around Gemma and kissed the side of her head.

Lincoln wiped his eyes with his tiny fist, teetering a little. Gemma and Truman both reached into the crib, but Lincoln wobbled, then settled on his butt and yawned.

"Oh my gosh," Gemma whispered, so as not to wake Kennedy, who was snuggled up in her new Tinker Bell pajamas, hugging the stuffed Pooh doll Dixie had given her.

"Tru, your boy's growing up."

Our boy's growing up. He gave her a chaste kiss to keep the words from slipping free and lifted Lincoln out of his crib.

"We should have gotten a picture," Gemma whispered.

Truman didn't need a picture. He knew he'd never forget the look of love in Gemma's eyes, the sight of Lincoln sitting up for the first time—or the feeling of his heart expanding inside his chest at how very blessed he was to have so much love under one roof.

CHAPTER NINETEEN

ONE OF THE things Gemma loved most about Peaceful Harbor was how the community came together for holidays and events. The Halloween parade was one of her favorites. Children and parents alike were allowed to join in the march down Main Street and around the harbor. Truman and Gemma discussed the event being too much for Kennedy, but she was so excited about the idea of it, they decided to try. Tonight Crystal and the Whiskeys joined Gemma and Truman for the kids' first Halloween adventure. They all dressed up like characters from the storybook Truman had made for Kennedy, and Kennedy was delighted at the outcome. The girls had dressed at the boutique. Queen Dixie's dress was bright red, while Gemma's was green, and Crystal dressed as Snow White, which was hilarious since she was definitely a dark princess at heart. After taking far too many pictures of their group, they headed into town. It was still light out when they reached Main Street, where crowds had already begun forming.

Kennedy gripped Gemma's hand tighter.

Prince Truman held Lincoln, who was dressed as Winnie the Pooh, thanks to Truman's love for his little girl. He must have sensed Kennedy's discomfort, because he moved closer, putting a protective arm around Gemma. Before she realized what was happening, Bullet, Bones, and Bear, each dressed in full biker Lost Boy garb, fell into formation like bodyguards. Bullet walked behind them, scanning the crowd with his deep-set eyes. Bones moved beside Dixie, sandwiching her between him and Truman. Dixie was at least five nine, but she looked small flanked by the two formidable men. Bear took up residence beside Crystal. A bookend to Bones on the other side of the group. It was an oddly safe and wonderful feeling to know the kids were so well protected. The fact that Gemma had grown up feeling oppressed by the people watching over her wasn't forgotten. The difference—and it was a huge one—was that these were friends who genuinely loved Kennedy and Lincoln as much as they loved each other. In the few seconds it took for them to effectively surround their charges, Gemma realized how strong a family Kennedy and Lincoln now had. And as she glanced up at Truman, who leaned in for a kiss, she realized she had that big, warm family, too. And it struck her that her own family would have snubbed their noses at such an event.

"When I have kids, I want you to write their fairy tales," Dixie said to Truman. Her red hair was piled on her head and a few tendrils had sprung loose.

Truman laughed. "I think you can find better fairy tales than mine."

"Only if you mean *ours*," Gemma said, and tipped her head up for a kiss, admiring how handsome he looked in his costume. Then she said to Dixie, "I'm trying to convince him that we should write stories together and he should illustrate them."

Kennedy had insisted on reading her storybook every night. Truman had not only illustrated the entire book, but he and Gemma had written the story out as well, so she could read it to

Kennedy, too. It was a lovely story about family and friendship, and Gemma wondered if it was what Truman had always dreamed of, like she had, or if he had made it up solely for his little girl. Either way, she loved how he thought of everything for the kids. He worried over every little detail, like the Lost Boys stealing kids in *Peter Pan* and the father dying in *The Lion King*. He picked apart movies and books, afraid something would spark an underlying fear in the kids he hadn't yet discovered. Kennedy had never once asked for her mother. It was a heartrending realization to think about what that meant. While creating his own fairy tale might seem a bit overprotective to others, Gemma knew that everything he did was driven by love, not by the need for control.

Bear draped an arm over Crystal's shoulder.

"Um. Hello? There might be single guys here," Crystal complained, trying to move out from under his grasp.

Bear shot her a look that clearly told her not to bother trying to dislodge herself from his grip—and something much hotter that caused Gemma to shoot a curious look at her best friend. Crystal rolled her eyes, but there was a secret message there meant only for her. People said blood was thicker than water, but Gemma believed true friendship was thickest of all.

Kennedy slowed, and when Gemma reached down to lift her into her arms, she saw fear in the little girl's eyes. What was she thinking? This was far too much for Kennedy. She picked her up and stopped walking, and the others stopped with her, the men's eyes actively searching the crowd. Only Truman's eyes remained on his little girl and Gemma.

"She's frightened. It's too much," Gemma said.

Truman nodded with a serious expression. "Turn it around."

Like an army, the group turned. Crystal wasn't as quick on the uptake and Bear turned her by the shoulders and put his arm around her again.

"Do you mind?" Crystal said, but there was a sultry undertone to her words.

"Yeah, actually, I do," Bear said with a smirk. "We're heading back. Kennedy's scared."

"Oh." Crystal leaned forward and looked at Gemma. "Is she okay?"

"Yes. I wasn't thinking. She's not ready for crowds like this." Gemma kissed Kennedy's forehead, holding her tightly as they headed back toward their cars.

"Twick or tweet?" Kennedy asked.

"Do you still want to go trick or treating, princess?" Truman asked.

Kennedy nodded.

Gemma looked questioningly at Truman, whose jaw had gone tight.

"She's never done it before," Gemma reminded him. "The next block is a residential street. We could try a few houses and see how she does. She's excited over the promise of candy even though she's nervous." She lowered her voice and whispered, "Sometimes you've got to let her take a chance. I took one, and look how things turned out."

A smile lifted Truman's lips and he whispered, "What if it scares her?"

"Look around you, Tru. She's got an army of family to help her feel safe again."

Truman shifted his gaze to the men one by one. A telepathic message seemed to pass between them, and without another word, they headed toward the residential street.

IT TURNED OUT what Kennedy really wanted was for Truman to go trick or treating while she waited on the sidewalk, safely surrounded by the rest of their group. Truman had never gone trick or treating before, but that didn't stop him from standing on the front stoop of a house with Lincoln in his arms, towering over a handful of children.

The older woman who answered the door glanced at Lincoln and smiled up at Truman. "I don't think that little guy has enough teeth to eat candy yet. A little old to trick or treat, aren't you?"

"Are you ever too old to make your kids happy?" He pointed to Kennedy, safely nestled in Gemma's arms, with his friends standing sentinel around them.

The woman handed him a few candy bars. "You've got yourself a nice-looking family. Happy Halloween."

Warmed by her observation, Truman thanked her and joined the rest of his *family*.

"Here you go, princess." He opened his hand, revealing the candy bars.

Kennedy's eyes widened and she grabbed a candy bar. "More?" The *r* was soft. "Them get candy?"

In unison everyone denied their need for a sweet treat, and Kennedy's smile grew bigger. "Mine?"

"Yes, princess. That one's yours," he said, pleased and mildly worried that at her young age she thought of others so quickly. His mind spun back to the first night he'd found her, when Lincoln was crying and she'd patted his back, as if she knew no one else would. He wondered if she'd always think of others first because she'd learned at such a young age that she needed to care for Lincoln, the same way he'd known to protect Quincy. While he loved that she shared so easily, when he thought of what her life must have been like before he found her, sadness slammed into him.

He helped her open the candy and she took a bite. "More?" she asked again, around a mouthful of chocolate, and everyone laughed.

After they trick or treated at a few more houses, the others headed to Whiskey Bro's to catch the costume party, and Gemma and Truman took the kids home.

They'd forgotten to leave on the outside lights at the apartment. Truman turned on the flashlight app on his phone, illuminating the path around the building. He carried Kennedy in one arm, his other hand resting protectively on Gemma's lower back. Lincoln was fast asleep in her arms.

"He made a damn cute Pooh bear." He smiled down at Gemma. "And you put every princess, other than our little princess, to shame."

"Thank you." She stopped walking to pull him closer for a kiss. "This was so much fun. I'm glad I got to share the kids' first real Halloween with you."

"Me too, sweetheart." He glanced over her shoulder at movement in the grass. Stepping in front of Gemma, he lifted his phone, aiming the flashlight toward the shadows, and his world tilted on its axis.

Quincy lay facedown in the grass.

"Stay here." The few feet between them and Quincy felt like a mile. He crouched beside his brother, still holding Kennedy. *Please don't be dead. Don't you fucking die on me.* He rolled Quincy over, quickly grabbing his wrist in search of a pulse, feeling the slow beat beneath his fingers. *Thank God.* He did a quick visual inspection of his unconscious brother, looking for stab wounds or bullet holes. *Fuck.* He didn't know what he was looking for. Quincy's nose and mouth were bloody, his face bruised on the right side, with a gash over his right cheekbone. Truman rose to his feet.

"Get the kids in the car, Gemma." The command came out harsh as he walked swiftly with a hand on Gemma's back, moving her forward, scanning the property in case whoever beat up Quincy was lurking.

"What happened? Should we call the police?" The fear in her voice was palpable.

She looked over her shoulder, and Truman stepped behind her, blocking her view. He didn't want that ugliness anywhere near her and the kids. His fucking brother had brought his nightmare to his doorstep, and he had no idea what else might follow.

"No police. If I have any interaction with the police, I have to report it, and I've got no black marks on my record since my release. I'm taking him to the hospital." He put Kennedy in her car seat, then took Lincoln from Gemma, who seemed too stunned to focus, and strapped him in.

He pressed Bear's speed-dial number and lifted his phone to his ear while opening the driver's door for Gemma.

"Bro?" Bear answered.

"I need you."

"On my way."

"Truman!" Gemma demanded. "Talk to me. Why are we leaving? Is Quincy okay? What happened?"

He looked into her eyes and tried to slow his racing mind long enough to give her the answers she deserved. "I don't know what happened or how Quincy got here. All I know is that he's breathing, but he's badly beaten and unconscious. I've got to get him to the hospital. But if this was a drug deal gone bad, whoever did this could come back. I want you and the kids safe—and you can't be safe here until I know what happened. I don't even know if anyone's been in the apartment."

"Okay. Oh God, Truman. What about you? What if someone is here?" She looked around the yard. "I hope Quincy's okay."

"Me too. But you have to go."

She hugged him quickly. "I'll go, but I need the kids' stuff."

Two sets of headlights raced down the driveway. Bear's and Bullet's trucks skidded to stops and their doors flew open. Bear, Bullet, Bones, Dixie, and Crystal stalked across the parking lot. Crystal made a beeline for Gemma.

Truman filled in the others as quickly as he could. Bones went to help Quincy. Gemma told Bear what she needed, and he went to retrieve it from the apartment.

"Gemma, I know this is scary, but I have to get back to Quincy and get him to the hospital, and I can't do that until I know you and the kids are okay. Please go."

She looked around the yard with fear in her eyes and nodded. "Please be careful."

"I will, baby. I love you, and I'm so sorry." He glanced into the car at the kids, feeling like he was right back in the hellhole he'd grown up in. He was *not* going to fail them. Not tonight. Not ever. That shit was going to end here and now.

CHAPTER TWENTY

GEMMA AND THE girls put the kids to sleep in her apartment, with Kennedy on the bed and Lincoln in the playpen Bear brought over shortly after they arrived. Gemma was a nervous wreck, worrying about Truman and Quincy and feeling completely out of her element. She paced the living room, a million questions racing through her mind.

"I've never been through anything like this before," she said to no one in particular. Lifting her eyes to Bear, who was sitting on the couch next to Dixie with his elbows on his knees, she asked, "Is this what it was like when he was growing up? Are the kids going to be safe there? Is Truman safe?"

Crystal tried to embrace her, but Gemma pushed out of her arms.

"Sorry," she said to Crystal. "I'm too nervous to stand still."

Bear lifted serious eyes to her. "Truman knows what he's doing. He's been down this path with his mother."

"His mother," she repeated, feeling a mix of sadness and anger. "I should be there with him. He must be so scared for Quincy."

"Bones is with him," Bear assured her. "The best thing you can do is stay here with the kids. He'd be worried sick if you and the kids weren't safe. He's already texted me to make sure I don't let you go back to the apartment. As if I would." He scoffed. "We won't know what's really going on until we hear back from him. Bullet's at the apartment keeping watch. Nothing was touched inside, and there were no signs of a break-in, which is good."

She checked her phone, but there were no messages from Truman. "He texted you?" She couldn't hide the hurt in her voice.

"Watchdog texts," Dixie said. "That's what my brothers call them. It's what they do when they don't have time to talk but they want to make sure everyone's okay."

Bear rose from the couch and showed her the message from Truman. *I love them, man. Watch them as if they're your own. Keep them away from the apartment until we know what's up.*

She looked up at Bear, feeling like she was floating at sea without a raft. "I don't know how to do this. Or how to live this way." She thought of the kids, and fear spread through her.

"You don't have to," he assured her. "We do. And none of us would ever put you or the kids in harm's way."

She looked at Crystal, who said, "I believe him. He's handsy, and he's territorial with things that aren't his, but I believe the dude."

Bear laughed. "Sugar, you haven't *seen* handsy."

"And you worry about Crow around me?" Dixie scoffed. "*Please.*" She put an arm around Gemma and led her to the couch, sitting down beside her. "Gemma, Truman is one of the best, most loyal men I know. It's really hard to separate *him* from everything that's happened tonight, especially when you're so upset. But remember that Truman has never done drugs. He's spent his life protecting Quincy, and paid a heavy price for doing so. He doesn't know how to turn that off, no matter how much he loves you. And he does love you. Hell, that man is so in love with you, he built a bedroom and made sheet forts. But the truth is, you need to dig deep and think about whether you love him enough to deal with Quincy's drug issues. Because tonight could happen again. It might not, but it could, and only you can decide if it's too much for you to handle."

TRUMAN KNOCKED ON the door to Gemma's apartment bleary-eyed and exhausted. It was seven thirty in the morning and he'd been up all night. The door swung open and Gemma launched herself into his arms. He'd texted her a few hours earlier to let her know that Quincy was out of the woods, and her simple text—*Good. I love you*—had comforted him. But that was nothing compared to holding the woman he loved in his arms.

"I was so worried." She kissed his cheeks, his lips, then his cheeks again.

He soaked in every second of her attention, feeling his tilting world right itself. "Hey, sweet girl." He rubbed his nose over hers, needing their secret silent affections as much as he needed their verbal ones. "I missed you."

"Me too. Are you okay? Is Quincy okay?" She searched his face, and he knew he looked like hell. Until the second she was in his arms he'd felt like hell, too. Now he felt exhausted, but better.

"Yeah. Let's go inside and I'll fill everyone in."

He found Dixie sitting at the table with Lincoln on her lap and Bear on the couch, his head resting back against the cushion, eyes closed. He leaned down and kissed Lincoln as

Bear pushed to his feet.

"All good?" Bear asked, giving him a quick embrace.

"Yeah." He looked around. "Where's Kennedy?"

"Tooman!" Kennedy ran down the hall with Crystal on her heels. Both wore a ponytail secured with a big pink bow.

He scooped Kennedy into his arms and hugged her tight.

"She's got Gemma's love of all things frilly." Crystal shook her head, sending her long black ponytail swinging from side to side.

Kennedy wiggled out of his arms and went to Bear, freeing Truman up to claim Gemma again. "Thanks for everything, you guys."

Crystal put her hand on her hip and glared at him. "You're welcome, but we're not leaving until we get the scoop."

"I figured as much, but I gotta sit down. I'm beat." He sank down to the couch, pulling Gemma down beside him and pinching the bridge of his nose as he tried to figure out where to begin.

"Quincy's in rehab," he finally said.

"He is?" Gemma and Bear asked at the same time.

"He hit rock bottom." Glancing at Kennedy, he chose his words carefully. "He owed a guy money. He's lucky they didn't…" He didn't want to say *kill* in front of Kennedy. He finally had a shred of hope that Quincy would clean up his act and become the brother Truman believed he was destined to be.

"They know where you live?" Bear asked.

Truman shook his head. "They dumped him over the bridge. He walked the seven miles to my place and collapsed."

"So, is it safe to go back there?" Gemma asked tentatively.

"Yes, but I want to talk to you about that after I get some sleep."

"Okay." She touched his hand and smiled.

The simple show of affection warmed him all over.

"Is this forced rehab?" Bear asked.

"No. He went willingly. It was actually his idea. He said he's been thinking about it ever since I sent him away from the shop." He squeezed Gemma's hand. "He can leave anytime, but it's a thirty-day program with the possibility of extending it to ninety if he needs it."

"Dude, how are you affording that?" Bear asked.

"What good is money if you don't use it to help your family?" He'd used his savings, and even if he had to work twice as many hours, he'd figure out a way to get his brother the help he needed.

"I hear ya." Bear touched Crystal's arm. "Come on, sugar. Let's give these guys some privacy."

"I'm not your 'sugar,'" Crystal snapped.

Bear chuckled.

Crystal hugged Gemma. "Do you guys want me to take the kids for a few hours so you can rest?"

"No," Gemma said. "I think Truman needs to have them here."

She knew him so well. "Thanks anyway, Crystal. I appreciate the offer." He embraced her, then took Lincoln from Dixie. "Thank you all for staying over and helping out."

Dixie hugged him. "No worries, and ditto on the offer to babysit. When you guys need it, I'm around."

"Thanks, Dix."

After everyone left, Truman sank down to the floor with Lincoln sitting between his legs and Gemma beside him.

"How are you really doing?" she asked him sweetly.

He watched Kennedy playing with her toys and looked at

Lincoln's little fist curled around his index finger. "I'm relieved and hopeful, but I know how it is with addicts. They can *want* to be clean, and in a blink of an eye they're chasing the dragon again."

"I've never been through anything like this. I was pretty terrified last night. Is that what it was like for you growing up?" She went up on her knees and slid an arm across his shoulder.

It was embarrassing how much he craved and needed her touch. "I'm sorry, sweetheart. I hate that you and the kids had to go through that. When we were growing up, I was so focused on taking care of Quincy that everything else was a blur. Going to school was a reprieve, and coming home was a nightmare. Last night, when I saw Quincy lying there, I was thrown right back there, to finding my mother passed out after school, or coming home to an empty house and she'd show up sometimes *days* later."

He cradled her face in his hands and said, "I don't want you or the kids to ever see anything like that again. If Quincy doesn't get clean, I'll lay down the law with him, and he won't come back."

She shook her head, her eyes serious. "You can't do that, because even if he isn't ready now, one day he might be. And if you're not there to help him, he'll have nowhere to go."

"Jesus, Gemma. What did I do to deserve you?"

"I ask myself the same thing about you, Tru. Dixie said some things that really made me think about us last night. I don't want to change anything about you. I was honest when I said I was terrified, and I second-guessed everything for half the night, because I've never been around anything even remotely similar to drugs or alcoholism, or even biker guys."

She paused and nibbled on her lower lip, making his stomach knot up.

"But I've never been happier, or felt more loved, in all my life than I am when I'm with you. And I love your kids, and I know that when we're together, we're safe. You took care of us before taking care of your own brother. I don't know how to deal with what Quincy is going through, but you didn't know how to raise babies. I have to believe we found each other for a reason, and I know you'll help me figure out how to deal with Quincy if it comes to that."

Lincoln patted Truman's leg and they both looked at his sweet, smiling face.

"See?" she said. "Lincoln has faith in us, too."

"Come here, sweetheart." He held her close. "I'm so happy to finally be home."

"But we're at my apartment," she said. "We never spend time here."

"You and the kids are home to me, Gem. Wherever you guys are is where I want to be."

She pressed her lips to his in a tender kiss. "Me too."

"I've been thinking all night about the apartment. I don't think there's any risk to our being there, but I want you to feel safe wherever we are. So if you'd rather not stay there, I'll understand."

"I know you wouldn't put me or the kids in danger, so I'm okay staying there if you really believe we're safe. Besides"—she lowered her voice to a whisper—"those apartment walls hold the story of our secret sexy nights and all the things that led us to where we are in our relationship. And the paintings on the cars out back are the story of your life, which I know mean a lot to you, even if you painted them with the intent of never looking back. I can't imagine not being there."

CHAPTER TWENTY-ONE

GEMMA AND CRYSTAL sat at the table in the back of the boutique going over their schedule of events for the next week, but Gemma's mind refused to focus. It had been a little more than two weeks since Quincy went into rehab, and Truman had made arrangements for Dixie to watch the kids so he could visit him this afternoon. He hadn't said much about Quincy since Halloween night, and he'd kept so busy finishing and painting the bedroom, Gemma wondered if he purposefully didn't give himself time to slow down and think about it. The nights she worked late, she'd found him out back painting dark, stormy images again. She knew he was struggling, but when she tried to talk to him about it, it was as if he couldn't breathe. He didn't shut her out. He simply didn't have much to say beyond, *It's a waiting game. Only time will tell. It's up to him now.* She got the feeling it was killing him not to be able to step in and complete the rehab *for* his brother to ensure a positive outcome, and that broke her heart.

"I was thinking we should have penis cakes," Crystal said.

"Uh-huh." She hoped the visit went well and wished he'd allowed her to go with him, but he wanted to keep her *protected from the poisons of addiction.*

"I slept with Truman."

"Uh-huh," Gemma said absently.

Crystal grabbed her shoulders and shook her. "Woman! Go toward the light!"

Gemma shook her head to clear her thoughts. "What? Sorry. I was thinking about Truman's visit with Quincy."

"Well, you just approved penis cupcakes for the Cunningham party, and you didn't seem to care that I slept with your boyfriend."

"What?" Her eyes nearly bugged out of her head. "You did not!"

"Of course not, but boy do I wish I had *something* to confess, because you were totally out of it." She pushed the calendar to the middle of the table. "Want to talk about it?"

Gemma sighed. "There's nothing to talk about. I'm just worried about him. He cares so much, and I just hope Quincy doesn't let him down."

"He's a big boy. If Quincy fucks up, he'll go on, just like he has for the past however long it's been since Quincy's been using drugs, right?"

"I guess, but I hate that he might get hurt."

"That's because you L-O-V-E him." Crystal looked dreamily toward the ceiling. "You fell in love, and now you hurt when he hurts. That's how it happens, you know."

"I do, Crys. I really, truly love him. And I love his kids as if they were my own. And you want to know the greatest thing?" Gemma didn't wait for an answer. "He loves me just as much. It's crazy! He's all the goodness and all the love I've hoped for my whole life wrapped up in one delicious creature. And he's *all mine*."

Her cell phone rang, and her thoughts skidded. Truman was supposed to be at the rehab center in ten minutes. He'd been so worried about Quincy checking out early or refusing to see him, she hoped he wasn't calling with bad news. She pulled her phone from her pocket and groaned when "Mom" appeared on the screen.

"You still haven't told her?"

Gemma set the phone down on the table. "No, and I can't do it now. I'm too stressed."

Crystal picked up the phone and handed it to her. "Then it's the perfect time, because she's not ruining a great day."

"God, I hate it when you make sense." She took the phone and walked toward the stockroom as she reluctantly answered it. "Hi."

"Gemaline, darling. Did you get a dress for the fundraiser?"

Gemma should be used to the way her mother skipped over asking how she was and dove straight into checking in about the fundraiser, but even after twenty-six years, her lack of interest hurt.

"I'm fine. Busy at work. Thanks for asking," she said, despite her mother's disinterest. "I did get a very nice dress. How are you?" She pushed open the stockroom doors and paced, bracing herself for her mother's typical lengthy list of events she'd attended lately. God forbid her mother ever tell her how she feels or that she misses her.

"I'm doing well. Daddy and I just flew to San Diego for a retreat with the Merbanks, and the spa was magnificent—"

Gemma listened for a full five minutes before cutting her mother short. "Mom, I'm sorry to interrupt, but I'm at work, so…"

"Oh, dear. I'm sorry. I forgot you run that little-girl shop."

"Princess boutique." Just once it would be nice to hear that her mother was proud of what she'd accomplished instead of mocking it. She had a bank account that her mother fed money into the way normal parents doled out hugs, but as far as Gemma was concerned, it was dirty money. *Sugar daddy money.* Gemma had worked through college and saved nearly every penny to be able to afford to open the shop.

"Yes, well, you wouldn't have to do that if you'd go out with one of the eligible bachelors I've tried to set you up with over the years."

The annual stuck-up setup. Gemma drew in a deep breath and said, "About those guys, Mom. Please don't do that this year. I'm seeing someone, and I'd rather not have to turn away another friend of yours."

"Seeing someone? Is it serious? What does he do for a living? Would I know of him?"

"Yes, it's serious. He's a mechanic, and no, you definitely wouldn't know of him." *Thank God, because you might scare him away.*

"I'm sorry, darling. Did you say a mechanical engineer?" she asked hopefully.

Gemma rolled her eyes. "No, Mom. A *mechanic*, as in, he works on cars."

Her mother fell silent, and Gemma imagined the manipulative gears in her head grinding, trying to figure out how to get her daughter out of the clutches of a mechanic.

Gemma paced until the silence became unbearable. Sucking up the hurt she loathed feeling from her mother's disapproval, she said, "Is there anything else you needed?"

"Oh, Gemaline. You know what you're doing." The accusation came across loud and clear.

"What are you talking about, Mom?" She couldn't contain her annoyance.

"You're rebelling. Just like that little business of yours. You're trying to…to…*hurt me.*"

"*Hurt* you?" Gemma raised her eyes to the ceiling.

"You've always tried to prove your independence by denying what's best for you."

"Here's a news flash, Mom. I'm twenty-six years old. I don't have to prove anything to anyone but myself. And I've already proven that I'm smart, capable, and—" *Why the hell am I explaining myself to you?*—"I have to get back to work."

"Does this 'mechanic' have a name?" She said *mechanic* as if it were a disease.

Choking back the urge to tell her mother off for using that disgusted tone, she said, "My boyfriend's name is Truman Gritt, and please, Mother, the next time you say what he does for a living, don't make it sound like a dirty word. Perhaps you should have taken those *essential* etiquette lessons with me."

"Gemaline. Is that any way to speak to your mother?"

She closed her eyes, willing herself to be nicer than her mother deserved. *I learned from the beast—I mean best.* "I'm sorry, but Truman is important to me, and I wish you would show him the same respect you expect me to show Warren."

"*Daddy,*" she corrected her.

The man had never been any type of father to Gemma, though he wasn't awful to her like her mother was. He was rarely around, but when he was, he wasn't unkind. He had a wealthy air about him, the kind that kept his dollars close and warmth at bay, allowing only a few words to slip out now and again.

"Warren, Mother. My father committed suicide. You do remember my real father, don't you?" She knew she was being a bitch, but her mother was just plain pissing her off.

There was a beat of silence, and when her mother finally spoke, her tone was almost believably sad.

"Yes, of course. He chose to leave us, Gemaline."

Fisting her hand at her side, she refused to cry down memory lane with the woman who hadn't been there for her when she first took that painful walk. "Yes. He did. But he was still my father. As I said, let's try to be civil when speaking about our significant others."

"Yes, darling. Is this... *Truman* coming to the fundraiser?"

Not on your life. "No. It's just going to be me."

"What kind of man lets his girlfriend attend a function of this caliber alone?"

"The kind that has children to care for. I have to go, Mom. I'll see you next week." She ended the call, knowing her mother would stew over her last comment, but she didn't care. She checked her watch, relieved to see it was closing time, and stormed out of the storeroom.

"Luscious Licks. *Now*," she said as she gathered her purse.

Crystal grabbed her purse and did a fist pump. "Hate binge. I love it!"

Gemma gave her a deadpan stare, working hard to stifle a smile at her friend's support. "So much joy over my pain..."

"I mean..."

After a beat of silence they both burst into laughter and said, "Hate binge!" and headed out the door to bury the awful conversation below miles of ice cream.

TRUMAN STOOD STOCK-STILL while being searched at the rehab center. His heart pounded so hard he was sure the guy searching him thought he was hiding something. The urge to bolt was so strong he curled his fingers into fists, trying to squeeze the frustration out, and reminded himself he was doing this for Quincy.

"All right. You're clear."

Truman followed a woman down a sterile hallway. He focused on her feet, counting her steps, because if he didn't, he was afraid he'd turn and leave. The process was too reminiscent of his years in prison. He reminded himself he was there of his own free will. Hell, everyone was. No one here was a prisoner.

Except to their addictions.

Quincy is my addiction.

He entered a small, comfortable room that resembled a living room. His eyes sped over the couch against the far wall, a table and chairs to his right. It all blurred together, like the thoughts going through his mind as he paced. When the door opened, he stilled, lifting his eyes to his brother. A wave of apprehension swept through him, quickly followed by the relief he should have felt when he first announced who he was visiting. But he'd been too stressed to slow down and appreciate the fact that Quincy was still there. His biggest fear was that his brother would give up and check himself out of rehab before completing the program.

Quincy was no longer covered in dirt and grime. His skin was marred with yellowing bruises, and the gash on his cheek was nearly healed. His hair held the sheen of a fresh shampoo, falling just above his shoulders and shading one eye. Truman wasn't prepared for the overwhelming emotions engulfing him at the sight of his brother looking like, well, his brother. He stepped forward, opening his arms to the man whose dull, tortured blue eyes were full of warning, like his body language, both of which Truman chose to ignore.

"Quincy."

His brother took a step backward, holding Truman's gaze and sending a clear message. Truman dropped his hands to his sides, while disappointment, sadness, and anger battled inside him.

Quincy pulled out a chair and sank into it. Truman did the same, taking a moment to look at his brother more closely. Time had a way of playing tricks on the mind. All those years in prison he'd kept an image of thirteen-year-old Quincy in his head. Held on to it like a security blanket. Like if he believed he'd stay kind and good and *clean*, it would happen. But walls and bars and miles had created a vast, impassable sea, and a part of each of them had drowned in the space between. Quincy was no longer that boy—or maybe even the same person. He was a man, with stubble over a strong jawline, shadows of too many drugs marring his handsome face, and track marks up his arms. He was almost twenty, not much younger than Truman had been when he'd been hauled off to prison.

"Surprised?" Quincy said.

He'd never been good at hiding his emotions. Truman cleared his throat, grasping for something to say. He'd spoken to Quincy's counselor and had been advised not to bring up family drama, money, the future, or anything else that might be stressful. She'd said that Quincy needed to live "in the moment" and that added anxiety would hinder his recovery.

"No. I'm not surprised," he lied, and Quincy arched a brow. "Okay, yeah. I am. Man, I'm not sure how this is supposed to go."

"Think I do?" Quincy ran a hand through his hair and looked away, the muscles in his jaw bunching. "Man, this place sucks." He pushed to his feet and paced.

Truman rose with him, watching as he stalked back and forth across the room like a caged tiger, his hair curtaining his face. "I'm proud of you for doing this."

Quincy scoffed. "Proud of me? I don't need your approval."

"I didn't mean that." He didn't want to fuck this up, but he had no idea how to handle his brother's comment. "I meant I know it's not easy."

"When has life ever been easy for me?" He lifted angry eyes to Truman.

"I didn't mean to imply—"

"Is anything ever what you *mean*, Truman?" Quincy stormed across the room, stopping inches from him. "'Don't say a word, Quincy.'"

A chill ran down Truman's spine at hearing his own words from that fateful night being thrown in his face. The words he'd meant for Quincy to take comfort in. The words that had sent him to prison.

"'You're not taking the fall, Quincy. I've got this,'" Quincy said through gritted teeth. "You had it, all right. Six years of meals and a roof over your head. Six years of *not* watching your mother get fucked by every cretin under the sun."

"Quincy, you can't believe it was better to be in prison than to—"

"Can't I?" Quincy stormed across the room, his shoulders rounding forward. "Was it better to be thirteen fucking years old and handed a crack pipe?"

"You could have—"

Quincy turned, rounding on Truman fast. Truman took a step back. This was exactly what the counselor had said to avoid. He'd somehow managed to fuck his brother over again by riling him up.

"What? What could I do at thirteen? Call Social Services and go into the system after you spent years telling me why that wasn't the way to go? You were my *stronghold*. My straight arrow to follow. You *made sure* I relied on you, man, and you did such a good fucking job that when you left, I was fucking lost. I would have followed Satan straight to hell."

The air left Truman's lungs. The room vibrated with the demons of their past, alive and clawing at them, pitting them against each other.

"I was trying to help," he said sternly. "I wasn't supposed to be convicted. You were there. You heard what the public defender said. I was supposed to get off and then take care of you, like I always had. You *know* she lied on the stand." It killed Truman that he'd never know why she'd lied and sent him to prison, but that wasn't Quincy's cross to bear.

Quincy's silent stare cut like a knife.

Truman lowered his voice. "You know the truth, man. You're the only one on this fucking earth who knows the truth."

"I had to kill him." He shifted his eyes away. "He would have killed her."

Maybe that would have been better. Truman felt his heart break right down the center, and guilt poured out for the hateful thought. And in the next breath he realized their mother's death would have meant that Kennedy and Lincoln would never have been born. He uttered a curse, wishing he could take that initial thought back. He loved those kids.

Forcing those thoughts away, he focused on the brother standing before him.

"My only thought was that if you were there, you would have killed him." Quincy's words were laden with venom. "I did what I know you would have done to protect Mom despite everything she was. I did what you ingrained into my fucking head. *Protect family.*"

"You did what you had to." *I wish I had been the one to do it. Maybe then you wouldn't be so fucked up.* "I thought they'd try you as an adult. I couldn't even stand the thought of you in juvie. You were just a kid, and you were a good kid, smarter than anyone I knew, and by the time I realized they wouldn't have tried you as an adult, it was too late. But we don't know that Mom wouldn't have fucked you over like she did me, and I wouldn't have been able to stand that. You have to know I'd never do a damn thing to hurt you. Not *ever*. I'll take our secret to my grave to protect you."

"I can't escape the guilt, man. It's always there. I look in the mirror and I hate the person I see. Your life is fucked because of me," Quincy seethed.

Truman grabbed him by the arms, imploring him to hear the truth. "No, Quincy. My life was fucked because of *her*. But my life is no longer fucked." Thinking of his record, and of the kids, he said, "I've got restrictions and responsibilities, but I'm not fucked. My life is actually pretty damn good right now. I've got the kids, and I've got Gemma, who I love so much it's insane. And, Quincy, she loves me back, man. Despite the conviction, despite our fucked-up past, she *loves* me and the kids. I can't imagine my life without her. And your life can be just as good. Just as *normal.* You've never had normal. It's unfuckingbelievable. I'm telling you, bro, there's a whole world waiting for you that has nothing to do with Mom or her effed-up life. All you have to do is make it through rehab, and I'll be there to help you stay clean. I know you can do this."

Quincy twisted out of his grasp, pushing both hands into

his hair and fisting them with a tortured groan. "Just get out of here, man. *Please*. Get the hell out."

"Quincy…" What could he say? Beg him to talk it out? That's exactly what the counselor said *not* to do. He'd done enough damage. Hell, he'd done even more damage than he'd ever imagined.

CHAPTER TWENTY-TWO

WHEN TRUMAN ARRIVED at his apartment, he was surprised to see Gemma's car in the parking lot. She'd sent him a text earlier saying she'd had a crappy day and was going out with Crystal. He breathed a little easier knowing she would soon be in his arms. He felt like he'd been dragged through quicksand, and as he stepped from his truck, he was still knee deep in it. He'd spoken with the counselor before leaving the rehab center to fess up to the stressful confrontation with his brother so they would be prepared for any backlash. And more importantly, in case his brother tried to check himself out, they'd know why and try to reason with him. He wished there were someone he could talk to about Quincy's guilt. He'd tried, in a roundabout way, to discuss it with the counselor, and she said part of recovery was acceptance and making amends to all the people their drug use had affected and that was part of the therapeutic process. But Truman knew Quincy could never make amends for what he'd done. They were both locked into their lies forever. *Locked into my lie.* It was his genius idea to take the fall for his brother. Now his brother was mired down in guilt and he was stuck lying to Gemma for the rest of his life. And to top it all off, he was worried sick that Quincy wouldn't be able to deal with the guilt and he'd give up on getting clean.

If that happened, Truman would never forgive himself.

The counselor, though concerned, wasn't surprised that their visit had blown up. *It'll get worse before it gets better. Nature of the beast.* Truman absently rubbed his chest, wishing he could slay that fucking beast once and for all.

Needing a moment to get his head on straight before seeing Gemma and the kids, he went into the shop. He was working on a '69 Mustang, one of his favorite cars. He ran his hand along the sleek hood, remembering the first day he'd brought the kids into the garage with him. He'd had no idea what he was doing, just like when he'd taken responsibility for the stabbing. He'd thought he was doing the right thing and trusted that he'd figure out how to handle it as he went along.

He crossed the room to the playroom they'd renovated for the kids and flicked on the light. The bright yellow walls brought a smile. How could they not? They reminded him of the reason he'd been able to figure out how to handle the kids. *Gemma.* His pushy, sexy ray of sunshine.

Quincy's words slammed into him. *You were my stronghold. My straight arrow to follow. You made sure I relied on you, man, and you did such a good fucking job that when you left, I was fucking lost. I would have followed Satan straight to hell.*

He leaned against the doorframe, his chin dropping to his chest. Quincy blamed him for everything—*the killing, the drugs, my own prison sentence.* His mind turned to the kids. Was he going to fuck up the kids by trying to make things good for them? Was he *doing* instead of *teaching*? Was it wrong to buffer Kennedy from the dark parts of fairy tales? Would they be as lost without him as Quincy had been? Had it been wrong to do whatever it took to keep Quincy safe?

Footsteps on the floor above pulled him from his mental

interrogation. He gazed up at the ceiling and his answers became clear. He hadn't done the wrong thing. He just hadn't thought he'd go to prison. Maybe he should have turned his mother in to the authorities, or disappeared with Quincy, but he'd run on survival mode for so long, by the time Quincy was born, hiding from the authorities was already ingrained. His mother had convinced him that foster care would be worse than anything she could ever do.

As he ascended the stairs toward his apartment, he accepted that there was only one way he knew how to be. He opened the door, and Gemma looked up from the floor where she was busy packing something into a bag. Beside her Lincoln's arms bobbed up and down excitedly, his grin healing the fissures the events of the day had created.

"Tooman!" Kennedy ran over with her arms up in the air. "We going out!"

He lifted her into his arms and rubbed noses with his happy little girl, feeling guilty for the joy pushing past his heartache.

"Where are we going?" He knelt beside Lincoln, letting Kennedy toddle off to play with her dolls. He scooped the baby into his arms and kissed him before leaning in and kissing Gemma.

"I knew you'd be stressed after your visit, and I had a frustrating day myself. I thought a picnic in the field would do us all some good." She nodded toward a cooler on the counter. "Is that okay, or has your day been too difficult?"

She'd had a bad day, too, and here she was, selflessly lifting all of their spirits.

With a hand on her neck, he drew her to him. "Sounds perfect. You're incredible. You know that?"

"I may need a little more convincing."

He kissed her deeply.

He didn't know if it was right, wrong, good, or bad, but this was the only man he knew how to be. A man who *held* and *loved* and *protected*. If that was detrimental, then they all had a long hard road ahead of them.

TRUMAN LAY ON his back on the blanket beside Lincoln after they finished dinner while the baby repeatedly whomped him on the stomach, giggling like crazy each time Truman made an *oomph* sound. Kennedy, busy playing with her dolls and using Truman's legs as props, also gave in to fits of giggles at her silly brothers. Gemma sat back and took it all in, reveling in their happiness. It was a breezy, cool evening, but the kids were bundled up in sweaters and hats and were having too much fun to be taken inside. Gemma loved this time of year, when the leaves fell from the trees, reminding her that Thanksgiving was right around the corner. She and Crystal usually cooked a small Thanksgiving dinner together. She smiled to herself, knowing this year they'd need a bigger turkey.

Truman reached for her hand. He'd told her about his difficult visit with Quincy. Gemma was continually amazed at his ability to contain and separate his emotions. He never misdirected his anger, which was so different from how her father used to stalk around the house with smoke coming out of his ears.

"Are you ready to talk about your day yet?" he asked.

She hadn't wanted to talk about her conversation with her mother earlier, partly because she was embarrassed by her mother's ignorance and partly because she worried about how hearing it would make Truman feel. But he'd always been honest with her, and he deserved the same in return. She just needed to figure out a way to say it that wasn't hurtful.

"My mother called this afternoon."

"About the fundraiser?" He sat up, sliding one hand protectively around Lincoln as he did.

She nodded. "I told her about us, and she wasn't exactly supportive."

"I'm sorry, Gem. You told her about my conviction?"

She shook her head, feeling sick about the truth. "Are you kidding? The only question she asked was what you did for a living. She's shallow and mean-spirited. It's not a reflection on you personally, Tru. It's who she is."

"You mean she didn't like the idea of you dating a mechanic?"

She nodded, dropping her eyes out of shame.

Truman lifted her chin and smiled. "Sweetness, don't you know by now that we can't be judged by who our parents are? Christ, imagine if we were. Look at my mother." He leaned down and kissed Lincoln's head. "Their mother."

"I know, but it's embarrassing that she's that way. All the things she cares about mean nothing to me. Do you know she still calls me Gemaline? I've asked her to call me Gemma for as long as I can remember. She says Gemma is too common." She paused, thinking about how much she hated the snooty way Gemaline sounded. "I love Gemma."

"Gemma is a beautiful name. At least you're not named after a president. My mother wanted us to have memorable names because she knew our lives would be shit." He kissed Lincoln again. "Their lives will never be shit."

"Of course not. They have you. You've given me more than

my mother ever could. She and I are so different. She cares about things. I care about people. I don't ever want to be judged by the way she is. She's awful."

"If there's anyone who understands where you're coming from, it's me. What I don't understand is if she's that way, why do you put yourself through the fundraiser every year?"

"I've asked myself that a million times." She lifted Lincoln into her lap and scooted closer to Truman. "I don't know how to explain it. She's my mother, and even though she's terrible in so many ways, she's still my mother. I feel a sense of obligation to her. And she's my only connection to my father. Even though she's not someone I can talk to about him, and I think she despises him for committing suicide, she's still the only person who was there in the same house when he was alive. It doesn't make sense, and hearing myself say it makes me feel like an idiot for doing anything for her." She shook her head. "She's *not* a nice person."

"But you are." He gathered her in his arms and held her. "You're doing the right thing. When we start turning our back on family, we become the very people we don't like."

"You're not upset with me for going to the fundraiser alone?" Even though they'd talked about it, she wanted to make sure he was really okay with her going.

"Not at all. I'm not thrilled about other guys checking you out in that sexy dress. And I love that you didn't want the kids to be put in a sucky situation, but you have to know that if you want me to go, Dixie and Bear can watch the kids. I have no issue meeting your mother, regardless of what she thinks of me."

"Oh, Truman." She pressed her lips to his. "I care about you too much to put you through the wrath of that woman, but I love you even more for offering."

Kennedy crawled into Truman's lap and snuggled against him.

"We'd better get these guys to bed." Gemma began gathering their things.

"Do you think I'll screw up the kids? Am I too protective of them?"

The question came out of the blue, and it took Gemma a minute to process it. She lifted the bag over her shoulder and settled Lincoln on her hip, realizing the question hadn't come out of the blue. It was a reflection of his worries about Quincy.

"Are you going to start doing drugs?"

"No," he said with disgust.

"Are you going to start ignoring them, beating them, starving them, or…?" She paused as understanding dawned in his eyes. "I don't think you're in danger of screwing anyone up. You're not *oppressively* protective, Tru Blue. You're *lovingly* protective. There's a huge difference."

CHAPTER TWENTY-THREE

"I THINK THIS dresser is perfect," Gemma said, pointing to a tall dresser for Truman's new bedroom. "It has plenty of drawers, and the dark wood is very masculine, like you."

Truman wrapped his arms around her from behind, glad to have a few hours alone with Gemma, even if they were only shopping. He didn't like leaving the kids, but he knew they were in good hands with Dixie and Crystal. Tomorrow was the fundraiser, and they'd be apart for most of the evening.

"And what about my girl's dresser? Don't we need something feminine, too?" He gathered her hair over one shoulder and kissed the nape of her neck, feeling goose bumps chasing his lips.

"I don't mind keeping my stuff on the shelves in the closet, where it is now. Besides, I should really move some of my summer clothes to my place to free up more space for you guys."

He turned her in his arms and gazed into the eyes of the woman he'd met over diapers and baby food and fallen in love with one second at a time ever since. Strands of gold and brown framed her beautiful face, and her smile—*God, your smile*—sent warm, whirling emotions to the pit of his stomach. The pieces of his life were finally falling into place. It had been a week since he'd visited Quincy, and three weeks since Quincy had entered rehab. He'd spoken with the counselor earlier that morning, and she assured him that Quincy was making tremendous progress, although he was struggling with a few personal issues. Truman knew all too well what those issues were, as he struggled with the guilt of their secret on a daily basis. Lately, it was weighing even more heavily on him. Every time he looked into Gemma's eyes, he wanted to tell her the truth about what happened all those years ago. He hated having any secrets between them, but what was done was done. He'd never screw over Quincy just to clear his own conscience.

And now, as he held the woman who loved him despite his conviction, despite his terrible upbringing, he focused on the future rather than the past.

"I like your summer clothes in my closet." He kissed her lips. "And I like your things in my apartment." He backed her up against the dresser, moving his hand to her ass and pressing their hips together. They were alone in the back of the store. He kissed her again, longer and deeper than before, until he felt her go soft in his arms and the moan of appreciation he'd come to expect slipped from her lungs.

"And I love you in my bed," he said, kissing her jaw. She tipped her head back, giving him better access to the neck he wanted to devour. "I want you in my bed every night." He dragged his tongue along the sensitive skin just below her ear, earning a sexy little shiver. "And I want to wake up with you in my arms every morning." He continued kissing a path down her neck, her fingers tightening around his sides. Sealing his mouth over the base of her neck, he reveled in the feel of her erratic pulse against his tongue.

She grabbed his ass and rocked into him, whispering heatedly, "Tru, you're making me wet."

"Mm." He slid his hand down the back of her long cotton skirt, over the lace panties covering her perfect ass, and between her legs, stroking over her slick center. "*Christ.* Now I want to drop to my knees and make you come."

She shuddered against him and made a wanton noise that vibrated through his veins. He crashed his mouth over hers, pushing his fingers into her hot pussy. Taking advantage of their solitude, he furtively sought the spot that made her go wild, and her hips began moving with him. Man, how he loved the way she moved. The way she tasted. The way she got wet and hot and ready with a single touch.

"I love fucking you," he said. "With my mouth, with my hand, with my cock."

"*Ohmygod,*" she said breathlessly. "Yes, please. I want all of that."

A growl erupted from his lungs, and he took her in another cock-throbbing kiss. Her knee rode up his outer thigh, her hips rocked, and sweet, hungry moans sailed from her lungs into his.

She clawed at his back, arching her whole body into him. "There. *Oh God.* There," she panted out between kisses.

In the next breath, she shattered against him. He swallowed her cries, kissing her roughly and loving every fucking second of it. Of her. Of their life together.

Her head fell back again, and she gulped in air. "Truman," she said breathlessly. "Geez." Her eyes darted around the empty showroom. "You are *so* good at being bad."

He laughed and kissed her again. When he withdrew his fingers, she gasped, and when he sucked his fingers clean, she went boneless in his arms. He kissed her again, the taste of her mixing with the taste of them.

"Bathroom," he said urgently, unable to wait another second before being buried deep inside her. He took her hand, walking swiftly toward the restrooms in the back of the store.

They kissed, and she giggled as they pushed through the men's room door.

"I've never done this before," she said, wiggling out of her skirt as Truman locked the door. Her skirt puddled at her feet with her black lace panties, and she trapped that sweet lip again, her green eyes darkly seductive. With her hair tousled, her sweater hanging off one shoulder, and her sweet, glistening pussy bare for the taking, she was an intriguing mix of guileless innocence and savage temptress.

"Holy Christ, sweetness. You're sinful." He unzipped his pants and pushed them down past his knees, giving his cock a long, tight stroke before taking her in another greedy, demanding kiss.

Her back met the wall hard as the kiss turned wild and urgent, and his hands moved to her bare ass, lifting her up and guiding her legs around his waist. When she sank onto his cock, everything intensified. They fucked hard and rough, grunting and moaning with reckless abandon, the location of their tryst forgotten in the passion searing through Truman's veins, the lust coiling at the base of his spine.

Gemma was wild, crying out, "Yes! Yes! Yes!" as he clung to her hips and slammed into her, branding her from the inside out. Her head fell back and she cried out louder as she came, her erotic pleas dragging him over the edge in an explosion of fierce possession. His senses reeled, his heart so full of Gemma he couldn't think past its thundering beats.

"I love you, sweet girl," he panted out. Breathing too hard to form a real kiss, he touched his lips to hers. She was so beautiful, gazing into his eyes through a lustful, sated haze. "Move in with us. I want you with me, with us, always."

She trapped her lower lip between her teeth and he placed a series of light kisses over that perfectly plump lip until she released it *and* the sexiest sigh he'd ever heard.

"Really?" Sparks of excitement shimmered in her eyes.

He nodded, kissed her again. "You and the kids are my life. Let's make it official."

She wound her arms around his neck and kissed him deep and slow, bringing his half-mast cock back into the game. "I want that, too, so very much. I love you, and I love your kids."

"Our kids," he corrected her. "They've never been just mine. We've been together since the night I found them."

"Oh, Truman," she whispered, and her brows knitted. She shook her head and shifted her eyes away.

Her lips pressed into a hard line. His heart, and his cock, deflated as he set her down on her feet.

"Did I say something wrong?"

"No. You said something so very right I think I'm going to cry. Yes, I'll move in with you. But I come with a lot of books."

Thank fucking God. "Baby, I'll build floor-to-ceiling bookcases if that's what it takes." He kissed her again, her salty tears slipping between their lips like secrets, sealing their plans.

GEMMA WALKED ON air for the rest of the day. After the kids were asleep, they transferred their clothes from the kids' room to the new dresser in their bedroom. *Our bedroom.* Gemma smiled with the thought. This was really happening. Even though she already practically lived at his place, nothing could compare to seeing the love in his eyes, or the emotions on his face, as he asked her to make it official.

"I'll never be able to go to that furniture store again," she said, embarrassment flushing her cheeks as she remembered coming out of the bathroom and finding a salesman glowering at them.

Truman looked up from the drawer he was filling. "Because he probably heard every"—his voice rose several octaves—"*There! Yes! Yes!*"

She threw a pillow at him, and he tackled her onto the bed, kissing her until she was laughing, and then he kissed her some more, until those laughs turned to hungry moans.

"You've turned me into a sex maniac." She wiggled out from beneath him.

"One day I'll turn you into my sex-maniac wife."

She nearly choked. "Truman…?" He held her so tight she was sure he could feel her racing heart.

"Haven't you thought about it?"

"Well, sure, but…" Had she thought about it? Not in so many words. They were together and happy, and she just assumed they'd stay that way. Maybe one day they'd get married, but she hadn't been actively wondering when. Were they really talking about this?

"Not now, but one day. After my parole is over, when things with Quincy are figured out and the children are legally settled."

Suddenly it all made sense. While she saw herself moving through life in a constant flow, Truman saw himself riding in a boat along a river, making necessary stops along the way. Checking off boxes on his way to a more settled life. He was out of prison, but it still wasn't behind him. He never made a big deal of checking in with the parole office. It was just one phone call each week, and he did it in the privacy of another room, or stepped outside on the deck, which made it easy for Gemma to write it off as *just another phone call.* But to Truman it was obviously a dark cloud hovering over him with a clear end in sight. Another step in the right direction. She understood his wanting to wait until he was clear of those ties, and she knew he worried about Quincy making it through rehab and staying clean. Quincy would be a forever worry, as they'd already discussed. Addiction was a lifelong struggle. But his comment about the children confused her.

She sat up and asked, "What does that mean? 'Legally settled'?"

Truman moved to the edge of the bed, rested his elbows on his knees, and wrung his hands together. "They don't have birth certificates, and I'm not their legal guardian yet. I have to take care of those things."

"Oh," she said, relieved. "The way you said it, I thought there was something more to it. Isn't that just filling out a few forms at the courthouse or through an attorney or something?"

He shook his head, turning serious eyes toward her. "Not for me."

"Why not? I don't understand."

He took her hand in his and the air around them shifted, filling with unease.

"Gemma, they'll never give the kids to me with a conviction of voluntary manslaughter on my record. Why would they?"

"Because you're their brother and you're good to them. You served your time, and it wasn't like you randomly went out and committed a murder." She hadn't thought about his conviction with relation to his custody of the kids.

"That won't matter. I'm sure they'll go into the system. They'll take them away from me. I can't risk that."

She pushed from the bed, arms crossed. "No. No, they can't do that. You don't know that they'll do that."

"I can't chance that they will."

"What do you mean? How will you get custody?"

"I mean I'll do what I have to to keep them with me, where they belong."

She shook her head, still confused.

He rose to his feet and went to her, speaking more soothingly. "Bullet knows a guy who can get fake birth certificates so I can enroll Kennedy in school next fall, and—"

"What? You can't do that." This couldn't be happening. "Truman, you can't start their lives off with a lie. They'll have that hanging over their heads forever."

"They'll never know." His eyes filled with regret.

She took a step away, confused and upset. "But *we'll* know. I can't be part of something illegal. And you can't either." She reached for him, hoping to change his mind. When he took her hand, familiar electricity traveled between them, too strong to be overshadowed even by a disagreement this powerful.

"Tru, you need to think this through. You just said you're waiting to get through the rest of your parole period. But won't this count as doing something illegal? Can't they send you back to prison for breaking parole? And then what would happen to the kids?"

Tension brought out the veins in his neck. "What do you expect me to do?" He released her hand and paced. "They're my family. I can't let them go into the system to be raised by someone else."

"I know you can't." She went to him, and he reluctantly

stopped pacing, his mouth tight, eyes narrow. "But neither one of us can afford to break the law. There has to be another way."

"I will *not* risk having them taken away," he said with finality that came across loud and clear.

But Gemma wasn't done with this conversation.

"I can't be involved in any part of this, Truman. Do you understand that? I can't be part of something illegal, no matter how much I love you or them." She held his steady gaze, his jaw working overtime.

"Gemma," he pleaded. "They're my kids."

"And you're the man I love. They're the kids I love." She took his hands, softening her tone. "You're *my* Tru Blue, and for all intents and purposes, you're their father. Are you willing to risk going back to prison because you're afraid of what might happen if you try to do things the right way? The legal way?"

"I'm doing this for *them*," he insisted. "They've been through so much already."

"I get that, Tru. But manipulating the law isn't the right thing to do, no matter how you look at it. Can't you ask someone who knows about these things? If Bullet knows those kinds of people, maybe he also knows an attorney who can help you figure this out. I just can't see jumping into this with your eyes closed when there might be another way."

"What if I lose the kids by trying to find out?"

They both fell silent.

"This is so fucked up," he finally said with a pained expression. "All I want is to take care of them."

"I know. But I can't do something illegal. I can't risk that, not even for the kids." Tears welled in her eyes at the heartache billowing off of him and the choices before them.

"I don't want to lose you, and I don't want to lose them.

Don't ask me to make that choice." He gathered her in his strong arms. His heart was beating as fast as hers.

"Don't ask me to look the other way," she said.

The sadness in his eyes nearly took her to her knees. "What if it's the only way I can keep them?"

Tension pressed in on her and she fell silent, unwilling to form an answer and hoping she wouldn't be forced to.

CHAPTER TWENTY-FOUR

TRUMAN FOLLOWED A woman down the hall of the rehab center hoping he was doing the right thing. After his and Gemma's perfect evening had turned into a shitty night, he hadn't slept a wink. He lay awake all night holding her and trying to figure out what to do. By the time she left this morning to go to work, and then to the fundraiser, he still didn't have any answers. But at least he had an idea, and an idea was better than nothing. He couldn't chance losing the kids, and he didn't want to lose Gemma, either. The way he saw it, Quincy was his only hope.

He stepped into the same room he'd been in the last time he'd visited Quincy, only this time it felt different. Because this time he was going to ask something of his brother that he wasn't sure he had the right to ask. Something he hoped would motivate Quincy to finish the program and stay clean.

Something that had the power to backfire.

Badly.

Quincy came through the door a few minutes later, and for a beat all the air left the room as they stared at each other. The counselor had told Truman that Quincy was doing great, making progress. *Past the worst of it doesn't mean any of it is easy.* Quincy's face was clear of bruises, his eyes were sharper, and his movements weren't as jerky and tense.

"Hey," Quincy said.

His friendly yet tentative tone took Truman off guard. He'd half expected him to still be angry and combative despite what the counselor had said.

"Hey." Still unsure of how to read him, he waited for his brother to make the first move.

Quincy stepped forward, lifted one arm, as if he were going to reach for Truman, then dropped it to his side again, his eyes coasting to the floor.

Truman couldn't leave it at that. He stepped forward and embraced him. Quincy's arms hung limply by his sides, and Truman's heart sank again. As he released him, his brother's arms came around him, bringing tears to Truman's eyes. *Figures.* If anyone could make him look like a pussy, it was Quincy.

They embraced for a second, maybe three. Long enough for Truman's gut to right itself again. Quincy stepped back and nervously waved toward the chairs. "We should…"

"Yeah." Truman took a seat, relieved by the change in his demeanor. "Listen, I'm sorry for upsetting you last time."

"No, man. It's all good." He tucked a lock of hair behind his ear.

That simple movement unearthed an avalanche of memories inside Truman. He sat back, feeling like he'd seen a ghost. Quincy used to hate it when Truman would try to get him to cut his hair, and he'd had a habit of tucking it behind his right ear. How could something so small feel like a good sign? A huge sign? A sign of his brother becoming the person he'd once known?

"How are the kids?" Quincy asked, taking Truman by surprise again.

"Good. Great, actually. They're why I wanted to see you."

Quincy nodded. "I've been thinking about them a lot. The way they lived. The way I let them live." He looked away. "I…"

"Quin, don't, man. Don't do that to yourself."

He lifted a sorrowful gaze to Truman. "Did I fuck them up forever?"

"No," he said emphatically. "You did not. They have good lives. They're happy, Quin. They're so fucking happy." Unexpected tears welled in Truman's eyes, and his brother turned away, his eyes suspiciously damp as well. Truman cleared his throat to try to regain control of his emotions.

"Good. She didn't use when she found out she was pregnant. There was this guy." He looked at Truman, his blue eyes serious and narrow. "You don't want to know what it was like, but she did it, man. This user was some kind of doctor turned crackhead or something. I don't know. He could have been bullshitting. But he knew what to do. He helped her through withdrawal, and when she gave birth"—he shook his head with a disgusted expression—"he was right there giving her drugs." Tears filled his eyes, and he swiped angrily at them. "But the babies were born okay. And they're okay now, right?"

"Yeah," Truman said, wiping his own tears—tears of anger for what their fucking mother had put Quincy and the kids, and *him*, through. He reached for Quincy, and his brother leaned willingly into his arms, crying openly.

"I'm sorry, Tru. I shoulda…You never would've…"

Truman grabbed his face and made him look into his eyes, as he'd done so many times when Quincy was a boy. "Don't. Not for a second. The past is the past, and nothing we do or say can change it. Your life starts *now*. *Here*. Your past will *not* define your future, little brother. You got that?"

Quincy grabbed his wrists, tears streaming down his cheeks. "How can you look at me after the way I ruined your life?"

It was all Truman could do to touch his forehead to Quincy's and close his eyes, when he wanted to shake him until he believed him when he said it wasn't his fault.

"Goddamn it." He pulled back, staring at the heartrending guilt looking back at him. "She did this. Not you. Not me. She did it. She brought that fucker and a hundred others like him into the house, and she put our lives in danger. Do you get that, Quin? Do you understand that is where the blame belongs?"

He nodded, gritting his teeth and sucking in one ragged breath after another. "Yeah. But I still feel guilty as fuck."

Truman pressed a kiss to Quincy's forehead, then released him.

Quincy laughed and shook his head. He swiped his forearm over his tears and blew out a breath. "Man, we're a couple of pussies."

They both laughed, and boy did it feel good. His brother was coming back. He'd come out from under the cloud of drugs and he was right there within reach. Truman hoped what he had to ask would motivate him to keep moving in the right direction. It had to. For all of their sakes.

"Want to relieve your guilt?"

Quincy cocked a brow. "Fuck, yes."

"Then do me and the kids a favor. Get clean and stay clean. I need your help, man."

"You've never needed anyone's help."

Truman sat back and crossed his arms. "I have. When I got the kids I needed help. A lot of it. The Whiskeys stepped in, but Gemma saved us. She's been right there the whole time, and I love her, Quin. I love her so damn much, and if I don't figure this out, I'm going to lose her."

He told Quincy about his dilemma with the birth certificates. "I need you to get clean, get a job, and make a stable life so you can apply for guardianship of the kids. I'll still take full responsibility for them, but at least they'd have legal paperwork and remain in the family. They won't have to live a life built on lies, like we have."

"Man, bro. No pressure there, huh?" Quincy blew out a breath.

Truman's heart sank. "I know it's a lot to ask. But Gemma loves me despite what she believes I did. She believes in me, Quin, and I want to do right by her. I want to do right by the kids."

Quincy swallowed hard. "This would be so easy if I had fessed up to killing that prick in the first place."

"We can't go back, and I wouldn't even if we could. I'm not throwing you under the bus, Quincy. Not now, not ever. She'll never know the truth, no matter how much I love her."

"That's gotta be killing you."

A chill ran down Truman's spine with his brother's challenging stare. "If leaving you with Mom didn't kill me, nothing will."

Quincy was quiet for a long moment, his eyes moving over the table, the floor, everywhere except meeting Truman's gaze. When he finally did, it was with worry etched into his expression. "What if I fuck up? I can't make any promises. You of all people know that."

Truman had been over the possible outcomes so many times since last night he had them memorized. "I'm not going to fill your head with bullshit. I believe in you, and I want to believe that you have faith in yourself, but we both know it's a crapshoot. It's going to be a daily battle of willpower, and I'll be right there to help you through. I'll get a bigger place so you can move in until you're on your feet or feel strong enough that you won't need me there. Whatever it takes, Quin. I'll be there for you."

"For the kids," Quincy uttered, shifting his eyes away again.

"For them and for you." Truman leaned forward, grabbing Quincy's attention again. "And for me, bro. I want my brother back, and I'll do whatever it takes to help you stay clean."

"All of this for Gemma." Quincy held his gaze. "She must really be something."

He couldn't deny that asking him to apply for guardianship was because of Gemma, but that wasn't why he wanted him to get clean. "It's not just for her. It's for all of us. She's right about the kids. I don't want them growing up worrying about fake papers. Clean slate, bro. That's what they deserve. That's what you deserve."

Quincy sat in silence for a beat too long, making Truman's gut twist tighter. Then he rose to his feet and said, "And what about you, Truman? What do you deserve?"

That was a loaded question. His lie had spurned Quincy's guilt and separated them for six grueling, life-changing years, which had allowed their mother to get him into drugs. Truman knew he deserved more than he was born into, but what that was exactly, he wasn't sure.

"Who the hell knows?" he finally answered. "But I know what I want."

The side of Quincy's mouth quirked up, amusement reaching his eyes. Damn, did that look good on him. So much better than the darkness he'd been haunted by when he'd first arrived at the rehab center.

"A normal family life and peace of mind that you're okay." He hugged Quincy and gave him a manly pat on the back. "Think about it. That's all I'm asking. If it's too much pressure, then I'll figure something else out. What matters most is you getting clean. I can figure out the rest." Truman reached for the door.

"Where are you heading now?"

"The courthouse."

Quincy's face blanched.

Truman patted his hand over his heart. "To the grave, bro. I'm just going to ask some hypothetical questions about guardianship to see what I'm up against."

Before Gemma left this morning he'd asked her if he was going to lose her over this. As he left the rehab center, her answer sailed through his mind. *I hope not.*

He was going to do everything in his power to make sure he didn't.

CHAPTER TWENTY-FIVE

IF THERE WAS one thing her mother did well, it was hosting black-tie events. Gemma stood beside one of many marble columns in the majestic ballroom of her stepfather's mansion, taking in the grand affair. Every detail had been attended to. From the valet parking to the shine on the marble floors and the quartet playing at the head of the room, the event was perfectly executed. Elegant candelabra graced every table alongside fine china and the best silver money could buy. Handsome men dressed in sharp black tuxedos with crisp white collared shirts and perfectly slicked-back hair sipped champagne with gorgeous, gown-wearing women draped on their arms—women who had undoubtedly spent hours in spas preparing for their evening out while their children were cared for by hired help. Gemma's stomach turned at the memories that chased that thought. She remembered those days all too well. Her mother would come home looking radiant, with every strand of her golden hair in place and makeup that made her look young and beautiful. *Friendly*, even. Gemma had been mesmerized by her mother's transformation on those nights. *Mommy, you look so beautiful*, she'd say with hopes that the makeup had truly brought out a more pleasant side of her mother. *Yes, thank you, darling. Don't touch*, she'd say on her way to wherever was more important than giving Gemma five minutes of her time.

The children, who were pointedly invited to this event for publicity purposes only, had been quickly swept away to another ballroom, where they were cared for by the nannies who accompanied them as well as by several staff her mother had hired solely for this occasion—after publicity pictures had been taken, of course.

Not for the first time, Gemma wondered why she'd traveled almost two hours to attend the event, when she had more important things on her mind. Like trying to convince Truman to do the right thing with the kids. When they'd parted that morning, things were tense and uncomfortable. She'd been on a dead run all day at the boutique, which was a great distraction. But here, all she could think about was how different Truman was from all those pretentious people who probably jetted off every other weekend for adults-only events. Truman would never leave the kids behind. Was she fighting for the wrong things? She had a real birth certificate showing her true lineage, and look how her family life had turned out. She'd have given anything to be raised by a man as loving as him. Maybe Truman's idea wasn't the worst, even if it was illegal.

She glanced at her mother standing across the room with a group of younger men, her smile painted on as thickly as the makeup mask she wore, as she reveled in their feigned attention. She was the *It Woman*, the wife of one of the most renowned defense attorneys in the world, Warren Benzos, and she was perfect for the role.

"She looks radiant, doesn't she?"

Gemma turned toward the familiar, rich voice of her stepfather. "Yes, she does parties well."

Warren nodded, a wry smile on his thin lips. He was in his

early sixties, a decade older than her mother. He had a long face and an angular nose that reminded Gemma of a weasel and puffy white hair that looked hard to tame. He wasn't an unfriendly man. He wasn't much of anything to Gemma. He'd married her mother and swept her away to one vacation and event after another, leaving Gemma behind. She couldn't blame him, really. Who was *she* to him? Baggage of the woman he chose to have on his arm.

"Your mother is quite good at convincing people to part with their money."

Something in his tone made Gemma's stomach twist a little tighter, but she couldn't get a read on what he really meant.

"Yes, well. At least she has some talents."

"Mothering was never one of them," he said more kindly.

Gemma glanced at him, his attention still on her mother across the room. He had the look of a contented man: a small smile that almost reached his eyes, deeply tanned skin, and no telltale signs of stress anywhere on his face. This never failed to surprise Gemma, given whom he was married to.

She chose to let his mothering comment go rather than ask the nagging questions it spurred. Namely, *Why? Why wasn't I enough for her?*

"The dress was a nice touch." He didn't look at her as he said it, but his smile widened, like he was in on her little rebellious secret. "She noticed."

Gemma smiled inwardly at her small triumph, though she wouldn't have known her mother had noticed if he hadn't told her. Her mother hadn't said more than, *Good to see you, Gemaline*, before moving on to brownnose the guests.

"That's a surprise," she said evenly. Why did she put herself through this every year? She was unhappy here, and even though her stepfather wasn't being unkind, just being in the presence of her mother made her unhappier by the second. Sadly, she always hoped her mother would change. That just once she'd show up at one of these events and her mother would actually be happy to see her. She should leave and go back home to Truman and the kids, where she was happiest. *Where I belong.*

"Is it?" Warren nodded toward a group of younger men who had been eyeing Gemma all evening and arched a thin brow.

A sarcastic laugh slipped out before she could stop it. "She noticed because attention was drawn away from her."

"Perhaps. Or perhaps because it's the first time you've crossed her on her own turf." He paused as his comment settled in like lead.

Her mother started across the floor in their direction. Jacqueline Benzos knew how to work a room. Her black silk gown clung to her curvaceous figure as she moved, blinking long, fake lashes and flashing practiced smiles.

Warren lowered his voice and said, "For what it's worth, the dress suits you far better than this environment does. Thank you for making the effort and coming tonight." He leaned down and kissed her cheek, disappearing into the crowd before her mother reached them.

Her mother's smile remained in place as she took up the space beside Gemma, sucking all the air from the room. "Darling."

An asp. That's what her mother's voice reminded her of, a slithering creature full of poison.

"Mother." She tried to hide her distaste but feared she'd failed.

"I've abided by your wishes and did not try to set you up with any of these gorgeous, wealthy men."

Though she'd been visually devoured by many of the men here all night, Gemma had noticed the lack of direct come-ons. "Thank you. I appreciate you respecting my request."

Her mother lifted her chin and her champagne glass to a woman passing in front of them and said under her breath, "Yes, well. We don't need these people catching wind of the derelict you're rebelling with, now, do we?"

Ice chilled Gemma's veins. "Excuse me?"

"Oh, Gemaline. Surely you didn't think I would let you see a man without having him thoroughly checked out. I can only assume you didn't know about his felony conviction." Her mother did not look at her as she spoke with maddening casualness. She was too busy nodding and smiling at her guests.

Anger assailed Gemma, stomping over the mild embarrassment that came with her mother's unveiling of Truman's dark past. "You would *let* me?"

"Of course, darling. You *are* my daughter. Someone has to watch out for you."

When have you ever watched out for me?

"The man is a convicted murderer. You're not safe with him, Gemaline. Now, you've had your little rebellion. It's time to move on and find a more suitable man."

Gemma's stomach plummeted, not at her mother's newfound knowledge or the casual way she delivered it, but at her mother demeaning her relationship with Truman. "And you were *so* worried about me, you chose to wait and tell me this at your fundraiser, where you thought I wouldn't make a scene," she seethed. "The truth is, *Mother*, I'm *very* safe with him. Safer with him than I ever was with you, because he's a good person.

He knows how to love with his whole heart, and he cares about *me*, not what I look like or what anyone else thinks of me. Do you even know why he was in prison, or don't you care?"

"*Murder*, Gemaline. Nothing matters beyond that."

Gemma stepped in front of her mother, forcing her to see her, maybe for the first time in her life. "His mother was being *raped*. He *saved* her. *That* matters. That's the *only* thing that matters. Do you know what *doesn't* matter, Mother?"

Her mother's jaw tightened. She lifted her chin and looked down her nose at Gemma in cold silence.

"My dress," Gemma said through gritted teeth, tears of anger and hurt filling her eyes. "What these people think of me, or—and it pains me to say it, even though it shouldn't—what *you* think of me. None of that matters, because none of it is real. I've spent my life attending these functions because they're important to you, and on some level I always hoped I'd become just as important. But it's clear that all you see when you look at me is someone to marry off so you can throw a wedding or be connected with another rich family. Well, guess what? I'm done." She held her mother's steely gaze. "I'm done with trying to do the right thing by you when you have *never* done right by me."

"Don't you take that tone with me. What would your father say?"

Gemma scoffed, a bitchy, loud, attention-grabbing jeer. "How would I know what he would say? He never talked to me. And neither did you, except to tell me the litany of things I needed to improve. And you know what? I grew up just fine *despite* the two of you and your rampant need to be stoic and oppressive."

Too carried away with the truth to stop, despite the guests

now gaping at them, she continued her rant. "I *know* how to love, and I'm *lovable*, which I wasn't really sure of for a good part of my life. I'm done coming to these ridiculously snobby events, and next time you speak to me, you *will* call me by my name. *Gemma*. And you'll ask me how I am, or you won't call me at all." Under her breath she added, "Maybe a fake birth certificate isn't the worst thing a child can have."

"What?" her mother snapped.

"Nothing. Goodbye, Mother."

On shaking legs, she made a beeline for the exit before her mother could misinterpret her tears for anything other than what they were—final acceptance of how little she meant to the woman who had given birth to her and finally moving on from it.

Waiting for the valet to bring her car was hell. She threw herself into the driver's seat, and sobs erupted as she scrambled to pull her phone from her purse. What was she thinking, making Truman decide between keeping his children and doing what *she* thought was the right thing? *He* was the right thing. For the kids and for her.

She drove out of the parking lot and powered up her phone, intending to call and tell him just that, when her phone vibrated with a call and Truman's face appeared on the screen, bringing more sobs.

"Tru—"

"Quincy's gone missing. He checked himself out of rehab an hour ago. I have to go find him. The kids are staying at Bear's."

How much more could one man endure?

Before she could find her voice, he said, "It's my fault. I begged him to stay in the program so he could apply for guardianship and the kids could stay in the family. It was too much pressure. I'm a fucking idiot."

"No," came out like a plea. This wasn't his fault. It was hers.

"Go to your place in case he gets high and shows up at mine. I'll call you when I know something."

"Tru—" The line went dead.

CHAPTER TWENTY-SIX

TRUMAN FLEW DOWN the driveway at breakneck speed. He'd been out looking for Quincy for hours when Gemma had called and said she was with him. *He's at your place. Come home.* He slammed on the brakes in front of Whiskey Automotive, cut the engine, and bolted toward the back of the building.

Gemma stood in the yard facing away from him. She turned as he approached. His eyes moved past her to Quincy, though he spoke to Gemma. "I told you to go home."

"I didn't listen," she said with a shaky voice, drawing his attention from his brother, who stood rigid and tense before him, to her.

Gemma's eyes were red and puffy, and fresh tears streaked her cheeks. Fire flamed inside Truman. He took a step toward his brother, ready to wring his neck if he'd touched her. "What have you done?"

Gemma grabbed his arm, stopping him from advancing on Quincy. "He told me. He told me everything."

Truman's gut wrenched, stealing the air from his lungs. "What…?"

"*Everything*, Tru." She tightened her hold on his arm.

Truman couldn't breathe. He'd gotten the best news of his life only a few short hours earlier at the courthouse, and now his world was crashing down around him again. He glared at Quincy, disbelief weighing down every word. "What have you done?"

Quincy stepped into the path of the porch light. His eyes were damp, his expression sorrowful and unmistakably relieved. "I couldn't do it, bro. I can't let your life fall apart because of me. Not anymore. Not if I want to stay clean."

Truman's world shifted on its axis. He sank to the steps and buried his face in his hands. "You have no idea what you've done. Now she's part of it."

"No," Gemma said. "He's going to the police tomorrow. He'll tell them everything. I won't get in trouble."

"Why, Quincy?" Truman implored, unable to look at Gemma, afraid his lie had ruined everything. "Why would you do this? I told you I'd figure something out."

Quincy drew his shoulders back, holding Truman's gaze with confidence and determination Truman had never seen. "Because you are still my stronghold, my straight arrow to follow, man. Because if I don't get this shit out of my head, I'll turn back to drugs to escape it. Why do you think I tried them in the first place? It's too much, knowing I fucked up your life. And, bro, it's the right thing to do."

"You can't do this, Quin," Truman pleaded. "I'll go back to prison for perjury. So will you. God knows how long they'll put you away for what happened, *and* I'll lose the kids. Then what? What happens to them? What happens to you?"

"I don't have all the answers," Quincy said. "But I need to do this. And I'm not done with rehab. Not by a long shot."

"I can't save you or help the kids if you do this," Truman said more to himself than to Quincy.

"You can't save me, Truman. Don't you see? Don't you get

it? Only I can save myself," Quincy said. "And I've been thinking about the kids. Maybe Bear or Dixie can raise them if this goes south."

"You won't need Bear or Dixie. I'll step in. You know I will." Tears slid down Gemma's cheeks as she crouched before Truman, who was still sitting on the steps. "You didn't commit the crime." It was a statement, not a question, said with awe, not accusation.

He shook his head.

"But you were willing to risk your freedom *again* to protect and raise the kids. To risk *everything*. Including me."

Truman shook his head. "No. I wasn't willing to lose you. I went to the courthouse to find out the process, like you suggested. You were right, Gemma. There is another way." He glared at Quincy again. "*Was* another way."

Gemma covered her mouth, fresh tears tumbling down her cheeks. "You went to the courthouse?"

He nodded again, trying to calm the storm within him long enough to tell her what he'd learned before he'd been thrown into searching for his brother.

"Since the state's not involved and the kids have been in my care, all I have to do is submit a Complaint for Custody to the court. They said if I turn in our mother's death certificate and sign an affidavit stating the father can't be found, I should be fine. The court doesn't typically do investigations with custody complaints unless a party to the litigation requests it. There's no one to oppose this. They said it would typically be granted without a hearing in the normal course of the court's business. But now..."

He looked at Quincy, standing more confidently and clear-headed than he'd ever seen him. He was torn between his brother's sobriety and the cost to everyone involved.

OVERWHELMED DIDN'T BEGIN to touch on the emotions reeling through Gemma. Between her blowout with her mother and learning the truth about Truman's—*Quincy's*—crime, she could barely think. But it didn't take much thought to know that if Truman and Quincy had a chance in hell of coming out on top of this nightmare, there was only one way to handle it. And she wasn't even sure what she had in mind would help.

Or if I can make the call.

Truman reached for her hand. "I'm sorry for all of this. For lying to you about killing that man and for getting you involved in this situation at all."

God she loved him. She loved his loyalty, the depth of his love, and everything else about him. She wasn't about to let him feel bad for doing what he had to do to protect his brother, not when he had proven himself to be the best man she knew.

"Don't. I'm not upset with you about not telling me the truth. I know you couldn't." She glanced at Quincy, who had been carrying so much guilt it's a wonder he'd survived at all. How had he found the courage to come forward, knowing Truman would be livid, in order to give his brother the future he deserved? He'd confessed all his wrongdoings, with unabashed tears and doleful regret. He told her how the crime had happened, how Truman had stepped in to take care of everything, and how their mother had turned against him. The strength and conviction of these two men was immeasurable, and she knew that despite the long road ahead for Quincy to recover from his drug addiction, and the legal battles they would face, they were a family she wanted to be part of.

Returning her attention to Truman and their conversation, she said, "The same way you can't be mad at Quincy for wanting to do the right thing. You've shown me that the line between right and wrong can be blurred, but that protecting those you love is the right thing no matter what the cost."

She opened her purse and withdrew her phone.

"Who are you calling?" Truman asked.

"You need the best legal counsel money can buy, and my stepfather is the best."

"Sweetheart. I have no money left," Truman said regretfully.

Thinking of that huge bank account her mother had been dumping money into for her for more than a decade, she said, "I do."

EPILOGUE

GEMMA PICKED THROUGH a rack of dresses at a sidewalk sale with Crystal and Dixie, looking for something for Kennedy to wear to the Easter parade next weekend. She'd really come into her own over the past few months. They'd been slowly introducing her to crowds, taking her to the zoo, for walks on the beach, and out to the mall, and she was excited about the Easter parade. It had been five months since Quincy confessed, two months since the court granted Truman post-conviction relief and vacated his sentence, and five weeks since Truman had been awarded guardianship of the children. The state could have placed both Truman and Quincy on trial; however, the prosecutor had exercised what Warren had called his *prosecutorial discretion* and declined to prosecute either of them. Warren had said that Quincy's age at the time of the crime and Truman's prison sentence had factored heavily into that decision.

"How about this?" Dixie held up a pink dress with giraffes and flowers on it. "She loves wild animals and flowers." Kennedy's newest obsession was wild animals, and Truman had been working hard on new animal-centric fairy tales. Although they'd decided to start introducing her to more mainstream fairy tales, since she'd be starting preschool in the fall.

"Or this!" Crystal held up a tie-dyed dress with lace around the edges. Thanks to Crystal, Kennedy loved edgy clothing as much as she loved frills.

"Why don't we ask her?" Gemma suggested as Truman, Quincy, and the kids came out of Luscious Licks. As Truman's eyes caught hers, a sinful smile spread across his handsome face, inciting a flurry of butterflies in her belly. They'd been living together for months, and she still got fluttery at the sight of him. She knew that would never change.

He blew her a kiss and knelt beside the stroller to feed Lincoln a spoonful of ice cream.

"Dada." Lincoln waved his arms up and down excitedly. He'd been calling Truman Dada and Gemma Mama for the last two weeks, and although Truman had at first tried to correct him, he'd since given up. Both he and Gemma ate up the endearments. Lincoln was hitting all his milestones, waving bye-bye and pulling himself up to stand while holding on to everything from a coffee table to Truman's leg. His favorite game, besides pulling Uncle Bullet's beard, was peekaboo.

Lincoln reached for the spoon and Quincy laughed. "He's got my appetite."

Quincy had filled out in the past few months, rivaling his older brother's massive frame. After several stressful months, Quincy had completed rehab and was working full-time at a bookstore, which Gemma was thrilled about. It turned out that where Truman excelled at art, Quincy excelled at academics. He'd even aced his GED and enrolled in the community college and was doing exceptionally well in all of his classes. Two weeks ago Truman, Gemma, and the kids had rented a house on a residential street near the preschool, and Quincy had taken over Truman's apartment. His relationship with Truman had been up and down during those first few weeks, but now they were closer than ever.

As Gemma watched the two brothers teasing each other, she sent a silent thank-you to her stepfather, who had taken on their case pro bono despite the fact that her mother had tried to convince Warren not to help her *derelict boyfriend.* She'd never understand her mother, and as she watched the kids and Truman and Quincy, she realized that was okay. Not all parents needed to be understood, or even liked, for that matter. She had a stepfather with whom she was forging a relationship that felt mildly paternal and a family of friends she adored.

"Hey, Kennedy." Crystal held up the dress she'd found. "What do you think of this dress?"

"Pwetty!" Kennedy had ice cream all over her lips. Her little tongue made a wide circle to clean it up.

Dixie crouched beside her and showed her the pink dress she'd picked out. "How about this one?"

The roar of motorcycles drowned out Kennedy's response as Bear, Bones, and Bullet pulled up to the curb.

"Be-ah!" Kennedy squealed.

Bear took off his helmet and climbed off the bike, scooping the little girl into his arms. When her cone hit his chin, he rolled his eyes and shrugged his shoulders over the mess, which made Kennedy giggle.

"What are you guys doing here?" Gemma asked.

Bones and Bullet exchanged a look with Truman she couldn't read. Truman had been quiet today, she realized, and she wondered what was up with him.

"We heard there were hot babes hanging out here," Bear answered, setting a seductive stare on Crystal, who rolled her eyes. That had become their *thing.* He hit on Crystal, and for whatever reason—one she wasn't sharing with Gemma—Crystal continuously turned him away.

"And free ice cream." Bones lifted Kennedy into his arms and licked her ice cream.

"Boney!" Kennedy complained.

They all roared at the nickname she'd adopted for him. She wiggled out of his arms and went to Truman, who reached down and tousled her hair. He leaned down and whispered something to her. Her brows knitted in concentration.

"How's my littlest buddy?" Bullet lifted Lincoln into his arms, and Lincoln tugged on his beard. "That's coming off tomorrow."

"Really?" Dixie asked.

"Yeah. I've had enough beard pulling by this little dude." He kissed Lincoln's cheek and the baby gave his beard another tug, giggling wildly when Bullet growled at him.

Gemma's heart warmed at all the love these children had in their lives. At the love *she* had in her life. Her eyes sought Truman, as they always did, and she caught him looking at her in the way he had so many times over the past few months, with wonder and so much love, it felt like an embrace.

Kennedy held her cone up to Gemma, brushing the creamy treat along the front of Gemma's skirt. Gemma leaned down, passing up the ice cream, and going in for ice-cream kisses instead.

"Mm. Best kisses ever," Gemma said with a laugh. She might not be Kennedy and Lincoln's parent, but she sure loved them as much as any parent ever could.

"I'll get that, sweetheart," Truman offered, bending to wipe her skirt with a napkin. He tipped his face up with a beautiful smile—sending her stomach all aflutter again—and held up his waffle cone.

"No thanks. Those ice-cream kisses were enough."

Crystal and Dixie gasped, and Gemma looked around, wondering what they'd seen. Crystal pointed at Truman perched on one knee before her, still offering her his ice cream—with a beautiful solitaire diamond ring stuck in the top she'd somehow missed seeing.

"Ohmygosh. Truman?" She met his eager, loving gaze, and her heart swelled, taking up all the space in her chest.

"Sweet girl, I can't offer you glamour or glitz, but I can offer you ice-cream stains, homemade fairy tales, and midnight kisses." His blue eyes heated when he said *midnight kisses*, and she wondered if he was thinking about when they'd made love last night in their new home. A *real* home, where the kids could grow up and have friends over and live a safe, happy life. "And a family who adores you. If you'll have us. I'll even let you write that article you've been bugging me about if you will marry me. Will you be my wife, Gemma? Will you marry *us*?"

Tears tumbled free. "I don't want glamour or glitz. Everything I could ever want is right here on this sidewalk. Yes, Tru Blue. I'll marry you."

He rose to his feet, licking the ring clean before sliding it on her finger. "It's sticky, and small, but one day I'll replace it with something bigger."

"You'll do no such thing," she said, admiring the gorgeous proof of his love. "It's perfect."

Everyone whooped and cheered as his strong arms came around her and he took her in the most incredible kiss of her life—the kiss of her future husband.

Kennedy tried to squeeze between their legs, and they parted, laughing as Truman lifted *their* little girl into his arms.

"Now you be my mommy?" Kennedy asked excitedly.

Fresh tears filled Gemma's eyes. She shifted a curious gaze to Truman.

"I don't know what started it, but she's been asking if she could call us Mommy and Daddy all day." He shrugged with the sweetest, scxiest smile she'd ever seen.

Gemma must have been wrong all those months ago. Her ovaries couldn't have exploded the day she'd met Truman, because she was sure they just had.

"Yes, baby girl. I would be honored to be your mommy."

Each of the Whiskey family members will have their own stories. Sign up for Melissa's newsletter so you never miss a release.

www.MelissaFoster.com/News

Get Ready for TRULY, MADLY, WHISKEY

A new, emotionally riveting, sexy standalone romance by New York Times bestselling author Melissa Foster. Watch mysteriously sexy Bear Whiskey claw his way to his happily ever after with sassy, rebellious Crystal Moon.

Releasing April 12, 2017 (pre-orders available prior to release)

The Whiskeys were first introduced in

RIVER OF LOVE (The Bradens at Peaceful Harbor)

~ Now Available ~

River rafting and adventure company owner Sam Braden works hard and plays harder. He's fast, focused, and determined—and never at a loss for a willing woman to share his time with. The trouble is, the only woman he wants refuses him at every turn.

Physician assistant Faith Hayes escaped her painful past and built a safe, happy life in Peaceful Harbor. She's also put what she's learned to good use helping others by founding Women Against Cheaters, an online support group. When her boss's sinfully sexy brother sets his sights on sweet Faith, she knows the self-professed player is everything she shouldn't want, and she's determined to resist him.

Sam pulls out all the stops, proving to Faith that his past doesn't have to define his future. As she lets down her guard and begins to trust Sam, intense conversations turn to intimate pleasures. But when real life steps in and their pasts collide, it's Faith who's left with something to prove.

More Books by Melissa

LOVE IN BLOOM SERIES

SNOW SISTERS
Sisters in Love
Sisters in Bloom
Sisters in White

THE BRADENS at Weston
Lovers at Heart
Destined for Love
Friendship on Fire
Sea of Love
Bursting with Love
Hearts at Play

THE BRADENS at Trusty
Taken by Love
Fated for Love
Romancing My Love
Flirting with Love
Dreaming of Love
Crashing into Love

THE BRADENS at Peaceful Harbor
Healed by Love
Surrender My Love
River of Love
Crushing on Love
Whisper of Love
Thrill of Love

THE BRADEN NOVELLAS
Promise My Love
Our New Love
Daring Her Love
Story of Love

THE REMINGTONS

Game of Love

Stroke of Love

Flames of Love

Slope of Love

Read, Write, Love

Touched by Love

SEASIDE SUMMERS

Seaside Dreams

Seaside Hearts

Seaside Sunsets

Seaside Secrets

Seaside Nights

Seaside Embrace

Seaside Lovers

Seaside Whispers

The RYDERS

Seized by Love

Claimed by Love

Chased by Love

Rescued by Love

Thrill of Love

BILLIONAIRES AFTER DARK SERIES

WILD BOYS AFTER DARK

Logan

Heath

Jackson

Cooper

BAD BOYS AFTER DARK

Mick

Dylan

Carson

Brett

SEXY STANDALONE ROMANCE

Tru Blue

Truly, Madly, Whiskey

HARBORSIDE NIGHTS SERIES

Includes characters from the Love in Bloom series

Catching Cassidy

Discovering Delilah

Tempting Tristan

Chasing Charley

Breaking Brandon

Embracing Evan

Reaching Rusty

Loving Livi

More Books by Melissa

Chasing Amanda (mystery/suspense)

Come Back to Me (mystery/suspense)

Have No Shame (historical fiction/romance)

Love, Lies & Mystery (3-book bundle)

Megan's Way (literary fiction)

Traces of Kara (psychological thriller)

Where Petals Fall (suspense)

Acknowledgments

Thank you for reading Truman and Gemma's story. I hope you fell in love with them, along with sweet Kennedy and Lincoln and all of our warm and wonderful family members, Quincy, Bullet, Bones, Bear, Dixie, and Crystal, each of whom will be getting their own happily ever after. Please sign up for my newsletter to make sure you don't miss out on the upcoming Whiskey family releases: www.MelissaFoster.com.

If you enjoyed this story and want to read more about the Whiskeys and about Peaceful Harbor, try *River of Love* (The Bradens at Peaceful Harbor) or check out all of my alpha heroes and sassy heroines in my Love in Bloom series. Every book can be read as a stand-alone novel, and characters appear in other family series, so you never miss out on an engagement, wedding, or birth. You can find information on Love in Bloom here: www.MelissaFoster.com/LIB, and you can start five of my series free here: www.MelissaFoster.com/LIBFree.

There are so many people to thank for "circle talking" with me about Truman and Gemma. Alexis Bruce, Stacy Eaton, Amy Manemann, Natasha Brown, Elise Sax, and so many others. Thank you for always being there. A special thank-you goes to Nancy Stopper, for connecting me with attorney Aiden Smith. And heaps of gratitude to Aiden for helping me to understand the legal process. I have taken a few fictional liberties with the story, and all errors are my own, not a reflection of Aiden's excellent legal knowledge.

As always, thank you to my incredible editorial team for helping my stories be the best they can be for readers.

www.MelissaFoster.com

Melissa Foster is a *New York Times* and *USA Today* bestselling and award-winning author. Her books have been recommended by *USA Today's* book blog, *Hagerstown* magazine, *The Patriot*, and several other print venues. She is the founder of the World Literary Café and Fostering Success. Melissa has painted and donated several murals to the Hospital for Sick Children in Washington, DC.

Visit Melissa on her website or chat with her on social media. Melissa enjoys discussing her books with book clubs and reader groups and welcomes an invitation to your event. Melissa's books are available through most online retailers in paperback and digital formats.

Made in the USA
Monee, IL
13 January 2022

88834497R00152